黃玟君 著

用英文寫台灣

英文作文35篇

Act Local Think Global

《聯合報》教育版「笑談時事英語」專欄，

本土議題；道地英語；多元觀點；盡在其中

［必備］英檢 學測 指考 托福 研究所

隨書附贈 2CD

自序

　　在大學任教，我常常很好奇學生選讀英文系、或選修英文相關課程的目的。大部分學生告訴我，學英文的目的除了可以幫助考試、找工作、升遷，最重要的目的是以後出國旅遊或深造時，可以用英文在當地生活、與當地人溝通。

　　然而，許多針對台灣人使用英語的調查顯示，真正出國旅遊或念書的人畢竟是少數，而且用到大量英文的機會並不多，反而是在台灣這塊土地上，大家必須用英文與身旁的外籍同事、上司、友人溝通。然而，當台灣人必須向這些外國人介紹發生在這塊土地上的時事、文化、節慶、社會現象、甚至八卦時，卻常常覺得力不從心。我的許多學生也向我承認，學了那麼多年的英文，他們可以用英文說出美國「萊特兄弟」發明動力飛機的故事，甚至「美國侵伊」的點點滴滴，然而卻無法用英文告訴身邊的外籍友人，台灣的「爆料文化」有多猖獗、「詐騙電話」有多氾濫、「跨年晚會」有多勁爆……！

　　所以當《聯合報》教育版邀我寫個貼近台灣的英語專欄時，我毫不考慮就答應了。

在專欄「笑談時事英語」刊出的這一年間，我陸續收到許多讀者的來信，才發現讀者群分布之廣，超乎想像：中小學教師、大學教授、家庭主婦、上班族、公司老闆、檢察官、退休人士……。可見許多人還是很關心發生在這小島上的種種新聞，更希望藉由英文，與外籍人士分享有關台灣的一切。

當然，我也發現這專欄的許多讀者是準備大學升學考試的高中生、準備碩士班考試的大學生，以及關心孩子升學的父母。很巧的是，今年七月剛考完的「大學入學指定考試」英文科試題，其中許多題目都與新聞時事相關，例如 judge（法官）的 bribery scandal（收賄醜聞）、avian flu（禽流感）、news report（新聞報導）誤導大眾……等，而這些題目恰好也與這個專欄的許多內容不謀而合，更加凸顯了新聞時事成為未來台灣各類考試的趨勢及重要性。另外，此次指考的閱讀測驗文章既多且長，考生所需的單字量大增，因此平日加強自己的長篇閱讀能力及提升字彙量可說刻不容緩。

此外，由於英文「閱讀」與「寫作」的能力乃一體兩面、相輔相成，因此《用英文寫台灣——英文作文35篇》不僅是一本加強作文的書，還是一本訓練閱讀能力的書。本書除了原本刊登在《聯合報》專欄的文章外，還加上了單字、片語的解說與例句，每篇並挑出兩個難句作句型、文法的解析，並在最後附上造句練習，幫助讀者反覆練習文章中的重要句型及單字。最重要的，我

特別撰寫〈英文寫作技巧大公開〉一章，盼能對想要真正精進寫作能力的讀者有所幫助。

最後感謝「聯經出版公司」、《聯合報》駱焜祺先生及張錦弘先生，以及台灣師大吳美貞教授及呂燕妮小姐對此書的大力協助。

英文寫作技巧大公開

在英文聽、說、讀、寫四項能力裡，最令大家頭痛的應該就屬「寫作」了。一般人一聽到要上英文寫作課，或工作上需要交英文報告，通常是一個頭、兩個大。就算已在大學念英文系了，還是常常追著老師問：

文章怎樣可以寫得長？

為什麼下筆時都腸枯思竭？

為什麼老師總說我的英文作文沒結構？

為什麼我的作文總是「滿江紅」？

英文作文要好，是不是要背範文、背名句？

既然「寫作」帶給大家這麼高的「痛苦指數」，現在就讓我們好好來破解寫作迷障！

英文作文結構

相信你還記得，小時候上國文課時，老師都會耳提面命，作文務必分四段，分別是「起」、「承」、「轉」、「合」。國文作文有一定的章法，英文作文當然也不例外！

首先我們要知道，英文是一種結構十分嚴謹的語言，不僅句

子本身如此（例如在英文句子中，一個句子只可以有一個主詞與一個動詞），寫成文章也是如此。在正式的英文文章中，哪一段該寫些什麼都有一定的規範，而這個規範通常在文章一開始就會點出來，清清楚楚、明明白白。

簡單來說，一篇英文文章通常分為三大部分，也就是「導論」、「內文」、及「結論」。以下就是一篇英文文章的「長相」：

導論（introduction）

內文（body）

結論（conclusion）

在這種「三段式」寫作中，「導論」與「結論」通常是自成一段，「內文」少則一段，多則好幾段，端看文章的長短而定，因此這種文章的字數通常不會少於兩、三百字。

對於台灣許多準備大學入學考試或其他類型考試的讀者而言，必須寫作的文章長度則在120-150字左右，這時便可以將剛

剛的「三段式」合成一大段，變成「段落寫作」，而非「文章寫作」，不過其架構還是一樣：

導論（introduction）

內文（body）

結論（conclusion）

在「段落寫作」中，「導論」不再是一段，而是一句話或兩句話；「內文」不再是好幾段，而是好幾句；同樣的，「結論」不再是一段，而是一、兩句話。

好，有了這個概念，讓我們來瞧瞧英文作文裡的這三大部分各自長得什麼樣子。

（註：這裡所舉的例子雖是以落落長的「文章寫作」為主，不過因為「段落寫作」與其寫作形式的道理相同，差別只在字數多寡，因此兩者是可以互通的！）

一、導論（Introduction）

一篇文章中最重要的部分是啥？當然是「導論」囉，因為它既能夠開宗明義，又能提綱挈領，可說是一篇文章的中心所在。不過第一段可能有很多句，哪一句通常最重要呢？第一句？第二句？最後一句？其實大部分的文章都不會一開頭便直接切入主

題，相反的，作者通常會在一開始稍微寒暄、暖場一下，利用問句、數據、典故、故事、笑話，或令人驚訝的用語來引起讀者的好奇心，點出文章的大概，讓讀者稍微熟悉文章的大方向後，再帶入文章真正的主題。

因此一篇文章的開頭幾句話通常是我們所謂的「開場白」(Opening Statement)。開場白後，才會正式導入文章的主題，也就是一篇文章中最重要的部分：「命題句」(Thesis Statement)。

通常「命題句」出現時，讀者都會很容易看得出來，因為寫作者一般都會利用「命題句」清楚點出這篇文章的結構、大意，與方向。導論中的「命題句」通常只有一句話，由這一句話負起闡揚整篇文章的大任。

（註：對於長度較短的「段落寫作」，寫作者通常會把「開場白」完全省略，在文章一開始便把「命題句」直接點出，毫不囉唆。）

那麼命題句到底長得什麼樣子呢？舉例來說，如果一篇作文的題目是 "Coping with Old Age"（面對老年），那麼這篇文章的命題句很可能長成這樣子：

> Since my parents retired from their jobs, they've had to cope with the physical, mental, and emotional stresses of being "old."（自從我父母退休後，便必須一直克服「老」所帶來的身體上、心智上、及情緒上的壓力。）

又如果一篇作文的題目是 "Aspects of Love"（愛情的種種面貌），那麼這篇文章的命題句很可能是這樣：

Love involves mutual respect, the desire to give rather than take, and the feeling of being wholly at ease.（愛情包括互相的尊重、寧願付出不計回報，以及全然自在的感覺。）

　　而如果一篇作文的題目是 "Three Common Ways of Losing Weight"（三種常見的減肥方法），那麼這篇文章的命題句很可能長這樣：

In my opinion, there are both advantages and drawbacks in the three common ways of losing weight: exercise, diet, and surgery.（我個人認為，運動、節食、手術這三種常見的減肥方法各有其優缺點。）

二、內文（Body）

　　我們之前說過，英文是一種結構十分嚴謹的語言，在正式的文章中，哪一段該寫些什麼，都有一定的規範，而這個規範通常在「導論」的「命題句」中就會點出來。有了「命題句」，我們便可以根據它來撰寫一篇文章「內文」的整個發展過程。為什麼呢？舉上面的例子，如果一篇文章的「命題句」是：

Since my parents retired from their jobs, they've had to cope with the physical, mental, and emotional stresses of being "old."

　　這時文章「內文」的第二、三、四段便會分別闡述作者父母的 physical（身體的）、mental（心智的）、emotional（情緒的）壓力。

　　如果導論的「命題句」是：

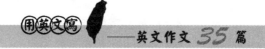

Love involves mutual respect, the desire to give rather than take, and the feeling of being wholly at ease.

則接下來的文章「內文」便會闡述愛情的三種面向：mutual respect（互相尊重）、the desire to give rather than take（寧願付出、不計回報）、the feeling of being wholly at ease（全然自在的感覺）。

當然，如果導論的「命題句」是：

In my opinion, there are both advantages and drawbacks in the three common ways of losing weight: exercise, diet, and surgery.

則接下來的文章「內文」便會闡述三種常見減肥法的優缺點。最後我們再舉一例。如果一篇文章的「命題句」是：

Car accidents are the number one killer of children, and several steps must be taken to reduce the serious dangers car accidents pose to children.（車禍高居幼兒死亡原因之首，要降低車禍對幼兒造成的嚴重傷害，我們一定要採取幾個步驟。）

則這篇文章的「內文」便會列舉一些可以預防幼兒車禍災害的方法。瞭嗎？

當然，長篇文章的「內文」有好幾段，且每段不可能只有一句話，因此「內文」的每一段其實包含了（1）主題句（Topic Sentence）及（2）支持此一主題句的細節（Supporting Details）。

「主題句」通常存在於內文中每一段的第一個句子，因此對於它所處的段落有領導的作用。不過，一個段落光有一個美美的

主題句還不夠，後面必須要接一連串支持這個美美的主題句的其他句子，也就是「支持細節」。

你或許會問，一個段落中既然有領導的主題句，為何還要囉哩叭唆的加上一串支持細節？其實一般寫作者這麼做的原因，不外乎是利用這些「支持細節」去詳加闡明「主題句」，幫助讀者更了解「主題句」所要傳達的訊息。

要注意的是，作者在寫這些「支持細節」時，態度通常十分嚴謹，即會緊緊扣住「主題句」、環繞「主題句」而寫，絕對不會離題！

舉例來說，如果一篇作文的題目是"Capital Punishment"（死刑），而且它的命題句是：

In my opinion, capital punishment is wrong in many aspects, and Taiwan should get rid of capital punishment, which is really just "legal murder."（我認為死刑在很多方面而言是錯的，而且台灣應該廢除死刑，因為它事實上是「合法的謀殺」。）

則這篇文章的「內文」就可能長得如下（內文中畫有底線的句子是「主題句」，其餘的則是支持此主題句的「細節」）：

First of all, I believe that it is wrong to kill. Only God has the right to take away life. Human beings should not kill human beings. Even if a criminal has committed horrible crimes, the government does not have the right to execute him.

Second, the threat of going to the electric chair or to the gas

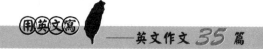
chamber does not stop criminals. When people commit a violent crime, they are not thinking about their punishment. In fact, many crimes happen when people are angry. They are not thinking about the consequences of their actions. According to a report in the *Chinatimes*, Taiwan executed 3 men in 10 weeks in the fall of 2002. During that same time period, the murder rate in Taiwan rose 15 percent. This shows that the threat of capital punishment does not stop crime.

The third and most important reason for abolishing the death penalty is that the government sometimes makes mistakes and executes innocent people. In fact, this has happened. According to an article in *Time magazine*, there were 6 executions of innocent people in Taiwan between 2002 and 2003. In my view, this makes the government itself guilty of murder.

（第一，我相信「殺人」是錯的。只有上帝有權力取走生命。人類不該殺其他人類。就算一個罪犯犯了罪，政府並沒有權力去殺死他。

第二，「上電椅」或者「進毒氣室」的威脅並不能阻止罪犯。當人們犯下殘忍暴力的罪行時，他們並不會想到隨之而來的懲罰。事實上，許多的罪行是人們在憤怒下犯的。而這些人在犯罪時，並不會想到他們的舉動會帶來何種後果。根據《中國時報》的一個報導，2002年秋天，台灣在十個星期裡執行了三個死刑。但在同一時期，台灣的謀殺率卻上升了百分之十五。這顯示死刑的威脅並不能阻止犯罪。

第三個、也是最重要的廢除死刑的理由是，政府有時會犯錯，而因著死刑誤殺了無辜的人。事實上，這種事的確發生過。根據《時代雜誌》的一篇文章，在2002至2003年間，台灣共有六個誤判死刑的案件。我認為這使得政府本身也犯了謀殺罪。）

　　而如果今天我們要寫的是一篇120字左右的「段落寫作」，這時上面許多的「支持細節」便會被削去，只留下各段的「主題句」及少數的「支持細節」來充當其「內文」部分(內文中畫有底線的句子是原本長篇文章中的「主題句」)：

First of all, I believe that it is wrong to kill. Even if a criminal has committed horrible crimes, the government does not have the right to execute him. Second, the threat of death penalty does not stop criminals. When people commit a violent crime, they are not thinking about their punishment. Many crimes happen when people are angry. They are not thinking about the consequences of their actions. The third and most important reason for abolishing the death penalty is that the government sometimes makes mistakes and executes innocent people. In my view, this makes the government itself guilty of murder.

　　(第一，我相信「殺人」是錯的。就算一個罪犯犯了罪，政府並沒有權力去殺死他。第二，死刑的威脅並不能阻止罪犯。許多的罪行是人們在憤怒下犯的。而這些人在犯罪時，並不會想到他們的舉動會帶來何種後果。第三個、也是最重要的廢除死刑的理由是，政府有時會犯錯，而因著死刑誤殺了無辜的人。我認為這使得政府本身也犯了謀殺罪。)

(註：因為「主題句」在各種形式的寫作中都占有極重要的地位，在接下來的35篇範文中，我們會特別將每段的主題句標示出來，讓你更清楚它們在文章中的位置。)

三、結論（Conclusion）

結論是一篇文章的總結。在正式的作文中，常見的結論形式有下列幾種：

‧**整理摘要及提供省思：**作者簡短重述整篇文章的主旨或要點，以及記錄個人的省思。

‧**提出引人深思的問題：**作者在結論時提出一個或數個問題給讀者，讓讀者有機會可以進一步思考文章的內容。

‧**提出預測或建議：**作者提出對所寫議題未來的預測、想法、建議，或解決方案。

‧**闡述文章可衍生的對策、呼籲讀者採取行動：**作者希望讀者藉由文章產生共鳴，並身體力行、採取行動、改變現狀。

一般而言，第一種「整理摘要及提供省思」是最常見的結論形式。不過，作者通常會依據文章性質及題目的不同，採用不同的結論寫法，有些作者甚至會將兩種或三種形式合併使用，寫出更豐富多變的結論！

好，在進入下一個主題前，讓我們把英文文章的結構詳細描繪一下：

| 導論
(**Introduction**) | 開場白 (Opening Statement) |
| | 命題句 (Thesis Statement) |

內文 (**Body**)	主題句 (Topic Sentence)
	支持細節 (Supporting Details)
	主題句 (Topic Sentence)
	支持細節 (Supporting Details)
	主題句 (Topic Sentence)
	支持細節 (Supporting Details)

| 結論
(**Conclusion**) | |

寫作的三大最高指導原則

在講完英文寫作的結構後,讓我們來瞧瞧英文寫作的三大最高指導原則:

一、統一性(Unity)

所謂的「統一性」是指一篇文章應該有一個、而且只有一個最主要的中心思想。

什麼意思呢?如果今天你要寫一篇有關「誠實」的文章,那你無論文章如何寫、例子如何舉,都必須與誠實的議題有關。如果你今天在文章中寫了這麼一句話:「台灣人每個人持有手機的比率居全球第一」,或者「大陸偷渡客猖獗,除台灣外,美、日、韓等國家也都深受其害」,那麼你這篇文章就沒有「統一性」,而且十之八九會離題(除非聰明的你可以掰得出手機與誠實、偷渡客與誠實的關係)!

好,一篇文章本身的「統一性」很重要,同樣的,一篇文章的每一個段落,尤其是「內文」的部分,一定也要一個段落一個主題,不可一個段落拉拉雜雜、扯一堆有的沒有的。

例如下面這段「結論」中,畫底線的地方便與主題不合,因為應該刪掉:

In summary, I had so much fun this summer touring around Taiwan, watching old movies, and playing with my friends. When the summer started, I was so worried that I would have to stay home studying for next year's Entrance Exam, but now I am really happy that I have done so much in these two months. "When there is a will, there is a way." I will never forget about my last summer vacation in high school.

（總而言之，我有個超好玩的暑假：環島台灣、看老電影、和朋友玩。當暑假開始時，我還很擔心我必須待在家裡準備明年的入學考，不過我現在真的很高興在兩個月中做了這麼多的事。「有志者，事竟成」，我永遠不會忘記我在高中的最後一個暑假！）

順帶一提，這些年我擔任過大學聯考與大學入學考試的閱卷委員，每次閱卷，總會在一本三、四十份的卷子裡，看到許多考生寫下賣力背誦的成語名句，例如：Better late than never.（亡羊補牢猶未晚）、The early bird gets the worm.（早起的鳥兒有蟲吃）、Actions speak louder than words.（事實勝於雄辯）、All work and no play makes Jack a dull boy.（一味工作不玩耍，聰明也會變笨瓜）、As you sow, so shall you reap.（種瓜得瓜，種豆得豆）等等。雖然這些都是大家苦背而來的精心傑作，但如果不分青紅皂白濫用，不僅會破壞文章的「統一性」，還會弄巧成拙哦！

二、支持性（Support）

「支持性」指的是文章中每一個論點或主題，都要有很明確的支持它的細節或例子。

大部分的人寫作時，通常都只有「論點」，卻沒有「支持」。舉例來說，如果你在一篇名為「有效減肥法」的文章寫了

以下的「主題句」：

> Liposuction is the most effective way of weight loss yet the most dangerous.
>
> （抽脂減肥是減肥法中最有效、但也是最危險的。）

那麼身為作者的你便必須在這句話後加上支持細節，因為如果你之後什麼東西也沒有寫，很多讀者便會問：「你憑什麼那麼確定？」、「我不覺得抽脂很危險啊！」所以在那句話後一定要有可供佐證的例子或數據，不然空口說白話，誰信誰呀！如果你在這句話之後補上一句：

> According to the U.S. Food and Drug Administration, some studies indicate that the risk of death is between 20 and 100 deaths per 100,000 liposuction procedures.
>
> （根據美國的「食品及藥品管制局」，每十萬件抽脂手術中，就有二十到一百個致死的案件。）

瞧，氣勢就完全不一樣了！而且加了這一句話，文章長度無形中又加長了一些，真是一舉兩得！

所以說寫文章時，在你的每一句論述後，最好都加些例子，這樣一方面可以取信於讀者，一方面也可以增加寫作篇幅。這些例子除了是一些有憑有據的數據，也可以是你個人的親身經歷及個人意見，或是奇聞軼事、研究報告、統計資料、專家意見等等，只要能讓你的論述看起來更有份量、更有誠信，你都應該寫

上去。

三、連貫性（Coherence）

　　所謂「連貫性」，就是一篇文章的結構必須有一致性。

　　例如說，如果你要寫一篇「我的求學經驗」的文章，那你寫作的流程必須是「國小→國中→高中→大學」，或者「大學→高中→國中→國小」（雖然這樣寫的人很少）。你不可以寫成「高中→小學→國中→大學」，因為這樣一來文章的連貫性就會被打亂。

　　為了讓文章結構含有連貫性，比較常用的組織方式有下列幾種：

　　（一）時間順序（time order）：如果你今天寫的文章是與時間的推移有關，則必須按照時間發展先後次序描述（無論是由前往後、或由後往前描述）；除非我們須強調某一時間發生的事，否則最好不要做跳躍式描述。

　　（二）空間順序（space order）：如果你今天寫的文章是與空間的推移有關，則我們需按照空間發展次序描述，如由左至右、由近到遠、由上到下、由前到後……；除非需強調某一空間，否則最好不要做跳躍式描述。

　　（三）重要性排序（emphatic order）：如果你今天寫的文章要提到一些論點、理由、陳述、例子……等，則要將自己覺得最重要的論點、理由、陳述、例子……等等放在最後。舉例而言，如果你要列舉你最喜歡的三位歌星（最喜歡周杰倫、其次孫燕姿、再

其次蔡依林)，並說明你喜歡他們的理由，這時你便可以先寫孫燕姿、再寫蔡依林、最後寫周杰倫。又如果我們今天要寫「找工作的三大指導原則」便可以這麼排序：事少—離家近—錢多，表示我們最重視「錢多」、再來「事少」、最後才是「離家近」。這就是所謂的「重要性2—3—1」(次重要、其次重要、最重要)排序法。

(四)歸納法(inductive reasoning)： 指的是由「特定細節」推論到「一般通則」。利用這種邏輯推理方式寫作文的人，通常藉著一系列的例證來歸納出結論。舉例來說，如果你想寫一篇論證「酒後駕車」的文章，便可以舉出許多實例或數據(此為「特定細節」)，說明很多駕車肇事者，事後均被發現喝酒過量，之後歸結出酒後開車的危險性(此為「一般通則」)、倡導駕駛人酒後不應開車，此即採用歸納法寫作的方式。

(五)演繹法(deductive reasoning)： 指的是先立下「一般通則」，再進行到支持此一通則的「細節」。利用這種邏輯推理方式寫作文的人，通常一開始即採取某個已被普遍接受的立場或觀點，再將本身的論點與之結合。舉例來說，如果你想寫篇文章告訴讀者吸毒的壞處，便可以先提出個已被一般大眾接受的觀點，例如「吸毒和身心耗弱具有關聯性」，闡述「一個人若吸毒」與「則身心耗弱」兩者的相關性，藉此闡述吸毒可能導致的問題，此即採用演繹法的方式。

(六)因果關係(cause and effect)： 利用因果關係寫作時，通

常有兩個方式：「先因後果」、「先果後因」，端看寫文章的需要。舉例來說，如果你想寫一篇有關時下年輕人的文章，便可以先在文章一開頭說：「我認為七年級生是草莓族」（此為「果」）然後再一一列舉為何七年級生成為草莓族的理由，例如：父母寵愛、同儕壓力、社會價值觀的改變等（此為「因」）；此即「先果後因」的寫法。

（七）**類比及對比（compare and contrast）**：很多人常以為「類比」（compare）與「對比」（contrast）兩者相同，事實上「類比」比較的是兩個事物的共同點、而「對比」則是比較兩個事物的不同點。如果你今天要比較「傳統發電廠」及「核能發電廠」的優缺點，這時便可以先從政治、經濟、環境三個角度敘述「傳統發電廠」的優缺點，之後再一樣從政治、經濟、環境三個角度敘述「核能發電廠」的優缺點。

寫作前的兩大功課

看完了寫作的三大最高指導原則，最後讓我們來瞧瞧寫作前務必要做的兩大功課。或許你會問：

「咦，寫作不就是拿起一枝筆，根據題目，從第一句拼命寫到最後一句嗎？為什麼寫作前還要做功課咧??」

事實上，這兩個寫作前的功課比起真正動筆寫作來說，重要性不遑多讓，甚至有過之而無不及呢！為什麼呢？因為你只要寫作前花點時間確實將這兩個功課做足，不僅可以讓你的文章有邏

輯性、結構性，還可以輕易解決「文章寫不長」的問題呢！

功課一：畫圖法（Mapping/Diagramming）

在你動筆寫作之前，必須先用「畫圖法」來幫助自己構思文章。怎麼進行畫圖法呢？首先請你找一張比較大的白紙，然後在紙的正中間畫個圈圈，寫下作文的主題，再將腦中出現的與題目有關的所有字詞寫下來，並將這些字、詞彼此間的關聯性，分成一叢一叢的。這種方法的好處是可以讓你很清楚的看出不同想法間不同的關聯。你可以從這些像是大樹枝幹的叢集中找出最多枝幹的（即代表你可以想出最多點子的），將之發展成一個段落，甚至是一篇文章。對於那些畫不出什麼圈圈的枝幹，就可以捨棄不用。

以下是一張利用「畫圖法」，根據作文題目 "Weight Loss"（減肥）而來的圖表：

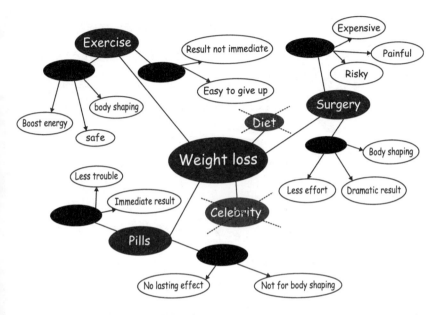

　　從上圖可知,「畫圖法」既清楚又明白,可以幫助我們在寫作前整理滿腦子內雜亂的思緒。另外,由圖可知,寫作者對於「運動」、「吃藥」、「手術」減肥方式的好壞處了解較多,也較有想法,而對於「減肥名人」及「飲食減肥法」則所知不多,所以當動筆寫文章時,就應將重點方向擺在「運動、吃藥、手術減肥方式的好壞處」方面。

功課二:列大綱(Outlining)

　　你在運用了上述的構思方法後,應該已經對所要寫的題目有許許多多的想法及點子,這時候便可以開始進入第二個功課:列大綱。

　　「大綱」(outline)是什麼呢?我們可以把文章的大綱想成支

撑人體的骨架。骨架負責將我們龐大的身軀撐起，讓我們經由透視對身體內部一目了然，也使內部的器官得以各居其位、各司其職。文章的大綱也有這種作用；由於它次序井然，因此可以幫助我們了解整篇文章的組織結構，對於較長或較複雜的文章尤其有幫助。

　　以上面的「**減肥**」為例，在做完功課一「畫圖法」之後，我們便可以依此列出大綱：

1. Exercise（運動）

　　(1) advantages（好處）

　　　　a. safe（安全）

　　　　b. good for body shaping（有助改善身體曲線）

　　　　c. boost energy and overall health（有助於精神提振及整體健康）

　　(2) drawbacks（缺點）

　　　　a. result not immediate（成果非隨即可見）

　　　　b. easy to give up（不易持之以恆）

　　　　c. hard to find time and space（很難找到合適的時間、空間從事運動）

2. Taking pills（吃藥）

　　(1) advantages（好處）

　　　　a. less trouble（方便、不麻煩）

b. immediate result（成果立即可見）

c. no time and space limitation（沒有時、空的限制）

(2) drawbacks（缺點）

a. harmful to health in the long run（長期對身體可能有害）

b. no long lasting effect（效果無法持久）

c. not for body shaping（無助於改善身體曲線）

3. Surgery（手術）

(1) advantages（好處）

a. dramatic result（效果明顯）

b. less effort（較不需額外費心）

c. good for body shaping（有助改善身體曲線）

(2) drawbacks（缺點）

a. expensive（昂貴）

b. risky（危險性高）

c. painful recovery after surgery（術後復原過程艱辛）

由此可知，藉由「畫圖法」而來的大綱雖然有點複雜，卻很有層次性，條理也超分明，有了這麼清楚的大綱，我們再開始下筆寫作，你說，寫出來的文章怎麼可能沒有章法呢！

最後，讓我們將這個大綱放回去我們一開始提到的「三段式」結構中，再加上適合的「題目」、「導論」、「結論」，便是一篇天下無雙、宇宙無敵的文章了！

題目：Three Common Ways of Losing Weight

導論

(命題句) In my opinion, there are both advantages and drawbacks in the three common ways of losing weight: exercise, taking pills, and surgery.

內文

(主題句一) There are both good and bad aspects in doing exercise to lose weight.

(支持細節)

(1) advantages:

    a. safe

    b. good for body shaping

    c. boost energy and overall health

(2) drawbacks:

    a. result not immediate

    b. easy to give up

    c. hard to find time and space

（主題句二）The advantages and disadvantages of taking pills for losing weight are as follows:

（支持細節）

(1) advantages:

　　a. less trouble

　　b. immediate result

　　c. no time and space limitation

(2) drawbacks

　　a. harmful to health in the long run

　　b. no long lasting effect

　　c. not for body shaping

（主題句三）Having liposuction has its strong and weak points in losing weight.

（支持細節）

(1) advantages:

　　a. dramatic result

　　b. less effort

　　c. good for body shaping

(2) drawbacks:

　　a. expensive

　　b. risky

　　c. painful recovery after surgery

結論

（摘要或其他方式的結尾）

　　其實若依照這樣一篇結構完整的大綱所寫出來的文章，其字數肯定在好幾百字以上、甚至上千字，因此畫圖法、列大綱不僅可以幫助我們寫得更有條理，還可以讓我們文章越寫越長，甚至到了欲罷不能的地步！

　　當然，如果你平日只需寫一、兩百字的「段落文章」，則可以把上面文章中的內文某一段抽出來單獨寫，例如專寫「運動減肥的好壞處」，一樣可以是篇條理分明的好短文喔：

導論

　　(命題句)There are both good and bad aspects in doing exercise to lose weight.

內文

　　(主題句)(1) The advantages of doing exercise to lose weight are as follows:

　　(支持細節)

　　a. safe

　　b. good for body shaping

　　c. boost energy and overall health

　　(主題句)(2) The drawbacks of doing exercise to lose weight are as follows:

　　(支持細節)

　　a. result not immediate

　　b. easy to give up

　　c. hard to find time and space

結論

閱讀與寫作

在這本書中，我們談了很多關於英文寫作的技巧及範例。最後要提醒你的是，在英文「聽」、「說」、「讀」、「寫」的四個技巧中，「讀」與「寫」就像雙胞胎一般關係緊密、不可分割。

因此我們可以說，「要怎麼閱讀、便那麼寫；要怎麼寫、便那麼閱讀」！

為什麼呢？因為如果你閱讀的東西越多，寫作時能從閱讀那裡「偷」到的句型、單字也越多。這些東西或許不是有意識偷到的，但所有很會寫作的人都可以作證：他們「嗜讀成痴」！我一些英文作文寫得很好的學生也可以作證：「有時候我下筆時，會莫名其妙的寫出一些連我自己都確定沒背過的精采句子，努力想才想起，啊，原來是前幾天在某篇文章中看到的句型！」

在接下來的35篇範文中，我們除了在每篇文章中標示段落的主題句，還附上單字、片語的解說及例句，並詳細分析解釋每篇的難句，讓你閱讀、寫作能力齊頭並進。每篇文章最後面的造句練習除了可以幫你複習文章中的重要句型及單字，也很適合當作目前大學入學考試學力測驗與指定考試翻譯題的練習。

事不宜遲，現在就讓我們為增進自己的閱讀與寫作能力努力！

東西節慶

新年新願望
New Year's Resolutions

　　過去幾年，台灣社會不斷在內耗中削弱力量：政府官員貪污腐化、政治人物輕忽誠信、政黨對立惡鬥、經濟走向窒息。曾高居「亞洲四小龍」之首的台灣，現在的地位已岌岌可危。

　　而在台灣無止盡的內耗同時，世界已經風起雲湧。台灣長久以來最大的敵人「中國」，已在和平中崛起；日本已從九○年代泡沫經濟破滅中站起來，經濟復甦的步伐穩健；「金磚四國」中的印度已成為IT委外重鎮，電腦軟體出口的規模世界第一；而「歐盟」已成為全世界前三大經濟體，在當地及國際事務中占有重要角色。

　　處於這樣一個一不小心便可能被「邊緣化」的全球化體系裡，台灣選擇「自欺欺人」地閉上眼睛、搗起耳朵，卻不知道自己已像是在熱水裡游泳的青蛙，再不警覺，很快便會燙死。

　　什麼？你問我新年的新願望是什麼？那當然是青蛙趕快變王子，跳出這一片「水深火熱」囉！

New Year's Resolutions (CD1-1)

The year 2005 was a year of **turbulence**. The world was plagued with a series of **terrorist attacks**. The number of **casualties** in the US war against Iraq was **incalculable**. The threat of a bird flu **pandemic looms** like a large shadow over the world. **Global** climate change is becoming even more **irregular**, causing **droughts** and floods everywhere... ❶

In spite of everything, the New Year is still exciting! You may choose to join tourists from all over the globe in a **countdown** in front of **Times Square**, or observe the first **sunrise** in New Zealand. You may also watch the fireworks display from the world's tallest building, Taipei 101, or join friends in **revelry** and attend New Year's Eve **festivities**. ❷

The New Year is also a time to make resolutions. Some people may have more **personal** resolutions such as losing weight, getting into college, getting **promoted**, or keeping healthy. At the same time, others may have **nobler** resolutions such as wishing for a **prosperous** and safe country, **favorable** weather, or world peace. No matter what your resolutions are, hope will make your dreams come true. HAPPY NEW YEAR!

新年新願望

2005年是個不平靜的年。世界各地恐怖攻擊事件不斷、美伊戰爭下的伊拉克死傷無數、禽流感威脅的陰影籠罩全球、各地氣候更加異常，乾旱、水患處處可見……。

不論如何，新的一年仍舊令人感到興奮！你可以在美國時代廣場前與來自全球的旅客齊聲倒數、到紐西蘭迎接新年第一道曙光、在全世界第一高樓台北101觀賞煙火，或是與朋友狂歡共飲、參加跨年晚會……。

新年也是大家許下新願望的時候。有些人的願望比較自我：減肥、考上大學、升遷、身體健康……；有些人的願望則比較崇高：國泰民安、風調雨順、世界和平。不管你的願望為何，有希望便會夢想成真。祝大家新年快樂！

主題句：　　　　單字：**加黑**　　片語：套色　　句型：❶❷

單字例句 ▶

◇ **resolution**(n.)決心；目標
You should not back down from your resolution.
你不該下了決心後退縮。

◇ **turbulence**(n.)騷亂
The terrorists caused turbulence worldwide.
恐怖份子在全世界造成了動亂。

◇ **terrorist attack** 恐怖攻擊

◇ **casualty**(n.)死傷(者)
Our aim is to reduce highway casualties.
我們的目標是要減少公路死傷。

◇ **incalculable**(adj.)無法計數的
The country suffered incalculable losses during the storm.
暴風雨期間這國家遭受無法計數的損失。

◇ **pandemic**(n.)(大規模的)流行病
One pandemic of Spanish flu took 22 million lives worldwide.
一場西班牙流感奪走了全球2200萬人的性命。

◇ **loom**(v.)(危險)迫近
A great black cloud looms over the city.
一朵大烏雲迫近城市。

◇ **global**(adj.)地球的；全球的
Obesity has become a serious global issue.

肥胖症已成為全球一個嚴重的問題。

◇ **irregular**(**adj.**)不合常規的
He worked irregular hours.
他工作時間不正常。

◇ **drought**(**n.**)乾旱
The drought kept the plants from growing.
乾旱使得植物無法生長。

◇ **countdown**(**n.**)倒數
The crowd gathered in the square for the final countdown.
群眾聚集在廣場做最後倒數計時。

◇ **Times Square** 紐約「時代廣場」

◇ **sunrise**(**n.**)日出
People flock to Mt. Jade to see the sunrise.
人們群聚到玉山看日出。

◇ **revelry**(**n.**)飲酒狂歡
The party crowd stayed up all night in wild revelry.
這舞會的人徹夜飲酒狂歡。

◇ **festivities**(**n.**)(複數)慶典；祝宴
The festivities went on all through the week.
這慶祝活動持續了一個禮拜。

◇ **personal**(**adj.**)私人的
The actor refused to answer any personal questions.
這演員拒絕回答任何私人問題。

◇ **promote**(**v.**)昇級；擢陞

His greatest wish for the New Year is to get promoted to regional manager.

他最大的新年願望是擢升為區經理。

◇ **noble**(**adj.**)清高的；高貴的

He is doing this for a noble cause.

他基於崇高的理想做這件事。

◇ **prosperous**(**adj.**)繁榮的

The prosperous little town attracts visitors from all over.

這個繁榮的小鎮吸引了各地的遊客。

◇ **favorable**(**adj.**)有幫助的；合適的

The hot weather is favorable to her plans.

這炎熱的天氣對她的計畫有幫助。

片　語 ▶

◇ **be plagued with... :**

plague(v.)是「折磨；得到災禍」，be plagued with... 是被動語式，意思是「被……所折磨」，例如：Our apartment is plagued with mosquitoes.(我們公寓深受蚊子之苦)。

◇ **war against... :**

against 是介系詞，意為「反對；反抗」，war against... 是「反抗……的戰爭」，例如：We're in war against terrorism.(我們在

打一場反恐戰爭)。

✧ **in spite of... :**
in spite of 是個慣用的片語，意為「雖然……；儘管……」，例
如：In spite of all his efforts, the enterprise ended in failure.(儘管
他竭盡全力，事業依然以失敗收場)。

✧ **in front of... :**
in front of...是「在……之前」之意，例如：He stood in front of
the teacher's desk.(他站在老師的桌子前)。

✧ **no matter what :**
no matter 是「不論……」，not matter what 則是「無論什
麼……」，例如：No matter what they say, don't do it.(不管他們
說什麼，別照做)。

句型分析 ▶

1. Global climate change is becoming even more irregular,
   causing droughts and floods everywhere.

   ◆ 這句話的主詞是 global climate change，主要動詞是 is
   becoming。句子逗點後面的 causing(造成……)原形為
   cause，意思是「引起」，不過因這句話已有主要動詞 is
   becoming，所以 cause 需「去動詞化」，變成 V+-ing。

   ◆ even more...是「更加……」之意。

2. You may also watch the fireworks display from the world's

tallest building, Taipei 101, or join friends in revelry and attend New Year's Eve festivities.

◆ 這句話的主詞是 you，主要動詞是 may (1) watch... or (2) join... and attend...，兩個動詞用「對等連接詞」or 連接。後面的另一個「對等連接詞」and 乃連接 join 與 attend 這兩個動詞 (加入……且參加……)。

◆ 句中的 Taipei 101 是當 the world's tallest building 的同位語。revelry (n.) 是「飲酒狂歡」，join friends in revelry 則是「加入朋友一起狂歡作樂」。

造句練習 ▶

1. 你的新年新希望是什麼？(New Year's resolutions)

----

2. 她的生活受到許多問題的折磨。(be plagued with...)

----

3. 恐怖攻擊造成廣大的恐慌。(terrorist attack / alarm)

----

4. 水災奪走了許多條性命。(flood)

----

5. 煙火表演奇妙地融合了不同的形狀與顏色。（fireworks display）

- -

2

吃尾牙囉！
It's Time for the Year-End Dinner!

　　說到尾牙，老一輩的人記憶最深的就是尾牙宴上的那隻雞頭。在以前那個工作不好找的年代，在寒冷的冬天被一隻雞頭對著，的確是蠻恐怖的一件事。不過時代在變，以前是老闆挑員工，現在則是員工挑老闆，因此許多公司紛紛祭出各項利多，以吸引員工上門。美國有許多大公司，便容許員工選擇在家或者在辦公室工作，這種辦公方式稱之為 flexplace（又稱為 flexiplace 或 flex-place）。現在網路如此發達，很多公司也推出 office-free（無辦公室）的制度，讓員工在家舒舒服服辦公，然後在一定時間內將成果透過網路傳回公司。

　　另外有些公司體認到「加班是企業不能避免的惡」，因此貼心地在公司裡弄個 nap nook（小歇角落），讓員工在超時工作之餘進去小憩一番，實踐「休息是為了走更長遠的路」的崇高理念。

　　不過這樣還不誇張，Google 位於美國加州 Mountain View 的總部，不僅公司占地廣大、建築新穎，對員工的福利也是樣樣不缺。據說 Google 提供員工早、中兩餐免費餐點，公司裡還有駐診的牙醫與家庭醫師，就連請育嬰假的員工也可照領四分之三的薪水，而且公司還發揮中國人的精神，補助員工「坐月子津貼」呢！怎麼樣，是不是很令人心動呢？

It's Time for the Year-End Dinner!

According to Taiwanese **customs**, the "year-end dinner" is the last chance to **worship** the **Earth God** before the year ends. It is also the time of the year when company owners reward their employees with **delicacies**. Families in Taiwan also enjoy **spring rolls** and **steamed sandwiches**, which **symbolize blessings** for the year to come and reward for their hard work.

In the past, employees were most afraid of the chicken head pointing straight at them during year-end dinners because this signified they were about to be fired. ❶ But as more and more employees have taken part in the **job-hopping craze** over the past few years, it is now the employers' turn to worry that their employees might say **farewell** to the company after having the year-end **feast** and receiving their **year-end bonus**!

High-tech companies have been turning in very **impressive** sales reports in recent years, and they hold big-time year-end dinners. Aside from **extravagant cuisine**, the events would also feature **variety shows** with movie and TV celebrities, **abundant raffle drawings**, and **generous** stock **giveaways**. ❷ But ever since the companies were accused of "earning much and paying little in taxes," the word is that these companies are planning to keep a low profile in their **gatherings** this year!

吃尾牙囉！

按照台灣習俗，「尾牙」是一年結束前最後一次祭拜土地公的日子，也是公司行號的老闆用佳餚犒賞員工的時候。在台灣，一般家庭也會在當天晚上吃潤餅和刈包，象徵來年祈福及慰勞自己。

以往吃尾牙的時候，員工最怕宴席上對準自己的雞頭，因為這意味著自己即將被炒魷魚。不過這幾年因為跳槽風氣盛，現在老闆們反而擔心員工們在吃完尾牙大餐、領完年終獎金後，就跟公司說拜拜！

這幾年高科技公司業績大好，每年的尾牙都很大手筆。除了豪華的菜色，還有影視明星的綜藝秀、豐富的抽獎活動，以及慷慨的股票大放送。不過自從有人高聲批評科技業「賺錢多、繳稅少」後，今年據說許多科技業者都打算低調舉行尾牙宴呢！

主題句： 　　　　單字：加黑　　　片語：套色　　　句型：❶❷

單字例句 ▶

◇ **year-end dinner** 尾牙

◇ **custom**(n.)習俗
Age-old customs are difficult to change.
古老的習俗很難改變。

◇ **worship**(v.)祭拜；尊敬
People go to temples to worship the gods.
人們到廟裡祭拜神。

◇ **Earth God** 土地公

◇ **delicacy** [ˋdɛləkəsɪ](n.)佳餚
People in Taipei like to enjoy all sorts of delicacies.
台北人喜歡享受各式的美食佳餚。

◇ **spring roll** 潤餅；春捲

◇ **steamed sandwich** 刈包

◇ **symbolize**(v.)象徵
A bird soaring in the sky symbolizes freedom.
在天空遨翔的鳥象徵著自由。

◇ **blessing**(n.)恩惠；祝福
It is a blessing to have friends and family nearby.
有朋友與家人在身旁的人是有福氣的。

◇ **job-hopping craze** 跳槽風（盛行）

◇ **farewell**(n.)離別；告別辭
The woman bade farewell to her friends.
這名女子與朋友道別。

◇ **feast**(n.)大餐；盛宴
The people stared hungrily at the feast before them.
人們飢餓地盯著眼前的大餐。

◇ **year-end bonus 年終獎金**
The biggest joy of the season is when we receive our year-end bonuses.
這季最令我們歡欣的是拿到年終獎金之時。

◇ **impressive**(adj.)令人印象深刻的
The museum has an impressive display of artwork.
這博物館的藝術品展示令人印象深刻。

◇ **extravagant**(adj.)奢侈豐盛的
The dress she has on is very extravagant.
她身上所穿的衣服非常的奢華。

◇ **cuisine** [kwɪˋzin](n.)菜餚
We enjoyed the wonderful cuisine served at the restaurant.
我們享受著餐館所提供的絕佳菜餚。

◇ **variety** [vəˋraɪətɪ]**show 綜藝節目**

◇ **abundant**(adj.)豐富的
Bananas are abundant in tropical countries.
熱帶國家盛產香蕉。

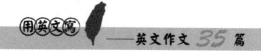

◇ **raffle drawing 抽獎**
The company holds a raffle drawing for its employees every year.
這公司每年為員工舉辦抽獎活動。

◇ **generous (adj.) 大方的**
The boss is very generous when it comes to handing out bonuses.
這老闆發放紅利時十分大方。

◇ **giveaway (n.) 贈品；免費贈送**
Everyone was very excited about the giveaway.
大家都對這免費的贈品十分興奮。

◇ **gathering (n.) 聚會**
The students had a gathering before school started.
學生們在開學前舉辦了個聚會。

片　語　▶

◇ **reward... with... :**
reward (v.) 是「酬謝」，reward... with... 就是「用……犒賞……」，例如：Alice rewarded her son with money. (Alice 用錢獎賞孩子)。

◇ **take part in :**
take part in... 是個常見的片語，意指「參加……；貢獻於……」，

例如：They all took part in the fund-raising event.(他們全都參加了募款的活動)。

◇ **someone's turn：**
turn(n.)是「輪流；順序」，someone's turn 則是「輪到……」，例如：It's your turn to wash the dishes.(輪到你洗碗了)。

◇ **turn in：**
turn in 這裡是「提交(文件；辭呈等)」，例如：She turned in her resignation today.(她今天提交辭呈)。

◇ **be accused of...：**
accuse(v.)是「控訴；譴責」，accuse... of...是「指責……；控訴……」，例如：She accused him of lying.(她指責他撒謊)。這裡的 be accused of...是被動語態，意為「被譴責為……；被控訴為……」，例如：He was accused of murder. (他被控謀殺)。

◇ **keep a low profile：**
profile(n.)是「輪廓；外型」，keep a low profile 則是「保持低調；有節制」之意，例如：Be sure to keep a low profile when traveling abroad.(到國外旅遊時記得保持低調)。

句型分析 ▶

1. In the past, employees were most afraid of the chicken head pointing straight at them during year-end dinners because this signified they were about to be fired.

◆ 這句話的主詞是 employees，主要動詞是 were afraid。後面的 because 引導「副詞子句」，用來說明原因。

◆ be afraid of...是「害怕……」，be most afraid of...則是「最害怕……」。point at... 是「對準……」，point straight at... 則為「直直地對準……」。

◆ 句中 signify(v.)是「意味；表示」。

◆ about 在這裡是副詞，意思為「即將……」，故 be about to be fired 是「即將被開除」。

2. Aside from extravagant cuisine, the events would also feature variety shows with movie and TV celebrities, abundant raffle drawings, and generous stock giveaways.

◆ 這句話的主詞是 the events，主要動詞是 would feature(會以……為特色)。這裡用「對等連接詞」and 列出三個主要的特色：(1)variety shows with movie and TV celebrities(2)abundant raffle drawings(3)generous stock giveaways。

◆ 句首的 Aside from... 是「除了……；除……之外加上；暫且撇開……不談」，這裡的 Aside from extravagant cuisine... 是「除了豐盛的菜餚外……」。

造句練習 ▶

1. 警察獎賞這個在路上發現錢、並且交給警察的人。（reward / turn in the money）

   ----

2. 這人將箭瞄準靶心。（aim at / bull's-eye）

   ----

3. 企業界最大的問題之一就是跳槽風的盛行。（job-hopping craze）

   ----

4. 週末時我們通常待在家觀賞綜藝節目。（stay home / variety show）

   ----

5. 這女演員試著保持低調。（keep a low profile）

農曆新年
Lunar New Year Holidays

　　說到過舊曆年，相信許多老一輩的人都會感嘆：台灣的「年味」越來越淡薄了！記得小時候過年，最期待的除了新衣新帽及紅包，還有一家子老老少少圍爐、擲骰子的熱鬧感。那時到處都有人放鞭炮，而且無論在哪個角落，都會聽到那「恭喜恭喜恭喜你呀」的新年歌。

　　現在則不同了。鞭炮不一定要放，大掃除不一定要自己掃，拜年不一定要親自登門，「團圓飯」不一定要在家裡吃，連「年」都不一定要在家過！

　　不過「新式的舊曆年」也未嘗不好，因為少了鞭炮聲，耳根至少清靜些；有了「鐘點清潔服務」，至少媽媽們不用為了掃除而累得半死；不用買見面禮，手機簡訊拜年既經濟又實惠；團圓飯在大飯店吃，既促進台灣經濟活動，又省掉婆婆媽媽的辛勞，實在一舉兩得！

Lunar New Year Holidays (CD1-3)

Taiwanese people are very **fortunate** in that they can celebrate New Year's Day twice a year, at both the **Gregorian New Year** and the **Lunar New Year**. In the past, very few Taiwanese celebrated the Gregorian New Year by staying up late on December 31 to count down to the New Year.

On the other hand, the Lunar New Year has been celebrated much more: **couplets** are seen on every door, and **firecrackers** are set off everywhere. New clothes and hats are also worn at this time of year. On Chinese New Year's Eve, all the members of the family gather to enjoy a **reunion dinner**, while **red envelopes** are given by the elders to the young ones. Children are told to **utter auspicious** words. Also, everyone gathers around to stay up late to welcome in the New Year.

However, as we enter the **millennium**, Taiwanese, who are **enthusiastic** by nature, are starting to celebrate the Gregorian New Year in **frenzied excitement** along with the rest of the world. ❶ The **spirit** of the Lunar New Year, on the contrary, is growing **dimmer** every year. Who knows— maybe in the coming years, our children and **grandchildren** may think that the true **essence** of the "New Year's Eve Party" is staying up late to bring in the new year, and that the **deafening** sounds of **cheering** and the colorful display of fireworks at the party are **produced** to scare away a **monster** known as "Nian" of the Gregorian year! ❷

農曆新年

幸福的台灣人每年可以過兩次新年：新曆年及舊曆年。過去很少台灣人會在12月31日的晚上熬夜不睡，迎接新曆年。

相反的，舊曆年則大大慶祝：家家戶戶貼春聯、放鞭炮、穿新衣、戴新帽。除夕時，全家會吃團圓飯，大人會發紅包給小孩子，小孩子則被要求講吉祥話，然後大家聚在一起守歲，迎接新的一年到來。

不過自從千禧年以後，天性熱情的台灣人開始跟著全世界一起瘋狂慶祝新曆年。舊曆年的氣氛反而一年比一年淡薄。誰知道？或許多年後，我們的子孫會以為新曆年的「跨年晚會」是為了守歲，而晚會上震耳欲聾的人群歡呼聲及五光十色的慶祝煙火，則是為了嚇走一種叫做「年」的怪獸！

主題句：　　　　　單字：加黑　　　片語：套色　　　句型：❶❷

單字例句 ▶

◇ **fortunate**(**adj.**)幸運的
We are fortunate enough to have a bed to sleep in.
我們很幸運有床可以睡。

◇ (**Gregorian / Western**)**New Year** 新曆年；新年

◇ **Lunarl / Chinese New Year** 舊曆年

◇ **couplet**(**n.**)對句，門聯
Couplets can usually be seen hanging from people's doors.
人們門上時常可見懸掛的對聯。

◇ **firecracker**(**n.**)鞭炮
The sound of firecrackers can be heard during the Chinese New Year holidays.
在舊曆年假期間常可聽見鞭炮聲。

◇ **reunion dinner** 團圓飯；年夜飯

◇ **red envelope** 紅包
Children look forward to receiving red envelopes from their elders.
小孩子們很期待從長輩那裡收到紅包。

◇ **utter**(**v.**)說出
The boy uttered his thanks and immediately ran away.
這男孩說了聲謝謝就馬上跑開了。

◇ **auspicious**(adj.)吉利的；吉祥的
I'm pleased that you've made such an auspicious start to the new semester.
我很高興你新學期就有個吉利的開始。

◇ **millennium** [mɪˈlɛnɪəm](n.)一千年的時間；千禧年
Babies born in 2000 are otherwise known as "millennium babies."
在西元2000年出生的寶寶又稱為「千禧寶寶」。

◇ **enthusiastic**(adj.)熱情的
The little girl is enthusiastic about starting school.
這小女孩很熱切地盼望上課。

◇ **frenzied** [ˈfrɛnzɪd](adj.)狂熱的
The frenzied crowd threw eggs at the stage.
狂熱的群眾將雞蛋投擲到台上。

◇ **excitement**(n.)興奮
Because of all the excitement, they forgot about the time.
他們興奮到把時間都忘了。

◇ **spirit**(n.)精神
People got into the holiday spirit and partied to their heart's content.
人們沈浸在假日的氛圍裡，狂歡到盡興為止。

◇ **dim**(adj.)暗淡的
I couldn't recognize anybody under the dim light.
在暗淡的燈光下，我認不出任何人。

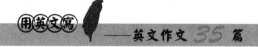
◇ **grandchild**(n.)孫子

The woman loves her first grandchild tremendously.

這女人超愛她的長孫。

◇ **essence** [ˈɛsn̩s](n.)本質

The true essence of the holiday is lost in all the merrymaking.

在盡情歡樂中，節日的本質被遺忘了。

◇ **deafening**(adj.)震耳欲聾的

A deafening noise silenced the crowd.

突來的一陣巨響讓群眾鴉雀無聲。

◇ **cheering**(n.)歡呼

Loud cheering reached my ears as I neared the building.

當我接近這建築物時，響亮的歡呼聲傳到耳中。

◇ **produce**(v.)製造；產生

The company produced several new products this year.

這公司今年生產了幾種新產品。

◇ **monster**(n.)怪物

Children are afraid of monsters under the bed.

小孩子都很怕床底下的怪獸。

片　語　▶

◇ **stay up :**

stay(v.)是「停留；留」，stay up 是「熬夜不睡」，例如：She

stayed up reading all night long.(她徹夜未眠地念書)。

◇ **set off：**

set off 這個片語有多種意義，這裡是「燃放……；發射……；引爆」，例如：The man set off the bomb.(這男人引爆炸彈)。

◇ **by nature：**

nature(n.)是「自然，本質」，by nature 是「生來；天生；生性」，例如：She is artistic by nature.(她生來就具有藝術氣息)。

◇ **on the contrary：**

contrary(n.)是「相反」之意，on the contrary 是強調反對剛剛所說的事，即「相反地；正相反」，例如：It wasn't a good thing; on the contrary, it was a huge mistake.(這不是件好事，相反的，它是個大錯誤)。

句型分析 ▶

1. However, as we enter the millennium, Taiwanese, who are enthusiastic by nature, are starting to celebrate the Gregorian New Year in frenzied excitement along with the rest of the world.

   ◆ 這句話的主詞是 Taiwanese，主要動詞是 are starting。句首的 However是「語氣轉折詞」，表示目前這句話與上面的那句話在語義上相反。

◆ 句中的 as... 是「當……；正當……」。who... 為「關係代名詞」，代替前面的 Taiwanese，形容「台灣人」的樣貌是 enthusiastic by nature，這裡的 by nature 是「天性」，意思是說「台灣人的天性熱情」。

◆ excitement(n.)是「興奮」，in frenzied excitement 則是「狂熱的興奮」。along with... 是「與……一起；伴隨……」，along with the rest of the world 是「與全世界一起」。

2. Who knows—maybe in the coming years, our children and grandchildren may think that the true essence of the "New Year's Eve Party" is staying up late to bring in the new year, and that the deafening sounds of cheering and the colorful display of fireworks at the party are produced to scare away a monster known as "Nian" of the Gregorian year!

◆ 這句話的主詞是 our children and grandchildren，主要動詞是 may think。that 後面引導的子句則是所「認為」的東西，這裡主詞認為的東西有兩個，用「對等連接詞」and 連接：(1)the true essence of the "New Year's Eve Party" is staying up late to bring in the new year (2)the deafening sounds of cheering and the colorful display of fireworks at the party are produced to scare away a monster known as "Nian" of the Gregorian year。

◆ 句首的 Who knows 是插入語，意為「誰知道？」

◆ essence(n.)是「本質」，the essence of...是「……的本質」，the true essence of... is...則為「……的真正的本質是……」。stay up late 是「晚睡；熬夜」。bring in...是「帶進來……」。

♦ scare(v)是「驚嚇」，scare away...是「把……嚇跑」。known as...是「以……著稱；以……為人所知」，所以a monster known as "Nian" 是「一隻名叫『年』的怪獸」。

造句練習 ▶

1. 學生通常熬夜準備考試。(stay up late)

----

2. 恐怖分子威脅如果政府不合作，他們就要引爆炸彈。(threaten / set off the bomb)

----

3. 人們在舊曆年假期與家人聚在一起吃團圓飯。(reunion dinner)

----

4. 他本性害羞且安靜。(by nature)

----

5. 這隻狗試著嚇跑陌生人。(scare away)

4

青年節與草莓族
Youth Day and the Strawberry Generation

在美國，一般人習慣以英文字母稱呼不同世代的人，例如 Generation X（X世代；指介於1965年至1977年出生的人）、Generation Y（Y世代；指1978年後出生的年輕世代）、Generation D（D世代；又稱為 Digital Generation，指的是超會用電腦及高科技數位產品的年輕世代）等。在日本，這幾年也流行所謂的freeter（飛特族），指的是沒有專長，選擇以打零工、兼職的方式度日的年輕人。因這種人口有快速增加的趨勢，許多日本專家預料會成為日本一項嚴重的社會經濟問題。

不知從何時開始，台灣也開始流行以「X年級生」或「X年X班」來稱呼不同年次的人，一時之間全國人民好像都成了校友般，互相有關係，親密得很。之後又有人以「新新人類」、「XYZ世代」、「e世代」、「水蜜桃」、「草莓族」、「卡債族」等名稱對特定族群貼以標籤。

因為工作關係，我每天接觸到的都是許多大人眼裡的「草莓族」。令我驚奇的是，有些「草莓」雖然真的不耐操，也很脆弱，可是有更多「草莓」卻聰明活潑，既肯努力，也充滿創意。這些「草莓」知道自己背負的 original sin（原罪），個個都奮發圖強，要讓看扁他們的大人眼睛一亮。這些「草莓」不但好看，也好吃，端看我們社會願不願意摒除刻板印象，給他們機會表現。「草莓」加油！

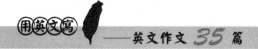

Youth Day and the Strawberry Generation (CD1-4)

March 29 is Youth Day, which serves to **commemorate** the lives of the **revolutionary** youth that were lost in the Guangzhou **Uprising**. Each year during this time, the government **honors** Ten Outstanding Youths and holds a series of youth-related **festivities**.

Speaking of which, today's youth have been **branded as** the "strawberry generation," to which many people would shake their heads and **heave** a sigh. ❶ And why not? The so-called "**Generation M**" loves pleasure, has low **resistance** and **stability**, and values personal interests over other people's **judgments**. They are just like strawberries: they look great on the outside but cannot **withstand** pressure, difficulties, and **frustration**.

As a matter of fact, who has not at one time been **viewed** by the earlier generation as being part of a "strawberry generation?" The following generation may not be any worse than the previous one, even though they may **uphold** different work ethics and values. Perhaps "strawberry" does not actually **pertain to** a single generation, but rather a **phase** that every person has to pass through! ❷ Such being the case, why don't we provide our youth with a little more **encouragement** and **appreciation**?

青年節與草莓族

3月29日是青年節，目的是為了紀念在「廣州起義」犧牲性命的革命青年。每年到了這個時候，政府會表揚「十大傑出青年」，並舉辦各種青少年相關的慶祝活動。

不過談起這一代被稱為「草莓族」的青年，很多人可能要搖頭嘆息。可不是嗎？這些所謂的「行動世代」重視享樂、抗壓性低、穩定度也低、只重視個人利益，不管他人看法……，就如同草莓一般，空有亮麗的外表，卻不耐風吹雨打。

其實，每個人在上一代人的眼中，不也都曾是「草莓族」？下一代不見得比上一代來得差，只不過擁有不同的工作觀與價值觀。或許「草莓」不是一個世代，而是每個人在一生中都必須經歷的一個階段罷了！既然如此，我們為何不給現在的年輕人多一點鼓勵及讚賞的眼光？

主題句：　　　　單字：加黑　　片語：套色　　句型：❶❷

單字例句 ▶

◇ **Youth Day** 青年節

◇ **strawberry generation** 草莓族

◇ **commemorate**(v.)紀念；表揚
We celebrate this day to commemorate the brave soldiers.
我們慶祝這一天，以紀念英勇的士兵們。

◇ **revolutionary**(adj.)革命的
The revolutionary improvement changed the course of history.
這革命性的進步改變了歷史的軌跡。

◇ **uprising**(n.)革命；叛變
There were many uprisings due to improper treatment.
因為處置不當，發生了許多次叛變。

◇ **honor** [ˋɑnɚ](v.)給予榮譽
You have to honor the vows you have made.
你必須遵守發下的誓言。

◇ **festivities**(n.)(複數)慶典；祝宴
There are a lot of festivities that promote the development of culture.
有很多慶典是用來促進文化的發展。

◇ **brand as...** 加註……(不好的)的名稱

◇ **heave**(v.)發出(嘆息)

He heaved a sigh of relief.
他放鬆地吐了一口氣。

◇ **Generation M** 「行動世代」；即 **Mobile Generation**

◇ **resistance**(n.)抵抗力
A poor diet lowers your resistance to illness.
不良的飲食降低你對疾病的抵抗力。

◇ **stability**(n.)穩定性
Stability in a relationship promotes mutual confidence.
穩定的關係有助提升彼此的信心。

◇ **judgment**(n.)意見；批評
Don't let your judgment be blinded by personal bias.
別讓個人偏見蒙蔽你的評判。

◇ **withstand**(v.)抵擋
Their love will withstand all the challenges life may bring.
他們的愛將能抵擋生活帶來的所有挑戰。

◇ **frustration**(n.)挫折；失敗
Don't let your frustrations get in the way of your future.
別讓你的挫折阻擋了你的未來。

◇ **view**(v.)看待；將……看成是
The foreigners view the local people as uncivilized beings.
這些外國人將當地居民視為不文明的人。

◇ **uphold**(v.)支持；舉起；維護
This is a committee that aims to uphold educational standards.

這個委員會致力於維護教育水準。

◇ **pertain** [pə'ten] **to...** 有關……；適合於……

◇ **phase**（n.）階段
Please be understanding; she is going through a very difficult phase.
請諒解；她正在經歷非常困難的階段。

◇ **encouragement**（n.）鼓勵
The teacher patted him in the back for encouragement.
老師拍拍他的背當作鼓勵。

◇ **appreciation**（n.）欣賞；尊重
Show some appreciation to the people around you.
對你身邊的人表達一點尊重。

片　語　▶

◇ **serve to... :**
serve（v.）是「服務；對……有用」，serve to...是「做……用途；當……用」，例如：This car accident serves to show what drunken driving can lead to.（這次的車禍可以顯示酒醉駕車會造成何種後果）。

◇ **value... over... :**
value（v.）是「給……訂價格；重視」，value... over... 是「重視……超過……」，例如：He values money over everything

else.(他重視金錢勝過任何其他東西)。

◇ **be just like... :**
like 是介系詞，為「像……的；如同……」，be just like...是
「就好像……」，例如：She is just like her mother.(她就像她的
母親)。

◇ **as a matter of fact :**
as a matter of fact 就是 in fact，乃「事實上……；實際上……」，
例如：She's very smart. As a matter of fact, she's almost a
genius.(她非常聰明。事實上，她簡直就是個天才)。

◇ **provide... with... :**
provide(v.)是「提供」，provide...with...是「提供……；
供應……」，例如：Our hotel provides our customers with
everything.(我們旅館提供客戶任何東西)。

句型分析 ▶

1. Speaking of which, today's youth have been branded as the
   "strawberry generation," to which many people would shake
   their heads and heave a sigh.

   ◆ 這句話的主詞是 today's youth，主要動詞是 have been
   branded(已經被冠上；已經被取名)。句首 Speaking of
   which 的 which 指的是文章上一段最後提到的 Youth Day(青
   年節)，意為「說到青年節……」。

- ◆ brand 當名詞用是「商標；品牌」之意，當動詞用為「加註名稱」(通常是不太好的名稱)，這裡用的是被動語態 be branded(被冠以……；被烙印……)，後面用的介系詞為 as，為「被冠以……稱號」。

- ◆ 逗號後出現的 which 指的是前面的 strawberry generation，to which many people would...(對「草莓族」，許多人會……)，這裡人們會做的動作有二，由「對等連接詞」and 連接：(1) shake their heads (2) heave a sign。

2. Perhaps "strawberry" does not actually pertain to a single generation, but rather a phase that every person has to pass through!

- ◆ 這句話的主詞是 strawberries，主要動詞是 does not pertain to。pertain to...是「與……有關；適合於……」，句中的 does not pertain to a single generation 是「與一個單一世代無關」。

- ◆ 句中由 that 引導子句 every person has to pass through 是用來形容前面的 phase(階段)，描述這個階段是「每個人都必須經歷」的。

造句練習 ▶

1. 3月29日是青年節，政府在這天舉行許多活動。（Youth Day）

   ----

2. 草莓族據說非常脆弱及怠慢。（the strawberry generation / inattentive）

   ----

3. 這間諜被他的同志稱作叛徒。（branded as... / traitor）

   ----

4. 她的忠告適合所有世代的人。（pertain to...）

   ----

5. 身為一個警察，你必須維護法律。（uphold the law）

清明掃墓節
Tomb Sweeping Day

　　多年前我在某工專任教時，曾湊合班上的同學與美國的高中生成為 e-pal（網友），利用 email 學習彼此的語言文化。有一次遇到清明節，班上一位同學因為必須隨家人回南部掃墓，故告知筆友可能有幾天不能通信，順便將清明節放假一天的由來及咱們「慎終追遠」的精神好好的向對方宣揚了一下。

　　沒想到對方回信時滿是驚訝，無法想像自詡注重傳統、孝道的我們竟然需要「國定假日」來提醒人民定期掃墓，而且一年竟然只有「一天」去墓園，不像美國人，可以隨時在思慕過世的親人時到墓園憑弔……。

　　這封 email 對我的學生震撼頗大，也讓我對長久以來不曾仔細探究的我國「傳統」有了新的看法。深入探究後，才發現咱們有些傳統雖值得保留，有些卻也值得三思，甚至揚棄。比方說，我們的祖先雖然溫柔敦厚，卻在許多古老習俗與觀念中歧視女性，尤其是出嫁後的女性；這些「傳統」不僅直接規範限制了女性在日常生活的行為，也間接導致台灣女權的不彰。

　　真正好的「傳統」應是能與時俱進的。或許下次我們沈醉在我國「悠久的歷史傳統」當中時，也可以深刻想想，哪些傳統可留、哪些可去！

Tomb Sweeping Day (CD1-5)

Our country is blessed with a long history, and its people honor **filial piety**. **Funeral rites** for the **deceased** are also carefully attended to. In general, people **worship** their ancestors in their homes all year round, and visit the ancestor's tombs on Tomb Sweeping Day.

Since most **cemeteries** are located on hills on the **outskirts** of town in Taiwan, families usually take advantage of this opportunity to go on a family **outing** after **completing** their Tomb Sweeping Day rites. ❶ These trips make the holiday even more meaningful.

Aside from observing the **virtuous** tradition of sweeping tombs, some **outdated** traditions should also be swept out the door. For instance, **immoderate superstitious** belief in **feng shui** may lead to over-**occupation** of land, or even **unlawful** burial that may disrupt the view and **spoil** our soil and water. **Inappropriate** customs in Taiwanese tradition that impose numerous **restrictions** and **taboos** on women should also be swept away. For instance, married women are traditionally **forbidden** from worshiping their side of the ancestors on Tomb Sweeping Day and from going back to their parents' homes on Chinese New Year's Day. ❷ In addition, women tend to be excluded from participating in several important **folk-cultural activities**.

清明掃墓節

我國歷史悠久，人民注重孝道，慎終追遠。一般人除了一年到頭在家中祭拜祖先，也會在每年的清明節掃墓。

在台灣，由於許多墓園位於山上郊區，人們多會利用清掃祭拜之餘，與全家人一起出遊踏青，讓這個節日更加有意義。

不過我們在遵循掃墓的傳統美德之餘，對於長久以來一些過時的傳統，也可以一併掃除。例如對於風水的過度迷信，導致墓地占地過大，甚至濫葬，破壞了景觀與水土保持。另外在台灣的習俗中，加諸女性的種種限制及禁忌，例如出嫁的女兒不能回娘家掃墓、不能初一回娘家、不能參與許多重要民俗活動……等的陋習，應該也一併掃除！

主題句： 　　　　單字：加黑　　片語：套色　　句型：❶❷

單字例句 ▶

◇ **Tomb Sweeping Day** 清明掃墓節

◇ **filial piety** 孝道
According to Chinese tradition, filial piety is the primary duty of all children.
根據中國傳統，盡孝道是所有晚輩最主要的責任。

◇ **funeral rites**（多用複數）葬禮儀式
Funeral rites are observed all over the world.
全世界的人都舉行葬禮儀式。

◇ **deceased**（adj.）死亡的；已故的
Chinese have much respect for the deceased.
中國人對已故者有很高的崇敬。

◇ **worship**（v.）祭拜
It is believed that ancient people worshipped the sun and the moon.
一般認為古代人崇拜日月。

◇ **cemetery**（n.）墓地
We are going to the cemetery to attend a burial.
我們要去墓地參加葬禮。

◇ **outskirts**（n.）郊外；邊界
Life is much simpler in the outskirts of the city.
在城外的郊區生活簡單多了。

⬥ **outing**(**n.**)郊遊；遠足
We plan to go on an outing this weekend.
這週末我們計畫要去遠足。

⬥ **complete**(**v.**)完成
When will the railway be completed?
鐵路何時完工？

⬥ **virtuous**(**adj.**)美德的
Many people strive to live a virtuous life.
許多人努力活出高道德標準的人生。

⬥ **outdated**(**adj.**)過時的；不合時宜的
The youth of today do not believe in outdated ideas.
時下的年輕人不相信過時的觀念。

⬥ **immoderate**(**adj.**)過度的
Try not to engage yourself in immoderate work.
試著別讓自己工作過度。

⬥ **superstitious**(**adj.**)迷信的
She always puts her left shoe on first; she's superstitious about it.
她穿鞋總是先穿左腳；她很迷信這件事的。

⬥ **feng shui** 風水
I need a feng shui expert to help me arrange my furniture.
我需要風水專家幫忙安置我的家具。

⬥ **occupation**(**n.**)占有
This area is under German occupation.

這地區由德國占領。

⬦ **unlawful**(adj.)非法的；不道德的
If you see anything unlawful, report it immediately.
如果你看到任何非法情事，馬上通報。

⬦ **spoil**(v.)破壞
I don't want to spoil a perfect date.
我不想破壞一個完美的約會。

⬦ **inappropriate**(adj.)不適合的
Anybody in inappropriate attire will be escorted out.
任何穿著不合宜服裝的人會被請出去。

⬦ **restriction**(n.)限制
There are no restrictions on the number of invitations.
邀請函的數量沒有限制。

⬦ **taboo** [təˋbu](n.)禁忌
Things that are acceptable in one country may be a taboo in another.
在一個國家可以被接受的事，可能是另一個國家的禁忌。

⬦ **forbid**(v.)禁止
We strictly forbid the presence of alcohol in the church.
教堂內嚴禁酒的出現。

⬦ **folk-cultural activity** 民俗活動
I enjoy attending the folk-cultural activities of this town.
我喜歡參加這城鎮的民俗活動。

片 語 ▶

◇ **be blessed with... :**
bless(v.)是「祝福；賜福」之意，be blessed with...是「被賜……福；使……享有……」，例如：They are blessed with good children.(他們有好的子女，真是福氣)。

◇ **be attended to :**
attend 是「招呼；照顧」，例如：I may be late; I have a couple of things to attend to.(我可能會遲到；我有兩件事要處理)。be attended to 為被動語態，是「被照料；被服侍」，例如：She is being attended to carefully.(她被細心地照護著)。

◇ **aside from :**
aside(adv.)是「在一旁；在旁邊」，aside from...是「除了……；除……之外加上；暫且撇開……不談」，例如：Aside from beautiful scenery, Switzerland also has a wonderful local music tradition that is not to be missed.(除了美景，瑞士也有很棒的地方音樂傳統，不容錯過)。

◇ **impose... on... :**
impose(v.)是「加諸於」，impose... on... 是「將……加於……；強迫……於……」，例如：Our teachers always impose heavy tasks on us.(我們老師總是給我們很重的課業)。

◇ **be excluded from... :**
exclude(v.)是「排除；拒絕」，be excluded from...是「被排除在……外；被拒絕在……外」，例如：The criminal is excluded

from entering the country.(這罪犯被拒絕入境)。

句型分析 ▶

1. Since most cemeteries are located on hills on the outskirts of town in Taiwan, families usually take advantage of this opportunity to go on a family outing after completing their Tomb Sweeping Day rites.

   ♦ 這句話的主詞是 families，主要動詞是 take advantage of...。句首由 Since...(因為……)引導的副詞子句用來修飾逗號後的主要子句，目的在提供理由。

   ♦ 句中的 be located...是「位於……」，on the outskirts of...是「在……的邊緣；在……的郊區」。

   ♦ 句中 take advantage of...是「利用……」，take advantage of this opportunity 則是「把握機會」。go on an outing 是「去遠足」之意。

2. For instance, married women are traditionally forbidden from worshiping their side of the ancestors on Tomb Sweeping Day and from going back to their parents' homes on Chinese New Year's Day.

   ♦ 這句話的主詞是 married women，主要動詞是 are forbidden(被禁止)。這裡用到一個片語 be forbidden from...(被禁止做……)，句子中不能做的事有兩件，由「對等連接詞」and 連接：(1)worshiping their side of the ancestors on Tomb Sweeping Day(2)going back to their parents' homes on Chinese New Year's Day。

♦　句首的 For instance 即 For example，意為「舉例來說」。

造句練習 ▶

1. 我們在清明掃墓節這天表達對祖先的尊敬。（ancestor）

   ----

2. 新任總裁馬上施行一些新政策。（president / impose...）

   ----

3. 小孩被排除在參與他們父母的對話之外。（be excluded...）

   ----

4. 酒在沙烏地阿拉伯是嚴格禁止的。（be forbidden / Saudi Arabia）

   ----

5. 讓我們善加利用今天的好天氣！（take advantage of...）

情人節
Valentine's Day

　　說到情人節，台灣人很幸福，也很可憐。對於有情人的人而言，一年可以過兩次情人節，真是甜甜又蜜蜜。對於沒有情人的人來說，一年有兩次要被商業廣告及身旁的親朋好友提醒自己的形單影隻，真是慘慘又淒淒！

　　現在社會觀念開放，各種交友方式層出不窮，除了有大夥兒幫忙介紹的 blind date（所謂的「盲目約會」，很類似台灣的「相親」），還有現在最流行的 online dating（網路約會）、speed dating（「快速約會」，即一男一女於限定的時間內快速相互交談，幾分鐘後換新的對象，如此輪一圈後，便可以在一、兩小時內與二、三十位異性見面交談）；宣告自己單身，似乎已不是件尷尬的事。

　　而科技的發達，更促使交友管道的快速增加。在國外現在已有所謂的 MoSoSo（Mobile Social Software）出現，你若加入這種服務，便可以將一堆朋友的名字或自己心儀對象的名字給經營 MoSoSo 的公司，當你到某些特定地方，如酒吧或俱樂部，便可以送個訊息給這家公司，要他們送訊息給你的朋友（在十條街內的距離），請他們加入你的活動。如此一來你可以隨時與朋友保持緊密關係，找到對象的機會當然也會大增。或許很快的，你也可以享受一年兩次的情人節喔！

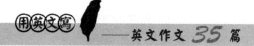
Valentine's Day (CD1-6)

On Valentine's Day, many lovers show their **mutual affection** by sending each other fresh flowers and chocolates or sharing a **candlelit dinner**. ❶ Yet according to Roman history, Valentine's Day is not only a celebration of love but also the **commemoration** of friendship, family, and human affection. Chinese Valentine's Day (the 7th day of the 7th lunar month), by **comparison**, is more romantic yet **heartrending**, because this is the only time of year when the **Cowherd** and the **Weaver Girl** meet each other across the **Milky Way**. ❷

Why is their path through love so **rough** and **bumpy**? Rumor has it that the Weaver Girl's father, the **Jade Emperor**, reached the end of his **patience** when he saw the two lovers' obsession for their **love affair**. They were so much in love that they forgot all their work **duties**. In his rage, he ordered that they be allowed to see each other only once a year. It turns out that even traditional Chinese love stories **convey** the importance of a **pragmatic lifestyle**: "Love is **dear**; but money is dearer!"

情人節

在西洋情人節這一天,許多戀人都會互贈鮮花、巧克力、共進燭光晚餐,向對方表達情意。不過根據羅馬歷史,西洋情人節慶祝的不只是愛情,也慶祝友情、親情,以及人與人之間的互愛。相較之下,中國七夕情人節(農曆七月七日)則更浪漫淒美,因為這是一年中,牛郎與織女唯一可以在鵲橋相會的日子。

為什麼這對愛人的命運如此坎坷?有一說法是織女的爸爸「玉皇大帝」受夠了兩人耽溺於戀愛情事,而將工作責任拋諸腦後,他一怒之下,下令兩人一年只能相見一次。看來在中國傳統的愛情故事背後,傳達的還是務實的生活態度:「愛情誠可貴、麵包價更高!」

主題句: ▨▨▨　　**單字:加黑**　　**片語:套色**　　**句型:❶❷**

單字例句 ▶

◇ **Valentine's** [ˋvæləntaɪn]**Day**（西洋）情人節

◇ **mutual**（**adj.**）相互的；共同的
They share many mutual interests.
他們擁有許多共同的興趣。

◇ **affection**（**n.**）愛；情感
He has great affection for the girl.
他對那個女生有強烈的情感。

◇ **candlelit dinner** 燭光晚餐

◇ **commemoration**（**n.**）慶祝；紀念
We are planning a trip to a foreign country as a commemoration of our love.
我們正計畫一趟國外旅遊，以慶祝我們的愛情。

◇ **comparison**（**n.**）比較
Singapore is an extremely clean country; China, by comparison, is a mess.
新加坡是個超乾淨的國家，相較之下，中國就比較髒亂。

◇ **heartrending**（**adj.**）斷腸的；令人悲痛的
"Romeo and Juliet" is a heartrending story.
「羅蜜歐與茱麗葉」是個令人悲傷的故事。

◇ **Cowherd**（**n.**）牛郎

- **Weaver Girl** 織女

- **Milky Way** 銀河（此指「鵲橋」）

- **rough**（adj.）崎嶇的；艱苦的
  The couples in love stories all undergo a rough time before ending up together.
  在愛情故事中的情侶們最後在一起之前，都經歷過艱苦的時光。

- **bumpy**（adj.）顛簸不平的
  We all felt uncomfortable as our car passed over the bumpy road.
  當車子經過顛簸不平的路時，我們都覺得不舒服。

- **Jade Emperor** 玉皇大帝

- **patience**（n.）耐性
  We need patience to succeed.
  要成功必須有耐性。

- **love affair** 戀愛情事

- **duty**（n.）責任；義務
  You should complete your duties before leaving for the day.
  結束今天之前，你應該完成你的責任。

- **convey** [kən`ve]（v.）傳遞；表達
  It is hard for me to convey my feelings through words.
  對我來說，要用文字表達我的情感是困難的。

- **pragmatic**（adj.）講求實際的

He is a pragmatic employer and requires a practical plan for the promotion of products.

他是個實事求是的老闆，講求務實的計畫來行銷產品。

◇ **lifestyle(n.)生活方式**

People can choose their own lifestyles.

人們可以選擇自己的生活方式。

◇ **dear(adj.)可愛的；珍貴的**

His little sister was very dear to him.

他很珍愛他的小妹。

片　語　▶

◇ **rumor has it(that)... :**

rumor(n.)是「謠言」，rumor has it(that)...是「傳聞說……；有風聲……」，例如：Rumor has it that she is over forty years old.(傳聞她已超過四十歲)。

◇ **obsession for... :**

obsession(n.)是「執著；著迷」，obsession for...是「對……的著迷」，例如：She has an obsession for Barbie dolls.(她對芭比娃娃著迷)。obsession for...與動詞片語 be obsessed with...同義。

◇ **in love :**

in love是「墜入愛河的」，例如：They are deeply in love.(他們深深相愛)。

◇ **in someone's rage：**

rage(n.)是「狂怒」，例如：In his rage he had all the farmers executed.(他在盛怒下處死所有的農人)。

◇ **turn out：**

turn out 有許多意思，這裡是「結果成為……；情況發展為……」，例如：The plan turned out to be a failure.(這計畫結果失敗了)。

句型分析 ▶

1. On Valentine's Day, many lovers show their mutual affection by sending each other fresh flowers and chocolates or sharing a candlelit dinner.

   ◆ 這句話的主詞是 many lovers，主要動詞是 show。句中 by 為介系詞，意味「藉由……方式」，這裡列出兩種方式，由「對等連接詞」or 連接：(1)sending each other fresh flowers and chocolates(2)sharing a candlelit dinner。

2. Chinese Valentine's Day, by comparison, is more romantic yet heartrending, because this is the only time of year when the Cowherd and the Weaver Girl meet each other across the Milky Way.

   ◆ 這句話的主詞是 Chinese Valentine's Day，主要動詞是 is。逗號後面由 because 引導的是副詞子句，補充說明主要子句。

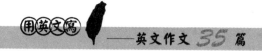

- ♦ comparison(n.)是「比較」，by comparison 是「相較之下」。

- ♦ 這裡的 yet 是連接詞，意為「但是；然而」，所以 romantic yet heartrending 是「浪漫但淒涼」。

造句練習 ▶

1. 情侶們在情人節享受燭光晚餐。(candlelit dinner)

- -

2. 有謠傳說她是個騙子，但我不相信。(rumor has it...)

- -

3. 青少年通常對流行偶像著迷。(be obsessed with...)

- -

4. 他與太太結婚前有一段美好的戀愛情事。(love affair)

- -

5. 你可以從他的臉上看到很大的怒氣。(rage)

- -

7

快樂母親節
A Joyous Mother's Day

　　在注重孝道的台灣，母親節一直是最被重視的節日之一。一般人慶祝母親節的方式不外乎幫媽媽作家事，或者請媽媽到餐廳大快朵頤。不過隨著社會的開放，越來越多人會送母親一些很「另類」的禮物，其中最匪夷所思的便是送媽媽各式各樣的 plastic surgery(整形手術)，例如 liposuction(抽脂)、face lift(拉皮)、face peel(換膚；又稱 chemical peel)、collagen injection(膠原蛋白注射)、laser hair-removal(雷射除毛)、eyelid surgery(拉眼皮手術)等等，林林總總，絕對可以滿足每位愛美母親的需要！

　　說到美容，現在還很流行一種稱之為botox injection(肉毒桿菌注射)的東西。大家都知道，注射肉毒桿菌的目的在於減少臉部皺紋，手術過程只需幾分鐘，不怎麼疼痛，傷口也只有針孔大小，加上幾乎沒啥 recovery period(恢復期)，因此在美國及世界各地已蔚為風潮。

　　除了不同的美容手術，孝順的你可以幫母親報名各種療程，例如 hydrotherapy(水療)、colon hydrotherapy(灌腸；大腸水療；浣腸治療)、detoxification therapy(排毒療法)、aromatherapy(芳香療法；香薰治療)等等，相信都會讓母親感受到你不一樣的心意！

A Joyous Mother's Day (CD1-7)

According to a **Jewish proverb**, "God could not be everywhere and therefore he made mothers." A widely known song among the Chinese goes like this, "Mothers are the best the world can give, and a child **blessed** with a mother is treated like a **treasure**." ❶

Mother's Day falls on different days around the world, but the respect that comes with the holiday does not **vary**. In Taiwan, many people express their **gratitude** for their mothers on the second Sunday of May by giving them **carnations** and presents, taking them to high-class restaurants, or helping with **housework**.

However, do keep in mind that behind the "joyous Mother's Day" **atmosphere** generated through commercial **speculation**, many Taiwanese mothers are still faced with a lot of problems and pressures: balancing work and family, suffering from **marital** violence, going through troubles with the **in-laws**, raising **single-parent families**, dealing with **sexual harassment** in the workplace, overcoming **sex discrimination**, etc. ❷

Without happy mothers, there would be no joyous families, nor would there be any joyous **communities** and countries. Let us work together to make every day a joyous Mother's Day for all of Taiwan's mothers!

快樂母親節

猶太諺云:「上帝無法照顧到每個人,所以祂創造了母親。」一首在華人地區廣為傳唱的歌也說:「世上只有媽媽好,有媽的孩子像塊寶」。

世界各國慶祝母親節的日子雖然不盡相同,然而賦予這個節日的崇高敬意卻沒有二致。在台灣,很多人會在五月的第二個星期日送母親康乃馨及禮物、請母親上高級餐館,或幫忙作家務,以表達對母親的感謝。

不過在商業炒作的「快樂母親節」氣氛之外,別忘了,許多台灣母親仍舊面臨了很多煩惱及壓力:工作家庭兩頭燒、婚姻暴力、婆媳相處問題、單親家庭、職場性騷擾、性別歧視……。

沒有快樂的母親,便沒有快樂的家庭,當然也沒有快樂的社區與國家。讓我們一起努力,讓台灣母親每天都可以享受真正的「快樂母親節」!

主題句 單字:加黑 片語:套色 句型:❶❷

單字例句 ▶

- ◇ **joyous**(adj.)高興的
  Mother's Day is such a joyous holiday for the whole family.
  母親節是個全家都高興的節日。

- ◇ **Mother's Day 母親節**

- ◇ **Jewish**(adj.)猶太人的
  The world adopts a lot of Jewish traditions.
  這世界採用許多猶太人的傳統。

- ◇ **proverb** [ˋprɑvɝb](n.)諺語；格言
  An old proverb says, "Hard work brings success."
  一個古老的諺語云：「愛拼才會贏」。

- ◇ **bless**(v.)祝福
  Thank the Lord that we are blessed with so much love.
  感謝上帝，我們擁有許多愛。

- ◇ **treasure**(n.)珍寶
  I consider my family the greatest treasure in my life.
  我將家庭視為我生命中的最大寶藏。

- ◇ **vary**(v.)改變；變化
  Life is more interesting if we vary our daily routines.
  如果我們改變日常生活的常規，生活會更有趣。

- ◇ **gratitude**(n.)感恩；感激
  I wish I could show you my real gratitude for you.

我真希望可以表達我對你的真心感謝。

◇ **carnation**(**n.**)康乃馨
Flower shops stock up on carnations for Mother's Day.
母親節時花店堆滿了康乃馨。

◇ **housework**(**n.**)家事
I spent the whole day at home doing housework.
我花了一整天的時間在家做家事。

◇ **atmosphere**(**n.**)氣氛
The atmosphere of the party is extremely jubilant.
聚會的氣氛超 high 的。

◇ **speculation**(**n.**)投機買賣
Some of their fortune is generated through speculation.
他們的一部份財富是靠投機買賣而產生的。

◇ **marital**(**adj.**)婚姻的
Please write down your marital status.
請寫下你的婚姻狀態。

◇ **in-laws**(**n.**)(多用複數)姻親
Some marriage problems stem from misunderstandings with the in-laws.
有些婚姻問題起因於姻親間的誤會。

◇ **single-parent family** 單親家庭

◇ **sexual harassment** 性騷擾
He was convicted by the court for sexual harassment.

他被法院定罪性騷擾。

◇ **sex/gender discrimination 性別歧視**
The company has been sued for sex discrimination.
這公司因性別歧視被告。

◇ **community(n.)社區**
This community is so peaceful and quiet.
這社區很平靜。

片　語 ▶

◇ **come with... :**
come with...是「伴隨……」，文章中的 the respect that comes with the holiday 意為「伴隨著節日而來的敬意」。

句型分析 ▶

1. A widely known song among the Chinese goes like this, "Mothers are the best the world can give, and a child blessed with a mother is treated like a treasure."

   ♦ 這句話的主詞是 a song，主要動詞是 goes。動詞的 go 是「歌曲、話語等的表現」，因此 A song goes like this...是「一條歌是這麼唱的……」，引號內的句子即為歌詞內

容。

◆ 句中 a child blessed with...是由 a child who is blessed with...
省略而來；be blessed with...是「被賦予……；享有……」，
這裡 a child blessed with a mother 是「擁有母親的小孩」。

2. However, do keep in mind that behind the "joyous Mother's
Day" atmosphere generated through commercial speculation,
many Taiwanese mothers are still faced with a lot of problems
and pressures: balancing work and family, suffering from
marital violence, going through troubles with the in-laws,
raising single-parent families, dealing with sexual harassment
in the workplace, overcoming sex discrimination, etc.

◆ 這句話是「祈使句」，由 do keep in mind...開始，do 為加
強語氣的用詞，意為「要確實謹記在心……」。必須謹記
在心的事情由 that 子句引出：behind the..., many Taiwanese
mothers are still faced with...（在……背後，許多台灣母親仍
然面臨……）。

◆ 句中 the atmosphere generated through...是由 the atmosphere
which is generated through...省略而來，意為「由……產生
的氣氛」。

◆ 句中提到台灣母親面臨的問題有六個，用「對等連接
詞」and 連接：(1)balancing work and family(2)suffering
from marital violence(3)going through troubles with the
in-laws(4)raising single-parent families(5)dealing with
sexual harassment in the workplace(6)overcoming sex
discrimination。其中 suffer from...是「遭受……」；go
through... 是「經歷……」；deal with...是「應付……；處
理……」。

造句練習 ▶

1. 古諺云：「人不可貌相」。(old saying)

   ----

2. 我今年帶母親上五星級餐館，慶祝母親節。(Mother's Day)

   ----

3. 很幸運地，我們的身體都擁有健康。(be blessed with...)

   ----

4. 單親家庭現在越來越普遍。(single-parent family)

   ----

5. 她控告公司性別歧視。(sex discrimination)

8

端午節
The Dragon Boat Festival

　　在台灣過傳統節日最好的一件事，便是有理由可以大吃大喝：新年吃那永遠吃不完的年夜飯、元宵節吃元宵、端午節吃粽子、中秋節吃月餅、冬至進補吃湯圓……。

　　不只台灣，美國人也喜歡在節慶大吃大喝，例如在復活節（Easter）時吃羊肉和火腿、在國慶日（Independence Day）烤肉野餐、在感恩節（Thanksgiving Day）吃火雞、在萬聖節（Halloween）及聖誕節（Christmas）吃各式各樣大餐等等，可見東西方對「在節慶吃美食」有志一同。

　　不過現代人平日已大魚大肉，碰到節慶若也卯起來吃，很快的體重便會無法控制。針對世界各地人們普遍肥胖的問題，WHO（World Health Organization，「世界衛生組織」）前幾年提出 globesity 這個名詞，用來凸顯問題的嚴重性。globesity 是 globe（全球）＋ obesity（肥胖症）的綜合體，指的是流行於全球、沒有任何地區可以倖免的全球化肥胖症。而且過度肥胖很容易引起糖尿病，導致一個人患有 diabesity（糖尿病加肥胖症）。這個字是由 diabetes（糖尿病）＋ obesity（肥胖症）而來，一個人兩種疾病都有，可說蠻慘的。因此下次在大吃大喝之際，別忘了注意一下自己的體重！

The Dragon Boat Festival CD1-8

The "**Dragon Boat Festival**" falls on the 5th day of the 5th lunar month. The **patriotic poet** Qu Yuan is said to have been a **minister** during the Warring States Period. Pushed by his **relentless** concern for his country and its people even while in **exile**, he **committed suicide** by jumping into a river on this day. ❶ In order to keep the fish from **consuming** his body, the locals **cast** rice, stored in bamboo tubes, into the water. These packages became what are now known as "**zongzi**" (or "**rice dumplings**"). Moreover, the act of beating drums and searching for his body in boats gradually became the present tradition of **dragon boat racing**.

In the **folktale**, "The **Legend** of the White Snake," the white snake almost **revealed** her snake form on this day after drinking "**realgar wine**," which is thought to remove **poison** from the body. It therefore became the custom for people to hang branches of **moxa**, drink realgar wine, and wear **sachets** to drive away **evil spirits**.

Judging from our current perspective, Qu Yuan chose to commit suicide solely because of his **frustration**, and is therefore not worthy of encouragement. In addition, the act of the locals casting food into the water is not only **wasteful**, but also not environmentally-friendly. The Dragon Boat Festival falls in the summer, the time of year infested with all sorts of **communicable** diseases. However, there is no cause for concern, as our **forefathers** were already **knowledgeable** in making use of traditional **herbs** to protect their bodies and **sterilize** their surroundings. ❷ What a remarkable display of wit!

端午節

農曆五月五日是「端午節」。相傳「愛國詩人」屈原是戰國時代楚國的臣子,因為被放逐,憂國憂民,最後在這一天投江自盡。當地民眾怕屈原的屍體被魚吃掉,所以用竹筒裝好米食投入江中,演變成今日的粽子。而當年敲鑼打鼓、划船尋找屈原屍體的舉動,也演變成今日傳統的划龍舟競賽。

在民間傳說「白蛇傳」中,白蛇也因為在這一天喝了被認為有消除疫病功用的「雄黃酒」後,差點現出蛇形。民眾因而在這天懸掛艾草、喝雄黃酒、戴香包,以驅邪避惡。

用今日的眼光來看,屈原只因不得志便選擇自殺,實在不值得鼓勵;而民眾將食物投到江中的舉動,不但浪費,也很不環保。倒是端午節正值夏日,是各種傳染病充斥的季節,老祖宗們卻毫不擔心,懂得利用傳統草藥進行身體及環境保健,其智慧令人佩服!

主題句: 　　　　　單字:加黑　　　片語:套色　　　句型:❶❷

單字例句 ▶

◇ **Dragon Boat Festival** 端午節

◇ **patriotic**（adj.）愛國的
The brave and patriotic soldiers fought the invaders.
這些勇敢且愛國的士兵與入侵者戰鬥。

◇ **poet**（n.）詩人
Everyone is a poet at heart.
在內心深處每個人都是詩人。

◇ **minister**（n.）大臣；部長
The minister agreed to come for a visit tomorrow.
部長答應明天來訪。

◇ **relentless**（adj.）不屈不撓的
The man was relentless in his pursuit of fame.
這人對追求名聲不遺餘力。

◇ **exile** [ˈɛksaɪl]（n.）流放；放逐
He went into exile to escape political imprisonment.
他為了逃避政治牢獄而流亡。

◇ **commit suicide** 自殺

◇ **consume**（v.）吃完；消耗
You should consume all the food on your plate.
你應該吃光你盤子內的所有食物。

- **cast**(**v.**)投擲
  The boy cast a stone toward the sea.
  這男孩向大海投擲石塊。

- **zongzi / rice dumpling** 粽子

- **dragon boat racing** 划龍舟競賽

- **folktale**(**n.**)民間傳說
  According to this folktale, humans evolved from apes.
  根據這個民間傳說，人類演化自猿猴。

- **legend** [ˈlɛdʒənd](**n.**)傳奇；故事
  The legend of the king will live forever in our hearts.
  國王的傳奇故事會永遠活在我們心中。

- **reveal**(**v.**)顯現；揭發
  The witness has something to reveal today in the hearing.
  這證人在今天的聽證會會揭發一些事情。

- **realgar wine** 雄黃酒
  Realgar wine is said to be beneficial to the body.
  雄黃酒據說對身體有好處。

- **poison**(**n.**)毒物
  The evil witch added some poison to the beverage.
  這邪惡的巫婆加了一些毒藥在飲料裡。

- **moxa** [ˈmɑksə](**n.**)艾草
  Branches of moxa can be seen hanging near the door.
  艾草枝掛在門旁邊。

◇ **sachet** [sæˋʃe] (**n.**) 香包
His mother insists that he wear a sachet for the trip.
為了這趟旅程，他母親堅持他帶香包。

◇ **evil spirit** 妖魔；「壞東西」
I sense a lot of evil spirits in this area.
我感覺到這地區有許多妖魔。

◇ **frustration** (**n.**) 挫折
Do not let your frustration get in the way of success.
別讓你的挫折阻擋了成功。

◇ **wasteful** (**adj.**) 浪費的
The children were scolded for being wasteful.
小孩子們因為浪費被罵。

◇ **communicable** (**adj.**) 可傳染的
Communicable diseases are among the main causes of death.
傳染性疾病是主要死因之一。

◇ **forefather** (**n.**) 祖先
Our forefathers may have prepared for the emergence of new diseases.
我們的祖先或許已準備好面對新疾病的出現。

◇ **knowledgeable** (**adj.**) 知識豐富的
I have never met such a knowledgeable child before you.
在你之前，我從未遇見這麼博學的小孩。

◇ **herb** (**n.**) 藥草

These herbs may be helpful in easing your pain.
這些藥草對減輕你的疼痛或許有幫助。

◇ **sterilize(v.)消毒；殺菌**
Make sure that all instruments are sterilized before the operation.
在手術前，要確定所有的器具都消毒過了。

片　語 ▶

◇ **be said... :**
be said...是「據說……；被認為……」，例如：He is said to be the richest man in the world.(據說他是世界上最富有的人)。類似的用法還有 it is said(that)...。

◇ **remove... from... :**
remove(v.)是「移除；移開」，remove... from... 是「將……從……移除」，例如：Reference books should not be removed from our library.(我們圖書館的參考書籍不該被移除)。

◇ **drive away :**
drive away 是「驅趕；遣散」之意，例如：They opened the window to drive away the summer heat.(他們開窗以驅散暑氣)。

◇ **a display of... :**
display(n.)是「顯現；表示」之意，a display of... 是「一種……的展現；……的展示」，例如：This new museum has a superb

display of porcelain.(這個新博物館有超棒的瓷器展示)。

句型分析 ▶

1. Pushed by his relentless concern for his country and its people even while in exile, he committed suicide by jumping into a river on this day.

   ♦ 這句話的主詞是 he，主要動詞是 committed。句首的 Pushed by...(被……所驅使)原本是 He was pushed by...；因為逗號前與逗號後的主詞都是 he，因此這裡將前面的 he 省略，並將其動詞「去動詞化」，以 pushed 起始。

   ♦ 句中 he(即屈原)所關心的事有二，以「對等連接詞」and 連接：(1)his country (2)the country's people。

   ♦ 句中的 while 是「當……時」，in exile 是「被放逐」，這裡的 even while in exile 是「甚至當他被放逐」。

   ♦ 逗點後的主要子句 he committed suicide by...表示「他用……方式自殺」，這裡是 jump into a river(跳河)。

2. However, there is no cause for concern, as our forefathers were already knowledgeable in making use of traditional herbs to protect their bodies and sterilize their surroundings.

   ♦ 這句話的主、動詞是 There is(there 為形式主詞)。句中的 cause(n.)是「原因；根據」，因此 no cause for concern 是「沒有擔憂的根據；不需擔憂」，後面接的 as...意為「之

所以不需要擔憂，是因為……」。

◆ knowledgeable(adj.)是「知識豐富的」，be knowledgeable in... 是「在……方面知識豐富」，這裡是make use of traditional herbs to(1)protect their bodies(2)sterilize their surroundings.(善用傳統草藥來保護身體、消毒四周環境)。

造句練習 ▶

1. 自殺的人不了解未來的希望。(commit suicide)

_____

2. 端午節時人們享用粽子。(rice dumpling)

_____

3. 划龍舟競賽總是既緊張又令人興奮。(dragon boat racing)

_____

4. 人們舉行一場儀式，試著趕走妖魔。(ritual / drive away / evil spirit)

_____

5. 請把這死掉的老鼠從房子裡移開。(remove... from...)

_____

9

月圓人團圓
Friends and Family Gather for the Full Moon

　　說來有趣，東、西方雖然思想文化相差甚大，但在「怪罪女性」上，倒是常常有志一同！於是可憐的夏娃多年來背負誘惑亞當吃下蘋果的罪名，而嫦娥因為背著丈夫偷吃長生不老藥，這些年來只好一個人淒苦的躲在月球懺悔……。

　　小時候讀到「嫦娥奔月」的故事時，相信很多人都很同情嫦娥的際遇，不過同情歸同情，還是怪罪她偷吃靈丹，後果當然只好自己擔！不過我們若將這則看似單純的民間傳說放在複雜的現代社會裡，則會很驚奇的發現，其實嫦娥一點都不可憐呢！尤其以現代女性的眼光來看，嫦娥的奔月可能是福不是禍！

　　想想看，如果一個女人嫁入豪門，卻發現自己原來嫁了一個不務正業、成天只知道射太陽的丈夫，那日子實在無趣得很。尤其如果丈夫又很愛叨念，說真的，倒不如一個人躲到廣寒宮來得清靜些呢！況且月亮上也不是真的空無一物，既有個身強體健的「吳剛」，又有隻可愛的寵物「玉兔」作陪；何況一年一度的中秋節，普天下華人都會到郊外翹首嫦娥的窈窕身影。眾星拱月，風華獨具，這樣的日子怎會不好過呢？

Friends and Family Gather for the Full Moon (CD1-9)

The **Moon Festival**, also known as the Mid-Autumn Festival, is one of the three major holidays in Taiwan. The most **prominent protagonist** of this holiday is none other than the lady who flew up to the sky to live in the **Moon Palace**, **Chang Er**. Luckily for her, she has had the **Jade Rabbit**, **Wu Gang**, and occasional **astronauts** from Earth to keep her company on the moon; otherwise she might **bitterly** regret having **swallowed** her husband **Hou Yi's elixir**. ❶

On this day of feasting on **moon cake** and **pomelo**, it is customary to hold a **barbeque** or throw a party with friends and family. Whether on the front **porch**, on the rooftop, or at the park, people can **devour** food while **gazing** up the moon, fantasizing about **waltzing** with Chang Er on top of the moon. ❷

But be careful! You may dance with Chang Er sooner than you think. All you have to do is go on using bleach-treated bamboo **chopsticks** and **aluminum foil** which releases **toxins** when heated. Also, if you **consume** too much of the **cancer-causing charred** meat from your numerous barbeque parties, believe it or not, you're already halfway from meeting Chang Er up in the sky!

月圓人團圓

中秋節是台灣的三大節慶之一。這個節慶最廣為人知的主角便是飛上月宮的嫦娥。幸好月亮上有玉兔與吳剛、以及偶爾從地球造訪的太空人與她作伴，不然嫦娥可能會很後悔當初偷吃了丈夫后羿的長生不老藥。

在這個可以狂吃月餅與文旦的節日，大家傳統上還會與親朋好友舉辦烤肉大會。不管是在家門前、在屋頂、在公園，大家都可以一邊狼吞虎嚥，一邊遙望滿月，幻想自己與嫦娥在月亮上共舞。

小心，你可能比想像中的更快與嫦娥共舞哦！只要大家在烤肉時繼續用加了漂白劑的竹筷、高溫會釋放毒素的鋁箔紙、以及多吃了含有致癌物質的燒焦肉，相信不久便可以與嫦娥在天上相見！

主題句：⬜　　單字：加黑　　片語：套色　　句型：❶❷

單字例句 ▶

◇ **full moon** 滿月
It is customary to enjoy moon cakes while gazing up at the moon during the Moon Festival.
傳統上，大家在中秋節時會一邊吃月餅、一邊仰望月亮。

◇ **Moon Festival**（又稱 **Mid-Autumn Festival**）中秋節

◇ **prominent**(adj.)著名的；廣為人知的
Shakespeare is very prominent in the literary world.
莎士比亞在文學界十分著名。

◇ **protagonist**(n.)主角；主人翁
The protagonist in the film, "The Lord of the Rings," is the hobbit Frodo.
電影「魔戒」中的主角是哈比人佛羅多。

◇ **Moon Palace** 月宮

◇ **Chang Er** 嫦娥

◇ **Jade Rabbit** 玉兔

◇ **Wu Gang** 吳剛

◇ **astronaut**(n.)太空人
Astronauts have to undergo rigorous training before making a trip into space.
在上太空前，太空人必須經歷嚴酷的訓練。

◇ **bitterly（adv.）悲痛地；難堪地**
The woman cried bitterly when her husband left her for another woman.
當她老公為了別的女人離開她時，這女人哭得很傷心。

◇ **swallow（v.）吞嚥**
You should chew your moon cake carefully; never swallow it whole.
你吃月餅時要小心嚼，千萬不要整個吞下去。

◇ **Hou Yi 后羿**

◇ **elixir** [ɪˈlɪksə]（n.）長生不老藥；萬靈丹
People in ancient times spent a fortune on elixirs for fear of dying.
古時候的人因為怕死，因此花很多錢在長生不老藥。

◇ **moon cake 月餅**
No Moon Festival is complete without eating moon cakes!
沒吃月餅，就不算完整的中秋節！

◇ **pomelo** [ˈpɑmələ]（n.）文旦；柚子
People usually send out boxes of pomelos to friends and family during the Moon Festival.
中秋節時，人們通常寄送一箱箱的文旦給親朋好友。

◇ **barbeque（n.）烤肉**
In Taiwan, many people celebrate special occasions by having barbeques.
在台灣，許多人舉辦烤肉來慶祝特別的事件。

◇ **porch**(n.)門廊

Americans usually keep their porch lights on during the night.

美國人通常讓門廊的燈整夜亮著。

◇ **devour**(v.)狼吞虎嚥

It is considered very impolite to devour food at the dinner table.

在餐桌上狼吞虎嚥被認為是很不禮貌的。

◇ **gaze**(v.)凝視

The little boy gazed longingly at the toy truck he wasn't allowed to buy.

這小男孩很渴望地凝視著那個他不准買的玩具卡車。

◇ **waltz**(v.)輕巧地跳；跳華爾滋

The young woman waltzed beautifully on the dance floor.

這年輕的小姐在舞池跳著曼妙的舞姿。

◇ **chopsticks**(n.)(多用複數)筷子

The art of eating with chopsticks looks difficult to foreigners.

對外國人來說，用筷子吃東西看起來是一項很難的藝術。

◇ **aluminum foil** 鋁箔紙

People place aluminum foil on the grill to keep the food from burning.

人們鋁箔紙放在烤肉架上，以防食物烤焦。

◇ **toxin**(n.)毒素

Excessive amounts of toxins can be fatal.

過量的毒素會致命。

◇ **consume**（v.）食盡；消耗
Humans consume large amounts of food every day.
人類每天吃很多的食物。

◇ **cancer-causing**（adj.）會導致癌症的
Cancer-causing substances are sometimes found in unlikely products.
會導致癌症的物質有時候存在於看起來不太可能會有的產品中。

◇ **charred** [tʃɑrd]（adj.）燒焦的
Health reports advised against eating charred meat.
健康報告建議大家不要吃燒焦的肉。

片　語 ▶

◇ **also known as... :**
known as... 是「以……為人所知」，故 also known as... 是「又以……為人所知」，即「又名……；亦稱……」，例如：Michael Jackson, also known as the "King of the Pop," has been accused of child molestation.（Michael Jackson；又名為「流行樂之王」，被控性騷擾孩童）。

◇ **none other than... :**
none other than... 是「正是……；就是……」，也就是「不是別的，而是……」之意，例如：She is none other than the queen.（她正是皇后）。

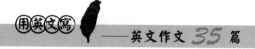
◇ **be customary to... :**

be customary to... 是「慣例的；習以為常的」，通常在 be customary 後還會加上 for...（對……人而言），例如：It's customary for me to get up at five.（我習慣五點起床）。

◇ **throw a party :**

throw a party 是「舉辦舞會、派對」的標準說法，後面可加 for...（為……人），例如：We threw a party for Jim yesterday.（我們昨晚為 Jim 舉辦派對）。

◇ **believe it or not... :**

這是口語的說法，意思為「信不信由你」，例如：Believe it or not, I will marry her.（信不信由你，我反正會娶她）。

◇ **halfway from... :**

halfway（adj.）是「中途的」，halfway from... 就是「在中途」，意思與 halfway to... 一樣，例如：Don't give up now; you're halfway to becoming proficient in English!（別放棄；你已在精通英文的途中了）。

句型分析 ▶

1. Luckily for her, she has had the Jade Rabbit, Wu Gang and occasional astronauts from Earth to keep her company on the moon; otherwise she might bitterly regret having swallowed her husband Hou Yi's elixir.

   ◆ 這句話的主詞是 she，主要動詞是 has had。前面的 luckily for her 是形容詞，修飾整句話，her 指的就是後面的主詞

she，也就是「嫦娥」。

♦ and 是「對等連接詞」，這裡連接三個東西：(1) Jade Rabbit (2) Wu Gang (3) astronauts。occasional 是形容詞，修飾 astronauts，意思是「偶爾造訪的太空人」。astronauts 後面的 from Earth 也是形容詞，同樣用來修飾 astronauts，意指「來自地球的太空人」。

♦ keep... company 是「與……作伴」，keep her company 便是「與她作伴」，意指「玉兔、吳剛、太空人與嫦娥作伴」。

♦ 句子裡分號後面的是另一個句子，主詞是 she，主要動詞是 might regret。otherwise... 是「要不然……」。

♦ 這整句話的重點為：She has had... to keep her company; otherwise she might regret having swallowed...（她有……陪伴她；不然她可就要後悔吞下……）。

2. Whether on the front porch, on the rooftop, or at the park, people can devour food while gazing up the moon, fantasizing about waltzing with Chang Er on top of the moon.

♦ 這句話的主詞是 people，主要動詞是 can devour。句首 Whether... 是「不管是……；任隨是……」，後面的 or 是「對等連接詞」，連接三個東西：(1) on the front porch (2) on the rooftop (3) at the park。

♦ while 是連接詞，意為「當……的時候；與……同時」，此為「一邊狂吃、一邊賞月」。gaze up... 是「凝視……」之意。

◆ 逗點後的 fantasizing about...(幻想……)是形容詞，fantasize
意為「幻想」，原本是動詞，但因這句話已有主要動詞
can devour，fantasize 只好「去動詞化」，加上 –ing，當形
容詞用。waltz 也是動詞，是「輕巧地跳；跳華爾滋舞」，
這裡因為接在介系詞 about 之後，所以加 –ing。waltz
with... 就是「與……跳華爾滋舞」。

造句練習 ▶

1. 他距完成工作還有一半的進程。(be halfway from...)

   -

2. 婚宴之前，新郎絕對不能見到新娘是許多國家的習俗。(be
   customary / the groom / the bride)

   -

3. 這小女孩要求母親與她作伴，因為她怕在黑暗中睡覺。(keep...
   company)

   -

4. 小孩子有時會幻想與卡通人物見面。(fantasize about... /
   cartoon character)

   -

5. 消基會警告不要用漂白過的筷子。

(The Consumers' Foundation / bleach-treated...)

- -

10

教師感嘆的教師節
A Teacher's Day Full of Sighs

現代孔夫子真是越來越難當了！先從國小老師說起。老師們除了要教育「國家未來的主人翁」，還得注意學生們的生活禮儀，有時回到家還要應付家長關切的電話，真可謂7-11(早上7點出門，晚上11點才得閒)。

國中與高中老師也不輕鬆，除了要應付教育當局朝令夕改的教育政策及令人一頭霧水的「一綱多本」、「多元入學」等，還要應付成長期的學生混幫派、泡網咖、吸毒、蹺課等一連串的問題。

大學老師雖然上課時數較少，可是教學研究外，還要關心學生的課業問題、感情問題、打工問題、生涯規劃問題……，一樣忙得團團轉。

其實有心為人師表的老師一點都不介意辛勤工作，因為老師們做的是最重要也最偉大的教育事業，那種成就感是旁人無法體會的。壞就壞在有心人士故意把老師當作只知享受、卻不繳稅的「米蟲」，或者是只知爭福利，卻不知民間疾苦的貪心鬼。這種污名化的賤招比起所謂「廢除18趴」、「取消免稅」等更加傷透老師們的心。要知道，如果台灣連老師們也罷工了，那麼整個社會就真的沒救了！

A Teacher's Day Full of Sighs <small>CD1-10</small>

September 28 is Teacher's Day, which is celebrated to **commemorate** the birth of **Confucius, "The Great Sage."**

On this day, **Confucian temples** all over Taiwan will hold a grand and **solemn ceremony** dedicated to Confucius. The ceremony is highlighted by a traditional **"eight-row dance"** to pay tribute to the Confucian **ideals** of "teaching without **discrimination"** and "teaching students in accordance with their **aptitude."** At the same time, it is also a day to honor our teachers and **acknowledge** their hard work over the past year.

For the many **diligent** teachers in Taiwan, Teacher's Day is indeed a holiday worth celebrating. Unfortunately, due to **constant** government policy changes in recent years, more and more teachers are left with nothing more than **lamentations** on this special day. ❶ The increase of **vagabond teachers**, the strict **retirement qualification** for senior teachers, the recorded **demerits** for student **corporal punishment**, the possible **elimination** of the **"preferential** 18-percent **interest rate** on **pension** savings" as well as the income **tax exemption** for teachers and **military personnel** are some sources of worry for teachers today. ❷ No wonder so many of our educators sigh, "It is not easy being a teacher!"

教師感嘆的教師節

每年的9月28日是教師節，也是「至聖先師」孔子的誕辰紀念。

在這一天，台灣各地的孔廟都會舉行隆重莊嚴的祭孔大典，特別是表演傳統的「八佾舞」，表達對孔子「有教無類」、「因材施教」理念的敬意。同時，在教師節這天，人們也會表彰及慰勞老師們整年的辛勞。

對許多辛勤的台灣老師而言，教師節的確是個值得慶賀的節日。只不過近年來，由於政府的政策改變，使得越來越多的老師在這一天感嘆不已。流浪教師大量充斥、資深教師無法核退、老師體罰學生會被記過處罰、再加上可能的「18趴優惠退休存款取消」及「軍教免稅取消」等，都是現代老師們的憂鬱來源。難怪許多老師要大嘆：「師道難為」！

主題句：　　　　單字：**加黑**　　片語：套色　　句型：❶❷

單字例句 ▶

◇ **Teacher's Day** 教師節

◇ **sigh**(n.)嘆息；嘆息聲
The girl sighed loudly and stared at the stars in sorrow.
這女生悲傷地盯著星星，大聲嘆息。

◇ **commemorate**(v.)紀念；表揚
The monument commemorates those who died in the war.
這紀念碑是用來紀念在戰爭中死亡的人。

◇ **Confucius** 孔子

◇ **The Great Sage** 至聖先師(或稱 **The Ultimate Sage**)

◇ **Confucian temple** 孔廟

◇ **solemn**[ˋsɑləm](adj.)神聖的；莊嚴的
The priest said a solemn prayer, signaling the end of the funeral.
牧師念著神聖的禱辭，意味葬禮結束。

◇ **ceremony**(n.)典禮；儀式
Many people attended the flag-raising ceremony on Double-Ten Day.
許多人在雙十節參加升旗典禮。

◇ **eight-row dance** 八佾舞

◇ **ideal**(n.)理念；理想

The "Pledge of Allegiance" upholds the American ideals of liberty and justice for all.
「效忠誓言」強調了美國自由與公平正義的理念。

◇ **discrimination** (n.) 歧視；差別待遇
Gender discrimination is still a big problem in the workplace.
職場的性別歧視仍是一個大問題。

◇ **aptitude** (n.) 性向；才能
This test is supposed to measure the scholastic aptitude of the students.
這個測驗是為了要測量學生的學術性向。

◇ **acknowledge** (v.) 承認；答謝
I acknowledge that he's a better athlete than I am.
我承認他在運動方面比我行。

◇ **diligent** [ˈdɪlədʒənt] (adj.) 勤勞的
Teachers enjoy teaching diligent students.
老師們喜歡教勤勞的學生。

◇ **constant** (adj.) 不斷的
The scar serves as a constant reminder of his rebellious childhood.
這疤痕不斷地提醒著他叛逆的童年。

◇ **lamentation** (n.) 感傷；悲歎
If you have time for lamentation, then you have time to change your ways.
如果你有時間感傷，那你便有時間改變自己做事的方式。

◇ **vagabond teacher** 流浪教師

Fresh graduates of teacher education programs face the threat of becoming just another vagabond teacher.

剛從師資教育學程畢業的學生面臨很可能成為另一個流浪教師的威脅。

◇ **retirement**(**n.**)退休

The man dreams of winning the lottery and applying for early retirement.

這男人夢想著中樂透，然後申請提早退休。

◇ **qualification**(**n.**)資格；條件

Qualifications such as educational background and related experiences are a must for getting a job.

教育背景及相關經驗在找工作時是必備的條件。

◇ **demerit**(**n.**)記過；缺點

Everyone has merits and demerits.

每個人都有優缺點。

◇ **corporal punishment** 體罰

Corporal punishment is no longer allowed in the classroom.

課堂上已不容許體罰。

◇ **elimination**(**n.**)取消

The elimination of the reward system made the employees less motivated.

獎勵制度的取消使得員工們比較不積極了。

◇ **preferential**(**adj.**)優惠的

Employees with influential relatives were given preferential treatment.
員工若有具權勢的親戚，便會得到優惠的待遇。

◇ **interest rate 利息**
People choose to buy stocks instead of saving money in the bank because of low interest rates.
因為利率低，人們選擇買股票，而非將錢存在銀行中。

◇ **pension (n.) 退職金；津貼**
His father has retired and is now collecting his pension.
他父親退休了，現在靠退職金過日。

◇ **tax exemption 免稅**
Before filing your tax returns, you should check if you are qualified for any tax exemptions.
在申報稅時，你應該先檢查是否符合任何免稅的條件。

◇ **military personnel** [ˌpɝsṇˈɛl] 軍方人員

片　語　▶

◇ **dedicated to... :**
dedicate (v.) 是「奉獻；獻給……」之意，常用過去分詞當形容詞用 (dedicated)，例如：This is a chapel dedicated to the Virgin Mary. (這是間奉獻給聖母瑪麗亞的禮拜堂)。

◇ **be highlighted by... :**

highlight(v.)是「強調」，be highlighted by... 則是「用⋯⋯強調」，例如：Two events have highlighted the tensions in recent days.(這兩個事件凸顯了最近這段期間的緊張狀態)。

◇ **pay tribute to... :**

tribute(n.)是「讚辭；尊敬」，pay tribute to... 是「向⋯⋯表達敬意」，例如：Members of Congress paid tribute to the departing Representative Johnson.(國會議員對即將離職的眾議員 Johnson 致敬)。

◇ **in accordance with... :**

accordance(n.)是「一致；符合」，in accordance with... 是「根據⋯⋯；按照⋯⋯」之意，例如：She completed the mission in accordance with your orders.(她按照你的命令完成任務)。

◇ **no wonder：**

wonder(n.)是「驚異」，no wonder 則是「難怪；果然；怪不得」，例如：They had a fight; no wonder he didn't come.(他們吵架了；難怪他沒來)。

句型分析 ▶

1. Unfortunately, due to constant government policy changes in recent years, more and more teachers are left with nothing more than lamentations on this special day.

   ◆ 這句話的主詞是 teachers，主要動詞是 are left。逗號前的 due to...(由於⋯⋯)是形容詞，告訴讀者後面主要子句的前

因後果。

◆ leave(v.)是「留下」的意思，這裡用被動式 be left with...，意思是「剩下……；留……給……」，teachers are left with... 是「留給老師們……；老師們剩下的只有……」。nothing more than... 就是「只有……」，所以 teachers are left with nothing more than... 就是「留給老師們的就只有……」。

2. The increase of vagabond teachers, the strict retirement qualification for senior teachers, the recorded demerits for student corporal punishment, the possible elimination of the "preferential 18-percent interest rate on pension savings" as well as the income tax exemption for teachers and military personnel are some sources of worry for teachers today.

◆ 這句話的主詞超長，幾乎占了整句話的四分之三，是從 the increase of...一直到 military personnel，主要動詞是 are。

◆ 主詞指的是現今老師們的憂慮，可以分類為下面五項：(1)the increase of vagabond teachers (2)the strict retirement qualification for senior teachers (3)the recorded demerits for student corporal punishment (4)the possible elimination of the "preferential 18-percent interest rate on pension savings" (5)the possible elimination of the income tax exemption for teachers and military personnel。

造句練習 ▶

1. 這位作家將他上一本書獻給他的女兒。（dedicate to...）

   ----

2. 這報導旨在強調老師們常會碰到的管教問題。（aim to... / highlight）

   ----

3. 他們舉辦音樂會，對老師們表達敬意。（pay tribute to...）

   ----

4. 學校提議依據學生的表現來付老師薪水。（in accordance with...）

   ----

5. 軍方人員享有許多福利，甚至直到退休。（military personnel / retirement）

11

雙十國慶！
Double Ten Day!

　　記得小時候，大人小孩似乎都很「愛國」，聽到國歌時會立正，看電影時會起立唱國歌，元旦時許多人會參加廣場前的升旗典禮，國慶日時島上也旗海飄揚，家家戶戶充滿著歡欣鼓舞的氣氛。

　　曾幾何時，大人小孩聽國歌就好像聽流行歌曲一樣沒反應，看到有人在戲院起立唱國歌還嫌人家太愛國，而元旦的升旗典禮變成只是跨年晚會後的「續攤」……，以往雙十節那種「國恩家慶」、「普天同慶」的熱烈，似乎已不復見。

　　有趣的是，在一般人認為最「隨性」的美國，唱國歌、向國旗致敬，可是很莊嚴神聖的事呢！在美國，一般體育賽事前都得唱國歌，而且大會還會費盡心思邀請有特殊事蹟的民眾或影視紅星蒞臨駐唱。國慶日時，大家在施放煙火前也都會不約而同起立唱國歌，有些民眾甚至引吭高歌、熱淚盈眶呢！而美國人在國慶日及非國慶日懸掛國旗的情形，也十分常見。最誇張的是，美國公立學校的學生，還必須在每天上課前站起來，將右手放到左胸前，朗誦一段Pledge of Allegiance（效忠誓言），表明愛國的決心呢！

Double Ten Day! (CD1-11)

On October 10, 1911, the **National Father**, Dr. Sun Yat-sen, led his **comrades** in the **Wuchang Uprising** (otherwise known as the Xinhai **Revolution**). ❶ As a result, the **then-corrupt** Manchu dynasty was **overthrown**. Consequently, the tenth of October was **thenceforth** known as Double Ten Day, which is also our nation's birthday.

In Taiwan, numerous **festivities** mark the celebration of every Double Ten Day. These include the **flag-raising ceremony** in front of the **presidential palace**, the **military review ceremony**, folk art performances, and evening events such as the National Day **fireworks display** and music **soiree**.

Although the festive air of the past few National Day celebrations has been **tinted** with **tension** over the **ongoing** debate of **unification** versus **independence**, most citizens do not really concern themselves with **slogans** like "One China," "One Country on Each Side," "One Country, Two Systems," or "ROC on Taiwan," just as long as the social **stability** and economic **prosperity** of Taiwan are **maintained**! ❷

雙十國慶！

在西元1911年的10月10日，國父孫中山先生領導同志發動武昌起義(亦即「辛亥革命」)，推翻了當時腐敗的滿清政府。也因此，每年的10月10日是「雙十節」，也是我們國家的生日。

在台灣，每年的雙十節都有許多慶祝活動，包括總統府前的升旗典禮、閱兵典禮、民俗技藝表演、晚間的煙火表演及國慶音樂晚會。

雖然這幾年的國慶日，因為持續辯論的統/獨的議題而蒙上濃濃的煙硝味，不過坦白說，對大多數民眾而言，只要社會持續安定、經濟繼續繁榮，管它什麼「一個中國」、「一邊一國」、「一國兩制」，還是「中華民國在台灣」！

主題句：　　　　單字：加黑　　片語：套色　　句型：❶❷

單字例句 ▶

◇ **Double Ten Day 雙十節**

◇ **National Father 國父**

◇ **comrade** [ˋkɑmræd] **(n.) 伙伴；同志**
His comrades pledged to fight alongside him until the end.
他的同志們誓言要與他並肩作戰直到最後。

◇ **Wuchang Uprising 武昌起義**

◇ **revolution (n.) 革命**
He led a revolution to topple the government.
他領導革命，以瓦解政府。

◇ **then-corrupt 當時腐敗的**
The then-corrupt government captured people who refused to cooperate with them.
當時腐敗的政府逮捕那些拒絕與之合作的人。

◇ **overthrow (v.) 推翻；毀滅**
The movement overthrew the slave system and freed millions of slaves.
這運動推翻了奴隸制度，使好幾百萬的奴隸自由。

◇ **thenceforth (adv.) 從那時以後**
On July 4, 1776, The U.S. declared its independence from Britain; the day was thenceforth celebrated annually as Independence Day.

1776年7月4日，美國宣布從英國獨立，從那時以後，每年的這一天就被慶祝為「獨立紀念日」。

◇ **festivities**(n.)(複數)慶典；祝宴
People enjoyed themselves at the festivities.
慶典中人們歡欣鼓舞。

◇ **flag-raising ceremony 升旗典禮**

◇ **presidential palace 總統府**

◇ **military review ceremony 閱兵典禮**

◇ **fireworks display 煙火表演**

◇ **soiree** [swɑˋre](n.)晚會；(正式的)社交聚會
The young woman dressed herself in a beautiful evening gown for the soiree.
這年輕的女人穿了件漂亮的晚禮服參加晚會。

◇ **tint**(v.)染色；使受影響
His answer was tinted by his prior knowledge.
他的回答受到他之前所知的影響。

◇ **tension**(n.)緊張狀態
The man tried to ease the tension by making lame jokes.
這男人試圖緩和緊張，講了一些無聊的笑話。

◇ **ongoing**(adj.)持續的；進行中的
The ongoing conflict shows no signs of easing up.
持續的衝突沒有任何緩解的跡象。

◇ **unification**(n.)統一

Mainland China promotes unification every chance it gets.

中國大陸只要一有機會就鼓吹統一。

◇ **independence**(n.)獨立

The people enjoy their independence and would like to stay that way.

這些人喜歡獨立，也喜歡一直保持如此。

◇ **slogan**(n.)口號；標語

The angry crowd yelled slogans, demanding that the government compensate for their losses.

憤怒的群眾高呼口號，要求政府補償他們的損失。

◇ **stability**(n.)穩定(性)

The treaty could threaten the peace and stability of the region.

這條約會威脅此地區的和平與穩定。

◇ **prosperity**(n.)繁榮；興旺

The people do not hope for prosperity but merely for stability.

人們不要求繁榮興旺，只求安定。

◇ **maintain**(v.)維持；保存

The government maintained its stance regarding the issue.

政府在這件事上維持既定的立場。

片　語　▶

◇ **then-(corrupt)：**

then(adj.)是「那時的」，要接在名詞前面，例如： the then
US President Richard Nixon。若 then 後面接的是個形容詞，則
必須在 then 後加上 -，將整個字當作形容詞，例如文章中的
then-corrupt 是「當時腐敗的」。其他用法如：the then-married
Cruise and Kidman(當時結婚的克魯斯與基嫚)。

句型分析　▶

1. On October 10, 1911, the National Father, Dr. Sun Yat-sen,
   led his comrades in the Wuchang Uprising(otherwise known
   as the Xinhai Revolution).

   ◆ 這句話的主詞是 the National Father，主要動詞是 led(「領
   導」的過去式)。逗號與逗號之間的 Dr. Sun Yat-sen 是主詞
   the National Father 的同位語。

   ◆ 句首的 On October 10, 是時間單位。句末括號中的
   otherwise known as... 是由 it is otherwise known as... 省略而
   來，意為「也因……為人所知；又稱為……」。

2. Although the festive air of the past few National Day
   celebrations has been tinted with tension over the ongoing
   debate of unification versus independence, most citizens do

not really concern themselves with slogans like "One China," "One Country on Each Side," "One Country, Two Systems," or "ROC on Taiwan," just as long as the social stability and economic prosperity of Taiwan are maintained!

◆ 這句話的主詞是 citizens，主要動詞是 do not concern。句子逗號前面的 Although... 為「副詞子句」，功能為講述本句的情況。

◆ be tinted with... 是「被……染上顏色」，這裡的 has been tinted with tension 是「已經沾惹上緊張的味道」。

◆ 句中的 versus 是介系詞，意為「……對……」，常被縮寫為 vs.；這裡的 unification versus independence 是「統一相對於獨立」。

◆ 主要子句中，concern oneself with... 就是「某人關心……」，這裡的 citizens do not concern themselves with... 就是「民眾們不關心……」。

◆ slogan 是「口號；標語」，like 是「如……；像……」，slogans like... 就是「像……的口號」。四個口號則接在 like 後面，用「對等連接詞」or 連接：(1) "One China" (2) "One Country on Each Side" (3) "One Country, Two Systems" (4) "ROC on Taiwan"。

◆ as long as... 是「只要……就好」，as long as... are maintained 就是「只要……有維持住就好」。這裡的「對等連接詞」and 連接的就是所要維持的兩個東西：(1) social stability of Taiwan (2) economic prosperity of Taiwan。

造句練習 ▶

1. 這法律是當時的工黨所頒布的。(enact / the then Labour Party)

   -

2. 人們聚在一起觀賞閱兵典禮。(military review ceremony)

   -

3. 小孩特別喜歡看煙火表演，因為煙火的顏色很漂亮。(fireworks display)

   -

4. 墮胎是個持續進行的辯論議題。(ongoing debate / abortion)

   -

5. 街上有一群憤怒的示威者呼喊著口號。(demonstrator / slogan)

   -

12

行憲紀念日與聖誕節
Constitution Day and Christmas

之前有一項調查，詢問大家對「七七」這兩個字的反應。結果大部分的受訪者認為「七七」代表巧克力棒(七七乳加巧克力)、或者代表喪葬習俗中的「七七佛事」，甚至是「七夕情人節」……講來講去，就是很少人將之聯想到「七七蘆溝橋事變」。

其實這種情形在以商業利益及消費為導向的現代社會中也越來越常見。例如，如果你問時下年輕人「12月25日」是什麼節日，大多數人都會回答「聖誕節」而非「行憲紀念日」。又如果你問他們「情人節幾月幾日？」大部分的人都會回答「2月14日」，而非「農曆七月七日」。至於「過年都做些什麼？」的問題，「參加跨年晚會」的答案恐怕要比「與家人一起守歲」要來得多！

傳統節日正在消失，西洋節慶卻日益受到重視，這是很多老一輩人的感嘆。但換個角度想，這種兼容並蓄，東西融合的特色，正是台灣寶島令人驕傲的地方。不管傳統或現代，本土或西洋，大家各取所需，各過各的節，又有什麼不好呢？

Constitution Day and Christmas

December 25th is our Constitution Day. In the past, Constitution Day had a great **significance**; **institutions**, schools, and even **households** would put out **national flags**.

December 25th is also Christmas, a very important day to **Christians** around the world. On this day, the birth of **Jesus Christ** is **celebrated**. Over the past few years, however, due to the **over-commercialization** of the holiday, many non-Christian Taiwanese, especially young people, started **exchanging** presents with friends, attending Christmas parties, and having Christmas **feasts**. ❶ Thus, Christmas is now a day when businesspeople rake in the dough while **turkeys** suffer great **calamity**.

In Taiwan, Constitution Day has no longer been celebrated these past few years. To most people, one less day **off** is **grim** news— not because the **solemnity** of Constitution Day has been lost, but for the reason that **Yuletide** celebrations have to be postponed until after work or after school! ❷

行憲紀念日與聖誕節

　　每年的12月25日，是我們的行憲紀念日。在以前，行憲紀念日具有非常重要的意義；各機關、學校、甚至住戶，都會在當天懸掛國旗。

　　12月25日也是聖誕節，是全世界基督徒慶祝耶穌誕生的重要節日。不過這幾年因為過度的商業炒作，很多非基督徒的台灣人、特別是年輕人，也開始在這天與朋友互贈禮物、參加聖誕節派對，以及吃聖誕大餐。因此聖誕節是個商人大發利市、而火雞遭受浩劫的日子。

　　在台灣，這幾年行憲紀念日已不再放假。對大多數人而言，損失了一天的假期，當然是個壞消息——倒不是因為行憲紀念日的莊嚴性喪失了，而是因為聖誕節的慶祝活動必須延至下班或放學後進行！

主題句：　　　　**單字：加黑**　　**片語：套色**　　**句型：❶❷**

單字例句 ▶

◇ **Constitution Day** 行憲紀念日

◇ **significance**(n.)重要性；意義
Few people are aware of the significance of the holiday.
很少人知道這節日的重要性。

◇ **institution**(n.)機構
The institution is famous for its good service.
這機構以好的服務聞名。

◇ **household**(n.)家庭；戶
Different households celebrate the New Year holiday in their own special ways.
家家戶戶以其特殊的方法慶祝新年佳節。

◇ **national flag** 國旗

◇ **Christian**(n.)基督徒
Most Christians go to church every Sunday.
大多數的基督徒每星期上教堂。

◇ **Jesus Christ** 耶穌基督

◇ **celebrate**(v.)慶祝
People all over the world celebrate Christmas Day.
全世界的人都慶祝聖誕節。

◇ **over-commercialization** 過度商業化

◇ **exchange**(v.)交換
The boy wants to exchange his book for my CD.
這男孩希望用他的書交換我的光碟。

◇ **feast**(n.)大餐；盛宴
The hosts prepared a magnificent feast for their guests.
主人準備了豪華大餐來招待他們的客人。

◇ **turkey**(n.)火雞
He had a turkey sandwich for lunch.
他午餐吃了火雞三明治。

◇ **calamity** [kə'læmətɪ](n.)災難；慘禍
The 9-21 earthquake was a major calamity for Taiwan.
九二一大地震對台灣是個大災難。

◇ **off**(adv.)停止；不工作
The boss gave us a week off during the holidays.
假期間老闆准許我們放一個星期的假。

◇ **grim**(adj.)冷酷的；面無喜色的
Their faces went grim when they heard the news.
當他們聽到這消息時，便面無喜色。

◇ **solemnity** [sə'lɛmnətɪ](n.)莊嚴；神聖
The solemnity of this religious occasion has been lost.
這宗教活動的莊嚴性已喪失了。

◇ **Yuletide** ['jul‚taɪd](n.)聖誕季節

片　語 ▶

◇ **put out :**

put out 有許多意思，這裡是「將……拿出放在外面」之意，例如：Remember to put the dog out before you go to bed.(睡覺前記得把狗放出去)。

◇ **rake in the dough :**

dough 原意為「生麵糰」，口語中是「金錢；現金」之意，rake in the dough 則是「賺進大筆鈔票」。

◇ **be postponed until... :**

postpone(v.)是「延遲；延擱」，be postponed until... 則是被動語式，意思為「被延期至……」，例如：The meeting was postponed until tomorrow.(會議被延到明天)。

句型分析 ▶

1. Over the past few years, however, due to the over-commercialization of the holiday, many non-Christian Taiwanese, especially young people, started exchanging presents with friends, attending Christmas parties, and having Christmas feasts.

　　◆ 這句話的主詞是 many non-Christian Taiwanese，主要動詞是 started。句中 however 是「語氣轉折詞」，表示目前這

句話與上面的那句話在語義上相反。

◆ due to... 是「因為……」，這裡的 due to the over-commercialization of... 是「因為……的過度商業化」。

◆ 句中逗號之間的 especially young people 是用來強調及修飾前面的主詞 many non-Christian Taiwanese，表示「許多非基督徒的台灣人，尤其是那些年輕人」。

◆ 句末的「對等連接詞」and連接了三個V+-ing，分別是：(1)exchanging...(2)attending...(3)having...（交換……、參加……、吃……）。

2. To most people, one less day off is grim news—not because the solemnity of Constitution Day has been lost, but for the reason that Yuletide celebrations have to be postponed until after work or after school!

◆ 這句話的主詞是 one less day off，主要動詞是 is。後面接的補充說明用的句型是：not because..., but for the reason that...（不是因為……，而是為了……的理由）。

◆ day off 的 off 是副詞，意為「停止；不工作」，因此 day off 就是「放假日」，而 one less day off 則是「少放一天假」。

◆ postpone(v.)是「延遲；延擱」，這裡用的是被動語態 be postponed until...「被延至……」。

造句練習 ▶

1. 12月25日是中華民國的行憲紀念日。(Constitution Day)

   ----

2. 特別場合節慶時國旗會升起。(national flag)

   ----

3. 節日的過度商業化扭曲了節日的真正意義。(over-commercialization / distort)

   ----

4. 節日是一年中商家賺大錢的好時機。(rake in the dough)

   ----

5. 這活動因為氣候不佳而延期。(be postponed)

政治外交

13

色彩繽紛的台灣選舉
Taiwan's Colorful Elections

　　美國著名人權牧師傑西・傑克森(Jesse Jackson)曾經說過，美國是個「彩虹國」，因為美國這個移民國度裡面各色人種都有，紅、黃、褐、黑、白("...our Nation is a rainbow, red, yellow, brown, black, white...")，就如彩虹一般美麗！

　　台灣近年來也成了「彩虹國」，其精神表現在兩方面：第一是年輕人頭髮的顏色：紅橙黃綠藍靛紫，好不美麗；另一個則是台灣人的政黨取向：藍綠橘黃紫，好不燦爛！

　　只可惜現在人們錯把顏色當成一切。以往善良的台灣人初次與人見面，第一個問的是：「甲罷未？」現在問的則是：「什麼顏色？」顏色錯了，一切免談！當然，有些人怕問顏色太直接，拐彎抹角問：「您認為兩顆子彈是真是假？」、「319廣場靜坐當天發的是排骨便當還是鰻魚便當？」、「三井日本料理有幾種套餐？」、「立委邱X到底是爆料天王還是台灣罪人？」答錯了，一樣一切免談！

Taiwan's Colorful Elections

Taiwan has "three **abundances**": people, money, and elections. The County **Magistrates** and City **Mayors** Election was believed to be not only a "blue **versus** green" war of **local authorities**, but also a **warm-up battle** for the 2008 **presidential elections**. ❶

On election night in the US, television **channels** display a map of the US and use red, blue, and purple to **mark** the **Democratic**, **Republican**, and **50-50** states. ❷ When compared with the US's, Taiwan's political colors are **undoubtedly** more **kaleidoscopic**!

On this color-**sensitive** island, everyone loves to **categorize** each other by using terms such as "**pan-blue**," "**pan-green**," or "pan-purple **alliance**." To **complicate** the situation even further, there are also "pro-**unification radicals**," "pro-independence radicals," "oranges that have turned green," and "yellow on the outside and blue on the inside," etc. Hey, why don't we make up our own "red party" and "**indigo** party?" Then Taiwan could become a colorful "**rainbow** country!"

色彩繽紛的台灣選舉

　　台灣有「三多」：人多、錢多、選舉也多。縣市長選舉被認為是「藍、綠」地方政權的攻防戰，也是2008年總統選舉的熱身戰。

　　美國在選舉夜時，電視台都會呈現美國地圖，然後用紅、藍、紫色代表共和黨、民主黨必勝的州，以及兩黨支持率呈五五波的州。比起美國，台灣的政治色彩便顯得繽紛燦爛、多采多姿！

　　在這個對「顏色」十分敏感的小島，大家最喜歡彼此亂扣帽子：你是「泛藍」、我是「泛綠」、他是「泛紫聯盟」。這樣還不夠，有人是「急統」、有人是「急獨」、還有人是「橘子綠了」、「外黃內藍」等等。嘿，我們何不自組「紅黨」及「靛黨」，這樣台灣便可以成為色彩繽紛的「彩虹國」！

主題句：　　　　　單字：加黑　　　片語：套色　　　句型：❶❷

單字例句 ▶

◇ **abundance**(n.)豐富；充裕
This year there is an abundance of mangoes and a shortage of strawberries.
今年芒果盛產，草莓短缺。

◇ **magistrate**(n.)長官；縣長
Magistrates are in charge of taking care of their people's needs.
縣長要負責照顧縣民的需要。

◇ **mayor**(n.)市長
The candidate for mayor has detailed a number of proposals.
這個市長候選人已列出一堆提案。

◇ **versus**(prep.)……對……
It is us versus them in this war.
在這場戰事中，是我們對抗他們。

◇ **local authority** 地方政權

◇ **warm-up battle** 熱身戰

◇ **presidential election** 總統選舉

◇ **channel**(n.)頻道
If you don't like the TV program, change the channel.
如果你不喜歡這節目，可以轉台。

- **mark(v.)標記**
  They used a red pen to mark their location on the map.
  他們用紅筆在地圖上標示他們的位置。

- **Democratic(adj.)(美國)民主黨的**
  The Democratic Party is one of the leading political parties in the United States.
  民主黨是美國主要政黨之一。

- **Republican(adj.)(美國)共和黨的**
  The President of the United States is a member of the Republican Party.
  這美國總統是共和黨的一員。

- **50-50 / fifty-fifty(adj.)呈「五五波」的；一半的**
  They started a business together, agreeing to split the profits fifty-fifty.
  他們一起創業，同意利潤對半分。

- **undoubtedly[kəˌlaɪdəˈskɑpɪk](adv.)毫無疑問地**
  This is undoubtedly the best piece of news I have heard today!
  這無疑是我今天聽到最好的消息！

- **kaleidoscopic [kəˌlaɪdəˈskɑpɪk](adj.)萬花筒的；五花八門的**
  The world of politics is definitely kaleidoscopic by nature.
  政治世界的本質絕對是千變萬化的。

- **sensitive(adj.)敏感的**
  Some politicians refuse to discuss sensitive issues such as

discrimination.

有些政治人物拒絕討論如歧視這種敏感的議題。

◇ **categorize**(v.)分類

The books have been categorized into three levels for ease of use.

為了方便使用，這些書已被分類為三個等級。

◇ **pan-blue** 「泛藍」

◇ **pan-green** 「泛綠」

◇ **alliance**(n.)同盟

Political parties set up alliances to garner more support.

政黨結交同盟以獲取更多的支持。

◇ **complicate**(v.)使複雜

To complicate matters further, another issue has been brought up.

另一個議題已被提出，使得事情更複雜了。

◇ **unification**(n.)統一

In Taiwan, politicians generally avoid discussing the question of unification.

在台灣，政治人物一般避免討論統一的問題。

◇ **radical**(n.)激進分子

People usually find it hard to agree with the proposals put forward by the radicals.

人們發現要同意激進分子所提出的提案往往很難。

◇ **indigo**[ˋɪndɪgo]（**n.**）靛色
The girl dyed her hair green with a hint of indigo.
這女孩將頭髮染呈成綠色，並帶點靛色。

◇ **rainbow**（**n.**）彩虹
I can see a rainbow now that the rain has stopped.
雨停了，我可以看到彩虹了。

片　語 ▶

◇ **compared with... :**
(when it is)compared with 是「與⋯⋯相比」之意(前面通常省略 when it is)，例如：The earth is a baby compared with many other celestial bodies.(和許多其他天體比較起來，地球不過是個小嬰兒)。

◇ （**color**）**-sensitive :**
sensitive(adj.)是「敏感的」，-sensitive則是「對⋯⋯敏感的」，例如 temperature-sensitive 是「對溫度敏感的」；sound-sensitive是「對聲音敏感的」。

◇ **pan-**（**blue**）**:**
pan- 表示「全⋯⋯；總⋯⋯；泛⋯⋯」之意，例如 pan-Asia 為「泛亞洲」，pantheist 為「泛神論者」。

◇ **pro-**（**unification**）**:**
pro- 是「贊成⋯⋯；親⋯⋯」之意，例如 pro-slavery 為「贊成

奴隸制度的」，pro-choice 為「主張女性有墮胎自主權的」。

◇ **make up：**

make up 有許多意思，文章中是「組成；形成」，例如：The committee is made up of representatives from every state.(這委員會是由每州的代表所組成的)。

句型分析 ▶

1. The County Magistrates and City Mayors Election was believed to be not only a "blue versus green" war of local authorities, but also a warm-up battle for the 2008 presidential elections.

   ◆ 這句話的主詞是 the County Magistrates and City Mayors Election，主要動詞是 was believed(被認為是……)。

   ◆ 句中的 versus 這個字即 vs.，因此 "blue versus green" 就是 "blue vs. green"，也就是「藍對抗綠」之意。

   ◆ 此句句中用到 not only..., but also... 的句型。not only a... war of..., but also a battle for... 為「不僅是一場……的戰爭，也是一場……的戰役」。

2. On election night in the US, television channels display a map of the US and use red, blue, and purple to mark the Democratic, Republican, and 50-50 states.

   ◆ 這句話的主詞是 television channels，主要動詞是 display...

(and)use...，以「對等連接詞」 and 連接兩個對等的動詞 (1)display(2)use。

◆ 句中的 mark 當動詞，是「標記；標註」，所標註的東 西有三個：(1)the Democratic states(2)the Republican states(3)the 50-50 states。

造句練習 ▶

1. 競爭對手們在比賽前一天碰面來個熱身賽。(contender / warm-up battle)

   -

2. 人們很關心總統選舉的結果。(presidential election)

   -

3. 她在已念過的書頁上做記號，然後闔上書。(mark the page)

   -

4. 他們贏得比賽的機會是一半一半。(competition / 50-50)

   -

5. 許多國家奮戰以保存獨立。(preserve / independence)

   -

14

馬屁文化
Brown-nosing Culture

　　台灣真是個生氣勃勃的小島！這個島上每隔一陣子便會流行一種新的文化，從以前的紅包文化(red-envelope culture)、送禮文化(gift-giving culture)、官場文化(political culture)、買票文化(vote-buying culture)，到最近的偷窺文化(peeping-Tom culture)、速食文化(fast-food culture)、甚至馬屁文化……，果真不負我國「擁有五千年悠久文化」的美名！

　　「馬屁文化」在寶島行之有年，從早期人們為了拍當權者馬屁所製作的一些「XX嘉言錄」，到這陣子還是為了拍當權者馬屁所引發的許多事件，在在都為「馬屁文化」下了最佳註解！

　　不過可別以為這種文化僅止於官場或政壇喔，舉凡職場、校園……都是馬屁文化的勢力範圍。君不見現在許多廠商為了能順利推動業務，每天照三餐送名畫紅包到官員家，許多公司員工也在下班後到老闆家幫忙澆花打掃接送小孩，或者將老闆的「墨寶」印成包裝紙四處分送。歪風傳到校園，現在許多學生家長也開始比照公家單位照「三節」送老師禮金。

　　唉，這種「君不君、臣不臣」、「上不上、下不下」、「師不師、徒不徒」的情形再惡化下去，恐怕繼「馬屁文化」後，台灣就要吹起「狗屁文化」了！

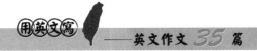
Brown-nosing Culture (CD1-14)

Last year Taiwan has been shrouded in a "**brown-nosing culture.**" Some examples of this are the so-called "brown-nosing questions," "brown-nosing bridge," and "brown-nosing **troops.**" With so much negative **wordplay** going around, it isn't hard to understand why former **Premier** Frank Hsieh is telling the general public to **mind** their "**personal hygiene.**" ❶

The rise of this brown-nosing culture can be **traced** to last year's senior examination for lawyers, where 78 out of 100 questions had something to do with President A-bian. Yet another brown-nosing drama is related to the Hsuehshan (Snow Mountain) Tunnel's temporary bridge, which was built on a NT$1.5 million budget, solely for the **transportation** convenience of A-bian and some **high ranking officials**. "Brown-nosing troops" refers to the Hsinchu air base troops who were forced to give up their holiday to **rehearse** songs and troop formation to welcome the president. ❷

It would be fair to say that the real **victims** here are the horses. There they were, living their lives without bothering anybody, and yet they are now associated with "brown-nosers." We can't help but wonder: do our **ancestors** hold a grudge against these creatures? You see, a lot of our negative idioms have something to do with horses, such as: "every ass likes to hear himself **bray**," "old and **unaccomplished**," "to give something away," "badly battered," and "to suffer an accidental **setback**"…

馬屁文化

去年台灣籠罩在一片「馬屁文化」中：馬屁題、馬屁橋、馬屁軍……，處處馬屁聲，難怪謝前院長要大家多注意「個人衛生」。

馬屁文化的興起可以追溯到去年的律師考試，其國文科試卷中，100分的考題竟有78分與阿扁總統有關。另一個與馬屁文化有關的「馬屁橋」，指的是雪山隧道的有關單位為了阿扁總統及一些高官的交通方便，特地花了150萬元所搭建的一座便橋。「馬屁軍」指的則是新竹空軍基地的官兵，他們為了歡迎阿扁總統視察基地，被迫犧牲休假排練歡迎歌曲和隊形。

平心而論，這些事件最大的受害者是可憐的馬兒。好端端的一隻動物，也沒招誰惹誰，現在竟然與「馬屁精」扯上關係。我們不禁要懷疑：我們的老祖先是否與馬有仇？不然怎麼有這麼多不好的成語，都與馬兒有關呢：「馬不知臉長」、「馬齒徒增」、「露出馬腳」、「人仰馬翻」、「馬失前蹄」……。

主題句：　　　　單字：加黑　　片語：套色　　句型：❶❷

單字例句 ▶

◇ **brown-nosing** (adj.) 拍馬屁的；諂媚的
brown-nose (v.) 拍馬屁
Lisa is always brown-nosing the boss, saying how smart she thinks he is.
Lisa 老是拍老闆的馬屁，說她認為他有多聰明。

◇ **troops** (n.) (多用複數) 軍隊
There is no news on when the troops in Iraq will be withdrawn.
沒有人知道駐在伊拉克的軍隊何時會撤退。

◇ **wordplay** (n.) 俏皮話
There is a lot of wordplay and puns in comic strips.
連環漫畫有許多俏皮話及雙關語。

◇ **premier** (n.) 首相；總理
The premier deals with important matters of the state.
首相處理國家的重大事情。

◇ **mind** (v.) 注意
Celebrities should mind what they say because people are always listening.
名人應該注意他們所講的話，因為人們總是很留意在聽。

◇ **personal hygiene** ['haɪdʒin] 個人衛生
Personal hygiene is a very important part of a person's image.

個人衛生是個人形象中很重要的一部分。

◇ **trace**(**v.**)追溯
The evidence could be traced back to the suspect's house.
這證據可以追溯回嫌犯的家中。

◇ **transportation**(**n.**)交通
The MRT is an indispensable transportation tool for traveling around Taipei.
在台北趴趴走時，捷運是個不可或缺的交通工具。

◇ **high ranking official** 高階官員
High-ranking officials seem to get a lot of benefits in addition to their high salaries.
除了高薪外，高階官員似乎還有許多福利。

◇ **rehearse**(**v.**)預演；演習
The actors need to rehearse that play.
演員們必須排演那齣戲。

◇ **victim**(**n.**)犧牲者
The people are the real victims of the politicians' reckless mistakes.
人民是政客魯莽錯誤的真正犧牲者。

◇ **ancestor**(**n.**)祖先
Some people are quite interested in reading about the history of their ancestors.
有些人對閱讀他們祖先的歷史很有興趣。

◇ **bray**(**v.**)(像驢子般)以高而沙啞的聲音說話

She brayed out her dissatisfaction while her husband tried to ignore her.
她高聲嘶叫著她的不滿，不過她老公試著不甩她。

✧ **unaccomplished（adj.）無成就的；無技能的**
We should not hire anybody who is unaccomplished.
我們不該雇用沒有本領的人。

✧ **setback（n.）挫折；倒退**
Do not let a single setback discourage you; more opportunities will come your way.
別讓一次的挫折使你沮喪；更多的機會將會到來。

片　語　▶

✧ **be shrouded in... :**
shroud（v.）為「遮蔽；覆蓋」，在句子中常用被動語態，後面接介系詞 in 或 by，例如：The airport was shrouded in a heavy mist.（機場籠罩在濃霧之中）。

✧ **... out of... :**
out of 這裡當介系詞，意思是「從某數當中……」，例如：one out of many 是「多數中的一個」，nine cases out of ten 是「十之八九」。

✧ **have something to do with... :**
此片語是「與……有關」之意，例如：She has something to do

with the murder.（她與這件謀殺案有關）。與此片語相反者為
have nothing to do with...，意思是「與……無關」。

◇ **solely for... :**
solely for... 意思是「完全為了……；只為了……」，例如：I
did it solely for his sake.（我完全是為了他才做那件事）。

◇ **be associated with... :**
associate(v.)是「與……有關連」之意，在句子中常用被動語
態，例如：We are associated with him in business.（我們跟他有
工作上的關係）。

◇ **can't help but... :**
can't help but... 是「不禁……；不得不……；不能不……」之
意，例如：I can't help but wonder.（我不禁納悶了起來）。

◇ **hold a grudge against... :**
grudge(n.)是「怨恨；宿怨」，hold(或用 have)a grudge
against... 是「對……懷恨」，例如：He's been holding a grudge
against me.（他對我懷恨已久）。

句型分析 ▶

1. With so much negative wordplay going around, it isn't hard
   to understand why former Premier Frank Hsieh is telling the
   general public to mind their "personal hygiene."

   ◆ 這句話的主詞是 it，主要動詞是 is。前面的 With so much

negative wordplay going around 是形容詞，修飾整句，一方面提供整句話所言的背景，一方面也帶出後面含有主詞與動詞的主要子句。With... 這裡是「隨著……」之意，around 形容 go，所以 go around 是「四處散播」。

◆ 主詞 it 是「虛主詞」，代替了後面的 to understand why...，意思是「要了解為什麼……」。因此 it isn't hard to understand why... 就是「要了解為什麼……並不困難」，簡言之，就是「難怪……」。

◆ general public 是「一般大眾」，tell the general public to... 就是「告訴一般大眾要……」。mind 這裡當動詞，是「注意」，用法較特別。personal hygiene 是個慣用語；mind one's personal hygiene 就是「注意個人衛生」。

2. "Brown-nosing troops" refers to the Hsinchu air base troops who were forced to give up their holiday to rehearse songs and troop formation to welcome the president.

◆ 這句話的主詞是 "Brown-nosing troops"，主要動詞是 refers。refer to... 是個常見的用法，意味「指的是……」。

◆ who 是「關係代名詞」，代替的是前面的 troops，所以子句中的動詞用的是複數形 were forced。這裡的 were forced to... 是「被強迫要……」，give up 是片語「放棄」。

◆ and 是「對等連接詞」，這裡連接的是兩個東西：(1) songs (2) troop formation。

◆ 句中 to rehearse... to welcome... 其實是 to rehearse... in order to welcome...，意思是「預演……以便歡迎……」。

造句練習 ▶

1. 報紙上充滿了有關那位政客的負面報導。(be full of negative...)

   ----

2. 一切都籠罩在霧雨之中。(shroud... in...)

   ----

3. 我總是把老闆與希特勒聯想在一起,因為他很殘酷。
   (associate... with Hitler...)

   ----

4. 人們聚集來觀賞廣場上的軍隊隊形表演。(gather to see...)

   ----

5. 一個好的領導者不該是個挾怨報復者。(a grudge holder)

15

凱子外交
Cash-for-Friendship Diplomacy

　　翻開台灣的外交史，簡直就是血淚斑斑的「斷交史」。自從咱們退出聯合國後，邦交國一路下滑，到現在只剩下二十多個，而且大多數還不太叫得出名字。

　　鑑於外交困境，台灣多年來一直奉行「金錢外交」、「凱子外交」政策，冀望高價「買」來的友邦們能在重要場合替咱們發言。不過灑錢不能保證邦交不墜，台灣的邦交國多游移在海峽兩岸，利用台灣與大陸的政治矛盾大賺其錢；也因此，台灣不惜重金維持的友誼，最後通常落得「國、財兩失」！

　　務實來說，台灣應該清楚，咱們再如何努力，也不可能買到進入聯合國門檻所需的邦交國數量。既然如此，多一國或少一國只是悵面好不好看、「奇檬子」好不好的問題而已；然而多「買」一個國家，台灣在財政及經濟上所必須付出的代價卻十分昂貴。

　　可憐的政府為免國人批評其「凱子外交」的政策，便以「獎勵投資」、「榮邦互惠」的名義加以美化。其實不論政府用什麼名義美化，凱子外交就是凱子外交，無底洞就是無底洞，就這麼簡單。

Cash-for-Friendship Diplomacy

President A-bian made **state visits** to **allied countries** in Central America last year, **announcing** a **pledge** of NT$8 billion for a "**co-prosperity fund.**" The **opposition camp** and local citizens accused the government of running another **episode** of "**money diplomacy.**"

Year after year, Taiwan spends millions on **public relations firms** just to get on the right side of **Uncle Sam,** but Taiwan is still no closer to gaining entry into the **United Nations**. Taiwan has continually been under pressure from Washington to buy **missiles** and other **weapons,** yet the U.S. claims that it has no **obligation** to help defend Taiwan in the event of an attack by China. ❶ Taiwan has also been investing **generous** amounts of money on its **allies,** which has only led to **monetary aid scandals**. The list of Taiwan's **woes** goes on and on.

Truth be told, the **expenditure** in question seems **minute** compared to our country's other **expenses**. ❷ It will cost us NT$80 billion to **strengthen** flood control and **drainage** functions, while **arms procurement** is also said to cost over NT$400 billion! On the other hand, what does NT$8 billion mean to Taiwanese people? All it really means is fewer cups of **pearl milk tea** and Louis Vuitton purses— what's all the fuss about anyway?

凱子外交

去年阿扁總統出訪中美洲友邦，宣布將以80億台幣成立「榮邦基金」，被在野黨及台灣人民罵到臭頭，認為又是一次「金錢外交」的戲碼。

台灣年年花大錢請公關公司向「山姆大叔」說好話，結果還是進不了聯合國；天天被逼著買飛彈武器，美國卻還說它沒責任在老共進犯時協防台灣；這幾年對友邦大肆灑錢，卻還陷入人家的金援醜聞……，說起台灣的悲情，那還真不是一天一夜說得完的。

其實比起其他花費，這些錢真的不算什麼。前陣子台灣治水的費用就要800億，軍購據說也有4000多億！不過台灣人也真是的，80億元算什麼？不過就是少喝點珍珠奶茶、少買個 LV 包包，吵什麼吵呢？

主題句：　　　　單字：加黑　　片語：套色　　句型：❶❷

單字例句 ▶

◇ **state visit 國事訪問**
Presidents usually make state visits to improve or maintain relationships with other countries.
總統通常進行國事訪問來增進或維持與其他國家的關係。

◇ **allied** [əˋlaɪd] **country 友邦**
Allied countries usually rely on each other for support.
友邦通常倚賴彼此的支持。

◇ **announce**(**v.**)**宣布**
The host announced the beginning of the party.
主人宣布舞會開始。

◇ **pledge** [plɛdʒ](**n.**)**保證；誓約**
The man signed a pledge to donate NT$1 million to charity.
這個人簽了一個約要捐獻一百萬元給慈善機構。

◇ **co-prosperity fund 榮邦基金**
The co-prosperity fund aims to provide financial aid to allies.
這個榮邦基金是為了要提供友邦財務援助。

◇ **opposition camp 反對陣營**
The opposition camp disagrees with everything the ruling party says.
反對陣營不同意執政黨所說的每件事。

◇ **episode** [ˋɛpəˏsod](**n.**)**插曲；情節**

It was only a matter of time before another episode of quarrels began.

另一個爭吵事件的發生只是遲早的事。

◇ **money diplomacy** [dɪˋplomǝsɪ] 金錢外交
Money diplomacy is another way of saying that we are paying countries to become our allies.

金錢外交只是我們付錢給他國，使之成為我們友邦的另一種說法。

◇ **public relations firm** 公關公司
Public relations firms help improve the image of the government.

公關公司幫忙改善政府的形象。

◇ **Uncle Sam** 山姆大叔（即美國）

◇ **United Nations** 聯合國

◇ **missile** [ˋmɪsḷ] (n.) 飛彈
Missiles cause massive destruction during attacks.

攻擊時，飛彈導致很大的破壞。

◇ **weapon** (n.) 武器
The military is stockpiling weapons to prepare for war.

軍隊正儲備武器，以準備戰事。

◇ **obligation** (n.) 義務；職責
You have an obligation to take care of your pet.

你有責任照顧你的寵物。

◇ **generous**(**adj.**)慷慨的；豐富的
The boss gave us a generous Christmas bonus this year.
老闆今年給我們很豐厚的聖誕節獎金。

◇ **ally**(**n.**)盟友
In the event of a war, your allies will come to your aid.
發生戰事時，你的盟友會來幫助你。

◇ **monetary aid scandal** 金援醜聞
The government is trying to win back the people's trust following the monetary aid scandal.
在金援醜聞後，政府正試著要贏回人民的信任。

◇ **woe**(**n.**)災禍；悲哀；苦惱
The man tried to drown his woes with a couple of beers.
這男的試著用啤酒抑制他的苦悶。

◇ **expenditure**(**n.**)花費；支出額
The manager advised the team members to limit their expenditures to essentials.
經理告誡隊員將花費控制在必要的支出上。

◇ **minute**(**adj.**)極少的
Don't bother too much with minute details.
別花太多心思在極小的細節。

◇ **expense**(**n.**)花費
The total expenses were more than they had anticipated.
總花費超出他們原先所預計的。

◇ **strengthen**(**v.**)強化；加強

You should drink more milk to help strengthen your bones.
你應該多喝牛奶，以幫助強健骨骼。

◇ **drainage** (n.) 排水
The government is working towards improving the drainage system of the city.
政府致力於改善城市的排水系統。

◇ **arms procurement** 軍購
The country is divided over the question of arms procurement.
這國家為了軍購問題而分裂。

◇ **pearl milk tea** 珍珠奶茶
An ice-cold cup of pearl milk tea feels especially refreshing on a hot summer day.
在炎熱的夏天，喝一杯冰冰涼涼的珍珠奶茶特別令人感到清爽。

片　語　▶

◇ **accuse... of... :**
accuse (v.) 是「控訴；譴責」，accuse... of... 是「以……理由譴責……」，例如：They accused him of cowardice.（他們指責他懦弱）。

◇ **gain entry into... :**
entry (n.) 是「入口；入場」，gain entry into... 是「取得……

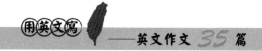

的入場權；加入……」，例如：Japan has gained entry into the WTO.(日本已取得進入世貿組織的權利)。

⬦ **the list... goes on and on：**

go on and on 是「持續不斷」，the list... goes on and on 是「……事情說也說不完」，例如：The list of government records removed from public access during the Bush administration goes on and on.(布希團隊主政期間，被移除掉的公眾可取得的政府紀錄多到說不完)。

⬦ **what's the fuss：**

fuss(n.)是「不必要的神經質；無謂的激動、煩惱」，例如：They want a quiet wedding without any fuss.(他們希望有個安靜的婚禮，不要無謂的煩惱)。文章中的 what's all the fuss about? 是「有什麼好大驚小怪的？」

句型分析 ▶

1. Taiwan has continually been under pressure from Washington to buy missiles and other weapons, yet the U.S. claims that it has no obligation to help defend Taiwan in the event of an attack by China.

   ◆ 這句話可以分為兩個子句，由「對等連接詞」yet 連接，第一個子句的主詞是 Taiwan，動詞是 has been；第二個子句的主詞是 the U.S.，動詞是 claims。

   ◆ 第一句話的 under pressure from... 是「處於來自……的壓

力」，這裡的 Washington 指的是「美國首府華盛頓」，也就是「美國」之意，所以 under pressure from Washington 就是「處於來自美方的壓力」。

◆ yet 是「然而」，表示前一個子句與現在這個子句在意義上有大轉變。it 指的是前面的 the U.S.。

◆ has obligation to help... 是「有義務幫助……」，加上 no，則變成「沒有義務幫助……」。in the event of... 是「在發生……事件時」，in the event of an attack 就是「在攻擊事件發生時」。

2. Truth be told, the expenditure in question seems minute compared to our country's other expenses.

◆ 這句話的主詞是 the expenditure，主要動詞是 seems。

◆ compared to... 是「與……相比」之意(前面通常省略 when it is)，所以這句話可看成：The expenditure seems minute when it is compared to other expenses.(與其他花費相比，這支出看起來其實很少)。

◆ in question 是「議論中的人、物；該人、物」，用來修飾前面的 expenditure，所以 the expenditure in question 就是「該項支出；所討論的這項支出」。

造句練習 ▶

1. 政府因為凱子外交被狠狠地批評。（be criticized for... / cash-for-friendship diplomacy）

   \-

2. 這經理處於必須增加銷售數字的壓力下。（under pressure / sales numbers）

   \-

3. 這男孩試著用棍子防禦這條狗。（defend... from...）

   \-

4. 這個新法律使得歐洲銀行得以進入新的市場。（enable / gain entry into...）

   \-

5. 別對不重要的事大驚小怪。（make a fuss about...）

   \-

16

政治酬庸
Political Compensation

「一人得道，雞犬升天」，這句話用來形容台灣的政壇真是再貼切不過！小至管家、特勤，大至總統府資政、國策顧問，這些雞雞犬犬，全都因為跟對了主子，一下子飛上了天。

有人辯說，「政治酬庸」在中國政壇由來已久：古代君王在得天下後，不也都會分封親戚、功臣、子弟為侯王，以換取他們的忠心嗎？

不過古代的帝王再昏庸也知道衡量輕重，將適合人選派駐在適合的地方，同舟共濟，同心協力，如此才能永保王朝的安康。現在的政治酬庸卻不然，只問「顏色」，不問「專業」。於是學文學的人可以擔任工程顧問公司的總管、駐外的特任官也非職業外交官出身，至於國營事業的董事長、電視台的總經理……，管它什麼專業，只要顏色對，通通有獎！不只如此，連大法官、監委、僑務委員會、蒙藏委員會的提名，也都有「政治酬庸」的影子，簡直把百姓當白癡看、把國家的前途當玩笑看。

治理國家不比扮家家酒，「只要我喜歡，有什麼不可以」，不可以就是不可以，台灣人民或許善良，但耐心總是有限度的！

Political Compensation (CD1-16)

The NT$40 million **stock bonus** awarded to the chairman of the China Steel Corporation (CSC) has created quite a **controversy**. The controversy has no doubt been **exacerbated** by the **recession** currently **plaguing** the local economy. While some students are **forced** to write lines on the chalkboard as **punishment** for paying **tuition** late, more fortunate individuals receive **honorary** positions and large **dividends** from **multiple corporations**. ❶ Who in his right mind wouldn't **blow a fuse**?

Although the chairman of CSC has **resigned** and **donated** his stock bonus to **charitable organizations**, the fact that the Taiwanese government is still offering high-paying **executive posts** to **cozy up** to individuals remains a reality. ❷

Indeed, the **nepotism** seen in Taiwanese politics goes well with an **instant coffee commercial**, which advises, "Share good things with good friends." Power should be **split** equally, and money should be **laundered collectively**! Well, "**absolute** power **corrupts** absolutely." This has not been the first case of "political compensation," and it will likely not be the last!

政治酬庸

中鋼董事長的4000萬分紅，引起許多爭議；而台灣目前經濟的蕭條，無疑地催化了這爭議。本來嘛，有學生窮到遲繳學費被強迫去罰寫黑板，卻有好命的人身兼多個榮譽職位、享有多家公司的鉅額分紅。哪個神智清楚的人能不大大生氣呢？

雖然這位中鋼董事長已宣布辭職，並將分紅捐贈慈善機構，但是台灣政府長久以來，利用高薪職務來拉攏特定人物的事實，卻沒有改變。

說起來，台灣這種內舉不避親的政治，正符合了某家即溶咖啡的廣告詞：「好東西要與好朋友分享」。有權大家分，有錢大家撈！唉，「絕對的權力導致絕對的腐敗」；這類「政治酬庸」不是第一次，當然也不會是最後一次啦！

主題句：　　　　　單字：**加黑**　　片語：套色　　句型：❶❷

單字例句 ▶

◇ **stock bonus** 股票分紅

◇ **controversy** [ˋkɑntrəˏvɝsɪ] (n.) 爭議
The controversy ruined the lawyer's reputation.
這爭議毀了這律師的名譽。

◇ **exacerbate** [ɪgˋzæsəˏbet] (v.) 使惡化
His illness was exacerbated by his not getting enough sleep.
他的病情因為睡眠不足而更加惡化。

◇ **recession** (n.) (經濟) 衰退；蕭條
Purchasing power declined during the recession.
經濟衰退時購買力便下跌。

◇ **plague** [pleg] (v.) 使受害；折磨
The new computer system has been plagued by many malfunctions.
這個新的電腦系統一直有許多故障。

◇ **force** (v.) 強迫
The mother forced her son to finish his vegetables.
這母親強迫她兒子吃完他的蔬菜。

◇ **punishment** (n.) 處罰
The boy was ordered to stay after school to clean the halls as punishment.
這男孩被命令留校清潔走廊，以做為懲罰。

◇ **tuition** [tjuˋɪʃən] (**n.**) 學費
Students work during the summer to earn money for tuition.
學生們暑假工作以賺取學費。

◇ **honorary** (**adj.**) 榮譽的
The influential man was given an honorary position in the company and enjoyed great benefits.
這個有權勢的人擔任此公司一個榮譽職位，且享有一拖拉庫的福利。

◇ **dividend** [ˋdɪvəˌdɛnd] (**n.**) 股息；紅利
The company distributed large amounts of dividends to its shareholders.
這公司分了許多股息給股東們。

◇ **multiple** (**adj.**) 多的
His new album includes multiple versions of the same songs.
他的新專輯包含了同一首歌曲的多種版本。

◇ **corporation** (**n.**) 公司；企業
The corporation owns a number of small companies.
這企業擁有一些小公司。

◇ **blow a fuse** 生氣；大怒

◇ **resign** (**v.**) 辭職
The man decided to resign after the boss refused to give him a pay raise.
當老闆拒絕給他加薪後，這人決定辭職。

◇ **donate** (**v.**) 捐贈

He donates blood regularly to help those in need.
他定期捐血以幫助需要的人。

- ◇ **charitable organization 慈善機構**

- ◇ **executive post 管理階層的職位；決策的職務**

- ◇ **cozy up**（口語）拉攏；博取歡心
  He tried to cozy up to his new boss.
  他試著博取新老闆的歡心。

- ◇ **nepotism**（n.）偏袒親戚；裙帶關係
  Most politicians practice nepotism, providing their family and friends with influential positions.
  大部分的政治人物都愛用裙帶關係，替他們的親朋好友弄到有權勢的職位。

- ◇ **instant coffee 即溶咖啡**
  To save time, I drink instant coffee instead of brewed coffee.
  為了節省時間，我喝即溶咖啡而非煮的咖啡。

- ◇ **commercial**（n.）商業廣告
  People are sometimes influenced by commercials to buy things they don't need.
  人們有時會受到廣告的影響而買了他們不需要的東西。

- ◇ **split**（v.）分裂；分開
  He used an ax to split the wood in half.
  他用斧頭將木材劈成兩半。

- ◇ **launder** ['lɔndə]（v.）洗（錢；贓款）

The drug dealers have used many methods to launder their money.

藥頭用盡各種方法洗錢。

◇ **collectively**(adv.)集體地

The nation needs to speak collectively in order to get more attention.

國家的人民必須集體發聲，以便引起更多的注意。

◇ **absolute**(adj.)絕對的；完全的

The people place absolute trust in their leaders.

人們完全信任他們的領導者。

◇ **corrupt**(v.)腐敗；墮落

They say power corrupts.

有一說「權力會腐化」。

片　語　▶

◇ **no doubt :**

doubt(n.)是「懷疑」，no doubt 是「無疑地」，例如：No doubt she will succeed.(毫無疑問，她會成功)。

◇ **who in his right mind :**

這片語的用法通常為 nobody in his/her right mind would + V，意思是強調「沒有哪個正常人會做……」。這裡的 who in his right mind 便是「哪個正常人會……？」例如：Who in his right mind would support such a program?(哪個頭腦清楚的人會支持那樣的方案?)

◇ **go well with... :**

go well with...是「與……合得來」,例如:White wines go well with seafood.(白酒與海鮮很合)。

句型分析 ▶

1. While some students are forced to write lines on the chalkboard as punishment for paying tuition late, more fortunate individuals receive honorary positions and large dividends from multiple corporations.

   ◆ 這句話的主詞是 individuals,主要動詞是 receive。句子逗號前的 While... 是引導讓步的副詞子句,意為「雖然……;儘管……」,與 although... 意思相近。

   ◆ be forced to... 是「被強迫要……」,as 這裡是「當成……」,所以 write lines on the chalkboard as punishment 是「在黑板寫字當作懲罰」。as punishment for... 是「當作……的懲罰」。

   ◆ 主要子句中的「對等連接詞」and 連接兩個東西:(1)honorary positions(2)large dividends。

2. Although the chairman of CSC has resigned and donated his stock bonus to charitable organizations, the fact that the

Taiwanese government is still offering high-paying executive posts to cozy up to individuals remains a reality.

♦ 這句話的主詞是 the fact，主要動詞是 remains。逗號前面的 Although...為「副詞子句」，功能為講述本句的情況。

♦ 副詞子句中的「對等連接詞」and 連接(1)has resigned(2)has donated。donate to... 是「捐獻給……」。

♦ 主要子句中的 that the Taiwanese government is still... to individuals是由 that 所引導的子句，補充說明前面的 fact，所以這個主要子句可以簡省為：the fact... remains a reality.(這個... 的事實沒有改變)。

♦ 由 that 所引導的子句中，high-paying post 是「高薪職位」，cozy up to... 是「拉攏……；博取……的歡心」。

造句練習 ▶

1. 政府又一次因為給予政治酬庸而被批評。(hand out / political compensation)

----

2. 他老爸因股票分紅賺了很多錢。(stock bonus)

----

3. 當她發現兒子蹺課時，發了一頓大脾氣。(blow a fuse)

----

4. 慈善機構尋找辦法替需要幫助的人募款。（charitable organization / raise money）

- -

5. Linda 已得到一個管理階層的職位，而且待遇超好。

（executive post）

- -

17

熊貓來台灣！
Pandas Coming to Taiwan!

　　自從中國宣布贈送台灣兩隻熊貓的消息曝光後，兩岸就陷入一股熊貓熱。在大家將這個議題泛政治化、甚至延請所謂「專家學者」閉門開會討論後，這兩隻熊貓仍是只聞樓梯響，不見人下來。

　　其實中國送咱們熊貓，說沒有私心，是騙人的。而台灣當局一直拒絕熊貓，說沒有私心，也是騙人的。不過熊貓哪管你藍綠，大家天天將「統戰」、「陰謀」等罪名往牠們身上灌，難怪可憐的熊貓吃不好睡不著，個個得了黑眼圈。

　　撇開政治因素不談，可愛的熊貓要被這麼「送來送去」，真的很可憐！台灣氣候炎熱，對性喜溫和氣候的熊貓是一大考驗，天天要牠們睡冷氣房，不僅花費多，也很不人道。另外，台北的木柵動物園究竟有無豢養熊貓的能力與場地，令人懷疑。就算這些問題都克服了，養熊貓還要大筆的經費與團隊的投入，龐大的照護費用在許多台灣學生都沒有營養午餐吃的情況下，似乎有點「不食人間煙火」……。

　　熊貓到底要不要來？讓我們政治擺一邊、務實擺中間！

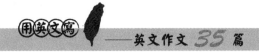
Pandas Coming to Taiwan! (CD1-17)

After **former** KMT **chairman** Lien Chan rounded off his trip to the mainland last May, China announced its big present to Taiwan: a pair of **pandas**, China's **national treasure**!

As soon as the news got out, a "Panda Effect" took over Taiwan. Some argued that the pandas are a **"communist conspiracy,"** so we should definitely not accept the gift. Some thought that pandas are **cuddly** and **rare**, and the government should not even think of **rejecting** them. The two sides argued so bitterly that a **referendum** was **proposed**. The poor pandas have become the **centerpiece** of a political **struggle**, although few people actually care about the **dilemma** the pandas themselves have been put under. ❶

The panda's **staple** food is **bamboo**, and it is fit to live in a **temperate climate**. They need wide open spaces to move about, not zoos where they will be kept in captivity. From the standpoint of **nature conservation**, the pandas' arrival in Taiwan will only speed up their process of becoming an **"endangered species!"**

Pandas are only black and white— they have no political **affiliation**. How could such a **creature** bring us peace? If we really are looking for peace, why don't the countries on the **opposite** sides of the **strait** just **trade** leaders? As for the question of who should be kept in captivity, the answer is none other than the **politicians** who are using these pandas as political **pawns**! ❷

熊貓來台灣！

去年五月國民黨前主席連戰結束大陸之旅後，中國便宣布送台灣一件大禮：一對國寶級熊貓！

消息一公布，「熊貓效應」馬上延燒全台灣。有人認為熊貓是「共產黨陰謀」，因此千萬不能接受。有人卻認為熊貓可愛又珍貴，政府萬萬不能拒絕。兩方人馬吵翻天，甚至祭出「全民公投」。可憐的熊貓，變成了政治角力的主角，卻很少人真正關心牠們的處境。

熊貓的主食是竹子，適合生長在溫帶氣候，且需要很大的活動範圍，而非在動物園內被囚禁。因此從自然保育的立場來看，來台灣的熊貓只會更加速變成「瀕臨絕種的動物」！

其實貓熊只有黑白，沒有政治，哪能換得和平？如果真要和平，那麼兩岸乾脆互贈領導人吧！至於誰最該被囚禁？當然是將熊貓當政治操弄的政客囉！

主題句： 　　　　單字：加黑　　片語：套色　　句型：❶❷

單字例句 ▶

- **former**(adj.)以前的
  The former president attended the ceremony today.
  前任總統今天參加了這典禮。

- **chairman**(n.)主席
  The chairman spoke in front of the whole company today.
  主席今天在公司所有員工面前講話。

- **panda**(n.)熊貓
  People flocked to the zoo to see the giant panda.
  人們聚集到動物園看大熊貓。

- **national treasure** 國家寶藏

- **communist** [ˋkɑmjuɔnɪst](adj.)共產黨的
  He is a loyal supporter of the communist party.
  他是共產黨的忠誠支持者。

- **conspiracy**(n.)陰謀
  They believe that the whole incident is a conspiracy.
  他們相信這整個事件是個陰謀。

- **cuddly**(adj.)可愛的；令人想擁抱的
  Children think that teddy bears are cute and cuddly.
  孩子們認為泰迪熊既可愛又令人想擁抱。

- **rare**(adj.)稀有的；珍貴的
  It is rare to see monkeys walking on the street.

看到猴子在路上走是很少見的。

◇ **reject**(v.)拒絕
His application has been rejected by the school board.
他的申請被學校董事會給拒絕了。

◇ **referendum** [ˌrɛfəˈrɛndəm](n.)公投
The government held a referendum to understand the preference of the public.
政府舉辦公投來瞭解大眾的喜好。

◇ **propose**(v.)提議
The manager proposed that we change our marketing strategy.
經理提議我們改變市場行銷策略。

◇ **centerpiece**(n.)最重要的部分
The product has become the centerpiece of the company's new plan.
這產品已成為公司新計畫中最重要的部分。

◇ **struggle**(n.)鬥爭；掙扎
His faith helped him through his struggle.
他的信念幫助他度過內心掙扎。

◇ **dilemma** [dəˈlɛmə](n.)左右為難的狀況
The problem put her into a dilemma.
這問題讓她陷入左右為難的情況。

◇ **staple**(adj.)主要的
Rice is the traditional staple food in Taiwan.

米是台灣傳統的主食。

◇ **bamboo** [bæmˋbu] (**n.**) 竹子
Chopsticks are made of bamboo.
筷子是竹子做的。

◇ **temperate climate** 溫帶氣候
Some animals are fit to live in a temperate climate.
有些動物適合在溫帶氣候生活。

◇ **nature conservation** 自然保育
The country is trying to promote nature conservation among its people.
這國家正試著向人民提倡自然保育的觀念。

◇ **endangered species** [ˋspiʃiz] 瀕臨絕種動物
Many animals are now considered to be endangered species.
很多動物現在都被認為是瀕臨絕種動物。

◇ **affiliation** (**n.**) 同盟；和……有關係
We help people without regard to their race, gender, or religious affiliation.
我們幫助人，不論其種族、性別、或宗教關係。

◇ **creature** [ˋkritʃɚ] (**n.**) 生物；動物
He cannot bear to harm living creatures.
他無法忍受傷害活著的動物。

◇ **opposite** (**adj.**) 相對的；相反的
She turned and walked off in the opposite direction.
她轉身往相反方向走去。

◇ **strait**(n.)海峽(此指台灣海峽)
The countries on the two sides of the strait have frequent disagreements.
海峽兩岸的國家常常有意見不合的時候。

◇ **trade**(v.)交換；做買賣
The man traded his watch for cash.
這人將他的手錶換成現金。

◇ **politician** [ˌpɑləˈtɪʃən] (n.)政客；政治人物
Politicians are known for being aggressive.
政客以好鬥聞名。

◇ **pawn**(n.)抵押物；卒子
Taiwan sometimes seems like a pawn in the political struggle between China and the U.S.
台灣有時似乎成為中國與美國政治角力的一顆卒子。

片　語 ▶

◇ **round off**：
round off 的意思是「圓滿的結束；愉快地度過」，例如：Let's round off the party with a song.(讓我們以一首歌，圓滿結束這次的聚會)。

◇ **take over**：
take over 是「接收；接管」，例如：This region was taken over

by the army.(這一地區由軍隊接收了)。take over 引申也有「席捲……」之意,例如文章中的 The effect took over Taiwan.(這效應席捲台灣)。

◇ **be fit to... :**

fit(adj.)是「適合的」,be fit to... 是「適合(做)……」,後接原形動詞,例如:The house is not fit to live in.(那棟房子不適合居住)。

◇ **move about :**

about(adv.)是「到處地」之意,常與動詞連用,例如:go about(四處走動)、move about(四處移動)、look about(環顧四周)等。

◇ **keep in captivity :**

captivity(n.)是「囚禁」,keep in captivity 是「使監禁;使囚禁」,例如:The animals in the zoo were kept in captivity.(動物園裡的動物都被囚禁了)。

◇ **from the standpoint of... :**

standpoint(n.)是「立場;觀點」,from the standpoint of... 是「從……的觀點來看」,例如:There is no point in studying history if we only see it from the standpoint of those in power.(如果我們只從當權者的觀點來看歷史,那就沒必要學歷史了)。

◇ **speed up :**

speed(v.)是「快速前進,」speed up 則是「加速」,例如:Let's speed up a bit.(我們加快一點速度好了)。

句型分析 ▶

1. The poor pandas have become the centerpiece of a political struggle, although few people actually care about the dilemma the pandas themselves have been put under.

   ◆ 這句話的主詞是 the pandas，主要動詞是 have become。句子逗號後面的 although... 是「副詞子句」，意為「雖然……」，功能為講述本句的情況。

   ◆ centerpiece(n.)是「最引人注意之處；最重要的部分」，become the centerpiece of... 則是「成為……最引人注意之處」。

   ◆ care about... 是「關心……」。put under 是「放在……處境」，這裡 be put under 用的是被動語態，代表「熊貓被放在……的處境」。

2. As for the question of who should be kept in captivity, the answer is none other than the politicians who are using these pandas as political pawns!

   ◆ 這句話的主詞是 the answer，主要動詞是 is。句首的 As for... 是「至於……」，As for the question of... 則是「至於……的問題」。

   ◆ captivity(n.)是「囚禁」，keep in captivity 是「監禁；囚禁」，這裡用的是被動語態 be kept in captivity(被囚禁)。

   ◆ none other than... 是「不是別人，而是……；就是；正是」，所以這裡的 the answer is none other than the politicians 為「答案正是這些政客」。

◆ 句末的 who... 為「關係代名詞」，代替前面的 politicians，說明這些 politicians 是 are using these pandas as...（將熊貓用來當作……）。

造句練習 ▶

1. 經過幾個星期成功的辯論，他們圓滿完成對談。(round off... / debate)

----

2. 熊貓被認為是中國最大的國家寶藏之一。(panda / national treasure)

----

3. 嫌犯在面對法庭之前會先羈押囚禁起來。(hold in captivity / face the court)

----

4. 請試著用旁人的觀點看事情。(from... standpoint)

----

5. 她必須多付費，好讓申請程序加速。(speed up / application process)

18

外資、港資、中資？
Foreign-, Hong Kong-, or China-Invested?

　　去年年底朝野為了 TVBS 到底是中資還是外資掀起一陣口水戰，結果新聞局認定 TVBS 股權百分之百屬外資，必須罰鍰一百萬元。不過 TVBS 後來提起訴願，行政院在今年五月決定撤銷原處分，要新聞局歸還那一百萬元。一場「X資」風波，似已告個段落。

　　撇開 TVBS 的案例不談，台灣多的是在維京、開曼群島等「避稅天堂」註冊，藉以逃避台灣稅制的不肖公司行號。這些公司吃台灣的、住台灣的，卻不用繳台灣稅。說實在的，政府在國家財務困窘的情況下，是否該認真查辦這個問題？這種隨便查都查得到的事不去追究，卻整天在吵外資還是中資，說難聽點，實在浪費口水又沒出息！

　　沒繳稅的不去查、有繳稅的又嫌人家資金來源不正確，這在邏輯上似乎有問題。

Foreign-, Hong Kong-, or China-Invested? (CD1-18)

Last year a TV station in Taiwan was suspected of having 100 percent of foreign **shareholdings**, and is thus in **violation** of the **Satellite Broadcasting Law**. All of a sudden, terms like "**foreign-invested**," "Hong Kong-invested," and "China-invested" are all over the place, leaving the general public completely **baffled**. ❶ Some say that "Hong Kong-invested" **equals** "China-invested," and the TV station should have its **license revoked**. Others say that if "Hong Kong-invested" equals "China-invested," then *Next Magazine*, the *Apple Daily*, and Watson's would all have to be shut down.

In truth, whether the station is foreign-, Hong Kong-, or China-invested is beside the point. The real issue is whether the **corporation** is "Taiwan-taxed," "foreign-taxed," or "untaxed." If a business is using foreign **capital** to earn money and paying its **taxes** in Taiwan, this is to be encouraged! ❷ But if a business rakes in money from Taiwan yet **registers** the company abroad to **avoid taxes**, it should be further **investigated**! Although with government **officials** so preoccupied with **campaign gimmicks**, who has enough energy left to tackle such a serious problem?

外資、港資、中資？

去年台灣某家電視台被質疑「外資持股達100%」，因而違反衛星廣播電視法的規定。一時之間，「外資」、「港資」、「中資」滿天飛，聽得老百姓一頭霧水。有人說，「港資」等於「中資」，這家電視台應被撤照。也有人說，如果「港資」等於「中資」，那麼《壹週刊》、《蘋果日報》、「屈臣氏」統統都應該關門！

其實這家電視台是「外資」、「港資」、「中資」都無關緊要，重點在於「台稅」、「外稅」，還是「沒繳稅」。如果一家公司拿外國資金在台灣賺錢、繳稅，其實值得鼓勵！但如果在台灣賺錢，卻將公司登記在外國來避稅，那才應該去追究！只不過政府官員搞選舉造勢花招都忙不完了，誰還有力氣去辦這種正經事呢？

主題句： 　　　　單字：**加黑**　　片語：套色　　句型：❶❷

單字例句 ▶

◇ **shareholding**(n.)持股
The government regulates the ratio of company shareholdings.
政府調整公司持股的比例。

◇ **violation**(n.)違背;破壞
He has to pay a fine for a traffic violation.
他駕車違規,必須繳罰款。

◇ **Satellite Broadcasting Law / Radio and Television Act** 廣電法

◇ **foreign-invested**(adj.)外資的
The foreign-invested company is said to have illegal operations.
據說這家外資公司有非法營運。

◇ **baffle**(v.)使困惑
The confusing news story baffled everyone who read it.
每個看了這則新聞故事的人都很困惑。

◇ **equal**(v.)等於;相等
Two plus two equals four.
2加2等於4。

◇ **license**(n.)執照
He has a license to own a gun.

他有擁槍執照。

◇ **revoke**(v.)撤銷
His driver's license was revoked after the accident.
意外事故後，他的執照被吊銷。

◇ **corporation**(n.)公司；企業
Big corporations hire celebrities to endorse their products.
大企業僱請名人為其產品代言。

◇ **capital**(n.)資金
The company is funded entirely by foreign capital.
這公司全為外資。

◇ **tax**(n.)稅
He has to pay thousands of dollars in taxes.
他必須繳好幾千元的稅。

◇ **register**(v.)註冊
His company is registered under his father's name.
他的公司註冊在他父親名下。

◇ **avoid tax** 避稅
It may be illegal to intentionally avoid taxes.
故意逃稅可能是違法的。

◇ **investigate**(v.)調查
The police are investigating the crime.
警察在調查犯罪。

◇ **official**(n.)官員
Government officials enjoy great benefits.
政府官員坐享許多福利。

◇ **campaign** [kæmˋpen](n.)(競選)活動
Election candidates always come up with new ideas for their campaigns.
選舉候選人總是為他們的競選活動想出新的點子。

◇ **gimmick** [ˋgɪmɪk](n.)噱頭；花招
The promises candidates make are usually no more than gimmicks.
候選人所下的承諾通常都只是噱頭罷了。

片　　語　▶

◇ **be suspected of... :**
suspect(v.)是「懷疑」，be suspected of... 是「被懷疑……」，
例如：These three people are suspected of involvement in the murder.(這三個人被懷疑涉及該謀殺案)。

◇ **in violation of... :**
violation(n.)是「違背；破壞」，in violation of... 是指「對法律或承諾等的違背、違犯」，例如：He is in violation of the traffic law.(他違反交通規則)。

◇ **shut down：**

shut down 是「暫時性或永久性的關閉店鋪、工廠」，例如：
He decided to shut down his company.(他決定關閉他的公司)。

◇ **beside the point：**

point 是「要點」，beside the point 是「離開本題」，引申有
「無關主旨」之意。例如：Being captured is beside the point; the
important thing is not to surrender.(被逮捕無關緊要；重點是不
要投降)。

◇ **rake in money：**

rake 是「以耙子耙……」，rake in money 是「耙進大把金錢；
大撈一筆」，例如：They put up an online shopping website,
hoping to rake in money.(他們架設了個網路購物網站，希望能
賺大錢)。

◇ **be preoccupied with...：**

preoccupy 是「使專注」，be preoccupied with... 是「全神專注
於……」，例如：They are preoccupied with their thoughts.(他們
個個心事重重)。

◇ **tackle a problem：**

tackle(v.)是「解決(問題)」，tackle a problem 即「解決問
題」，例如：There are many different ways you could use to
tackle this problem.(你有幾種不同的方法可以解決這個問題)。

句型分析 ▶

1. All of a sudden, terms like "foreign-invested," "Hong Kong-invested," and "China-invested" are all over the place, leaving the general public completely baffled.

   ♦ 這句話的主詞是 terms，動詞是 are。句子最前面的 All of a sudden 用來修飾全句，是「突然間，……」。

   ♦ like 這裡當「像……；如同……」，terms like... 意為「像……的語彙」，這裡舉出三個語彙：(1) "foreign-invested" (2) "Hong Kong-invested" (3) "China-invested"。

   ♦ 句中的 all over the place 是「到處都是」。leaving 的原形是 leave，這裡用 V+-ing 是因為這句話已有主要動詞 are，因此 leave 必須「去動詞化」。這裡 leaving... 的意思是「留給……；讓……」，leaving... baffled 是「讓……困惑」。

2. If a business is using foreign capital to earn money and paying its taxes in Taiwan, this is to be encouraged!

   ♦ 這句話的主詞是 this，主要動詞是 is。句子逗號前是以 If 引導的「條件句」，意為：「如果……」。

   ♦ 「對等連接詞」 and 在句子中連接兩個東西：(1) using foreign capital to earn money (2) paying taxes。

   ♦ 主要子句中的 this 是指條件子句中提的所有東西，即 "a business is using foreign capital to earn money and paying its taxes in Taiwan"。to be encouraged 是「可以被鼓勵的；值得鼓勵的」。

造句練習 ▶

1. 警察懷疑他與這犯罪有關。(suspect that... / crime)

   -

2. 政府關閉這家製造違禁藥的公司。(shut down / illegal medicine)

   -

3. 這公司很成功，賺進大把鈔票。(rake in money)

   -

4. 因為太專注於家庭問題，他的工作表現一直不佳。(be preoccupied with...)

   -

5. 我們必須解決手上的這個問題，之後再去擔心其他的事情。(tackle the problem)

   -

19

走開，損友！
Leave Me Be, Bad Company!

　　人在江湖混，最怕的就是交到一堆狐群狗黨的壞朋友；國家也一樣，就怕結交的盟友都是酒肉朋友，只能同享樂，不能共患難。

　　台灣所結交的友邦，多是政治不開明、經濟不發達的蕞爾小國。雖說咱們交朋友時，本不應該大小眼，斤斤計較朋友的身分地位，但是如果友邦頭目不勤政愛民，專門貪污受賄，將台灣納稅人的血汗錢拿去娶N個小老婆，或者供其數也數不清的子女胡亂花費，那咱們豈不是要背負「助紂為虐」的罪名嗎？

　　其實台灣對友邦及非友邦的好，真是沒話說。不僅常常派遣農耕隊、農技團、以及各種技術團幫助邦交國發展農、漁、觀光業，也常白白送錢給對方中飽私囊。若國際上發生任何災難，台灣也常義不容辭、給予不請自來的捐款及援助。無奈常常「熱臉貼冷屁股」、「妹有意，郎無情」。

　　俗語說，「出外靠朋友」，台灣身為地球村的一份子，固然有其應盡的責任與義務，不過長年這樣付出，卻得不到些許回報，或許大家應該仔細思考這樣的付出是不是值得？

Leave Me Be, Bad Company! `CD2-1`

An English **proverb** says, "A friend in need is a friend **indeed**." Confucius has also added that good friends should be "**straightforward, upright**, and **knowledgeable**." Poor Taiwan has been searching for friends around the world for years. It has even been offering cash **enticements** in exchange for friendship, only to end up **luring** those countries that are "poor, **deceitful**, and **materialistic**."

One friend of Taiwan, Senegal, is a perfect example. A decade ago, the country cut **diplomatic ties** with **mainland China** for **monetary** reasons, yet now it wants to **switch allegiance** to mainland China for the same reason. Not feeling **ashamed**, Senegal further adds that "between countries there are no friends, only **benefits**." ❶ **Alas**, we could certainly do without such friends!

With Senegal gone, Taiwan is left with only 25 friends. But we need not **despair**, for "when it comes to making friends, **quality** matters more than **quantity**." What's more, rather than **squandering** money year after year to provide for **corrupt** allies, wouldn't it be better if we used it to **fund** more nutritious school lunches for Taiwanese children? ❷

走開，損友！

西諺云：「在你需要時幫助你的，才是真正的朋友」。孔子也說，好的朋友必須「友直，友諒，友多聞」。可憐的台灣，多年來在世界各地辛苦尋找朋友，甚至不惜花大錢買朋友，遇到的卻偏偏都是「友貧，友詐，友現實」的傢伙。

台灣的朋友塞內加爾就是最好的例子。這傢伙10年前為了錢跟大陸斷交，現在又為了錢與大陸建交。此國不但不覺得羞愧，還進一步說「國家之間沒有友誼，只有利益」。唉，這種朋友不要也罷！

沒有了賽內加爾，台灣只剩25個朋友。不過大家別絕望，「朋友貴精不貴多」。而且與其每年灑錢讓友邦貪污，還不如將錢花在台灣學童的營養午餐！

主題句：████　　單字：**加黑**　　片語：套色　　句型：❶❷

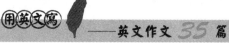
單字例句 ▶

◇ **company**(n.)伴侶

◇ **proverb**(n.)諺語;格言
Proverbs teach us lessons that are important in life.
格言教導我們生命中重要的課題。

◇ **indeed**(adv.)實在地;真正地
She is indeed the most beautiful girl in the party.
她真的是舞會中最漂亮的女孩。

◇ **straightforward**(adj.)直接的;坦率的
Good friends give straightforward answers to our questions.
好友對我們的問題坦率以答。

◇ **upright**(adj.)正直的;誠實的
Parents teach their children to always be upright in their daily lives.
父母親教導孩子們日常生活要保持誠實正直。

◇ **knowledgeable**(adj.)知識廣博的
He is very knowledgeable in the subject of politics.
他對於政治議題所知甚詳。

◇ **enticement**(n.)誘惑
He was offered cash and benefits as enticements.
他被誘以金錢及福利。

◇ **lure**(v.)引誘

Computer games are luring youngsters away from their lessons.

電腦遊戲引誘年輕人遠離課業。

◇ **deceitful** [dɪˋsitfəl]**(adj.)**詐欺的

Friends who are deceitful do not really care about your well-being.

不老實的朋友並不真的關心你的幸福。

◇ **materialistic(adj.)**物質主義的；現實主義的

People are becoming more and more materialistic.

人們越來越物質主義了。

◇ **diplomatic ties(多用複數)**外交關係

◇ **mainland China** 中國大陸

◇ **monetary(adj.)**金錢的

Impoverished countries were given monetary aid for support.

貧窮的國家接受金援。

◇ **switch(v.)**轉換

The salespersons convinced him to switch to using their brand of products.

銷售員們說服他換成他們品牌的產品來使用。

◇ **allegiance** [əˋlidʒəns]**(n.)**忠誠

National leaders have to pledge allegiance to their countries.

國家領導人必須宣示對國家的忠誠。

◇ **ashamed(adj.)**羞恥的

People who betray their friends should be ashamed of themselves.
背叛朋友的人應該感到羞恥。

◇ **benefits**(n.)(多用複數)利益;好處
Regular exercise brings great benefits to us.
規律的運動帶給我們極大的好處。

◇ **alas** [əˈlæs] 唉呀!

◇ **despair**(v.)絕望
The people despaired when they saw there was no hope.
發現沒有希望時,這些人感到絕望。

◇ **quality**(n.)品質
Consumers care about the quality of products.
消費者關心產品的品質。

◇ **quantity**(n.)量
Some companies produce large quantities of products to attract customers.
一些公司生產大量的產品以吸引消費者。

◇ **squander**(v.)浪費
We should strive to keep from squandering our resources.
我們要盡力不浪費資源。

◇ **corrupt**(adj.)腐敗的;貪污的
The corrupt judge has taken millions of dollars in bribes.
這貪污的法官拿了好幾百萬的賄賂。

◇ **fund**(v.)提供資金

The students saved their pocket money diligently to fund the trip.
學生們努力存零用錢，以籌措旅遊資金。

片　語　▶

◇ **in need：**
need(n.)是「需要」，in need 是「處於需要(幫忙)之中」，in need 後面的介系詞通常為 of，例如：He is in need of help.(他需要幫助)。

◇ **for years：**
for years 是「許多年」之意，例如：I haven't seen you for years.(我好多年沒見到你了)。

◇ **in exchange for... ：**
exchange(n.)是「交換」，in exchange for... 是「與……交換」，例如：The kidnappers demanded money in exchange for her safe return.(綁匪們要求以金錢換取她的平安回來)。

◇ **for... reason：**
for... reason 是「因為……的理由」，例如：He committed suicide for financial reason.(他因為財務上的理由自殺)。

◇ **do without：**
do 是「做」，do without 是「省去……；無須……；沒有」，例如：I can't do without you!(我不能沒有你！)

◇ **be left with... :**

leave (v.) 是「留下」的意思，be left with... 是「剩下……；留……給……」，例如：They were left with nothing to eat. (他們沒有任何食物可以吃)。

句型分析 ▶

1. **Not feeling ashamed, Senegal further adds that "between countries there are no friends, only benefits."**

   ◆ 這句話的主詞是 Senegal，主要動詞是 adds。句子逗號前面的 Not feeling ashamed (不覺得羞愧) 是用來形容後面的主詞 Senegal。

   ◆ further 是副詞「更進一步地」，用來形容動詞 add，表示「更進一步地加上……」。

   ◆ "...there are no friends, only benefits." 其實是："...there are no friends; there are only benefits." (沒有朋友，只有利益)，加上被省略的 there are 後，意思就清楚多了。

2. **What's more, rather than squandering money year after year to provide for corrupt allies, wouldn't it be better if we used it to fund more nutritious school lunches for Taiwanese children?**

   ◆ 這句話用的是 rather than..., wouldn't it be better if... 的句型，意為「與其……，如果……不是會比較好嗎？」最前面的 What's more, 用來修飾整句，意思是「更進一步說；更有

甚者」。

◆ 句中 wouldn't it be better 後面接了一個條件子句 if...，
意思是「如果……」。這裡的 fund 當動詞用，是「提
供資金給……」，所提供的東西接在 fund 後面，這裡
為 nutritious school lunches for Taiwanese children。此處的
nutritious(adj.)意為「有營養的」。

造句練習 ▶

1. 他提供服務以換取費用。(in exchange for...)

- -

2. 週末時我和另外五個同伴一起上山。(in the company of five)

- -

3. 台灣盡可能維繫最多的外交關係。(maintain / diplomatic ties)

- -

4. 唉呀，木已成舟！(alas)

- -

5. 需要援助時，我們冀望友邦能伸出援手。(ally / in time of
need)

- -

20

需要和平的和平紀念日
A Memorial Day in Need of Peace

台灣因為獨特的歷史原因，形成一個擁有多元族群的國家。一般來說，台灣有四大主要族群：原住民(aboriginal inhabitant，或稱 aborigine)、福佬人(Fukienese)、外省人(mainlander)、及客家人(Hakka)。近年來台灣因為外籍新娘的大量移入，漸漸形成另一股「新住民」(new inhabitant)的族群力量。

在以前，台灣的幾個族群彼此看對方不順眼，常互相取綽號、甚至醜化：「山地人」、「番仔」、「蕃薯」、「芋仔」、「阿山仔」、「客婆仔」……，多元族群塑造了台灣豐富多樣的文化，卻也因此造成各族群間的嫌隙與摩擦。

時至今日，台灣這個小島的人民因為通婚及雜居的結果，儘管意識型態或族群認同仍有差異，以往存在各族群間的差異已越形微弱。大家呼吸的是一樣的空氣，吹拂的是一樣的和風，面對的是相同的順境與逆境，實在沒有必要再去計較誰的祖先較有水準，誰的祖先濫殺無辜。過去的就讓它過去；逝者已矣，來者可追，只要明天比昨天更好，管他誰先來、誰後到！

A Memorial Day in Need of Peace

59 years ago, an important event happened in Taiwan that has been recorded in history as the "**2-28 incident.**"

In 1945, Taiwan shook off the **yoke** of 50 years of Japanese **colonial rule**, and the people rejoiced. However, the **Nationalist government** that took its place was both **corrupt** and **incompetent**. The public's hopes and expectations were **dashed**, and the mood of popular dissatisfaction **exploded** as the government clamped down on **contraband cigarettes**. After that **episode**, the Nationalist government proceeded to **capture** and murder many **petitioners** and even their families. It was from then on that the distinction between "Taiwanese" and "mainlander" **identities** was established.

The government has been vigorously pushing for **compensations** in recent years. Aside from offering a compensation to the victims and their families, the government is also helping to restore the **reputation** of those **defamed** in the incident. ❶ Moreover, a museum and a **monument** have been established, and memorial meetings have also been held to make up for the spiritual **scars** left behind by the incident.

Several surveys show that more than 70% of Taiwanese citizens— including relatives of the victims of the 2-28 incident— believe that we should just cast away our historical woes and live together in peace and **harmony**. ❷ Unfortunately, the Taiwanese political scene is still infested with politicians that **exploit ethnic conflict** as a weapon to improve their political chances for office. In truth, it is these people that are the **thorns** that **pierce** through the hearts of the peace-loving people of Taiwan!

需要和平的和平紀念日

59年前，台灣歷史上發生了重大事件，史稱「二二八事件」。

1945年台灣脫離日本殖民統治，人民歡欣鼓舞。然而當時取而代之的國民政府腐敗無能，導致人民對新政府由期望轉為失望；在一次政府取締私煙的行動中，人民不滿的情緒終於爆發。這次事件後，國民政府捕殺了許多請願的民眾及其家屬，使「台灣人」與「外省人」的認同從此涇渭分明。

這幾年政府積極從事各項補償，除了發放受難家屬的補償金、恢復受難者的名譽，並設立紀念館和紀念碑，舉辦追悼會，期望能減輕人民心中的痛。

據許多調查顯示，台灣七成以上的民眾，包括親人經歷過二二八事件者，都認為大家應該拋開歷史傷痛，和平相處。可惜的是，台灣政壇仍舊充斥著別有居心的政客，專以炒作省籍衝突來吸引選票。老實說，這些人才是愛好和平的台灣人心中永遠的痛！

主題句：　　　　　　單字：**加黑**　　　片語：套色　　句型：**❶❷**

單字例句 ▶

◇ **Peace Memorial Day** 和平紀念日

◇ **2-28 incident** 二二八事件

◇ **yoke**（n.）支配；奴役
Taiwan shook off the yoke of Japanese colonial rule at the end of the Second World War.
台灣在第二次世界大戰結束時擺脫了日本的殖民統治。

◇ **colonial** [kəˈlonjəl] **rule** 殖民統治

◇ **Nationalist government** 國民政府

◇ **corrupt**（adj.）腐敗的
Corrupt government officials should be expelled from office for abusing power.
腐敗的政府官員應該為濫用權力而被開除。

◇ **incompetent**（adj.）無能的
Some people believe that the police are incompetent and need further training.
有些人認為警察無能，需接受進一步的訓練。

◇ **dash**（v.）挫折；使沮喪
As time went by, his hopes were dashed by the reality of his poor financial situation.
隨著時間的流逝，他的希望因為財務不佳的現實狀況而受挫。

◇ **explode(v.)**(情感)爆發
At last his anger exploded.
他終於大發雷霆。

◇ **contraband cigarette 私煙**

◇ **episode(n.)插曲**
After another episode of talks, both sides still haven't reached a consensus.
經過另一段的對談，雙方還是無法達成共識。

◇ **capture(v.)逮捕**
The convicts were sent to prison immediately after being captured.
罪犯一被逮補後，便馬上被送到監獄。

◇ **petitioner(n.)請願者**
The petitioner respectfully delivered his request to the authorities.
請願者很恭敬地將他的要求遞給官員。

◇ **identity(n.)認同；身分**
Our identities are established during childhood.
我們的身分認同是在幼年時期建立的。

◇ **compensation(n.)補償**
They have already given compensation to the victim to show their sincere apology.
他們已經賠償受害者，表達他們誠摯的歉意。

◇ **reputation(n.)名聲**

I am glad to work in a company with a very good reputation.
我很高興可以在一間有良好聲譽的公司工作。

◇ **defame**(v.)破壞名譽；毀謗
He was fired from his job because of his attempts to defame our director.
他被開除了，因為他企圖破壞我們總裁的名譽。

◇ **monument**(n.)紀念碑
The monument was constructed to commemorate the event.
紀念碑已建立，用來紀念這事件。

◇ **scar**(n.)傷疤
I hope this scar on my leg will not last forever!
我希望腳上的疤不會永遠留著！

◇ **harmony**(n.)和睦；融洽
In the rainforest, plants and animals live in perfect harmony.
在雨林中，植物與動物和睦共處。

◇ **exploit**(v.)剝削；利用
Homeworkers can easily be exploited by employers.
家庭工作者很容易就被雇主剝削。

◇ **ethnic conflict** 族群衝突
In our history, there have been many ethnic conflicts caused by land disputes.
在我們的歷史中，許多族群的衝突都起因於土地爭論。

◇ **thorn**(n.)刺；荊棘
Beware of the sharp thorns on the rose.

小心玫瑰上的尖刺。

◇ **pierce（v.）刺穿；戳入**
She had her belly-button pierced.
她在肚臍穿洞。

片 語 ▶

◇ **shake off：**
shake（v.）是「搖動」，shake off 是口語用法，意為「擺脫（惡習）；去除（煩惱）；治好（疾病）」，例如：She can't seem to shake off her cold.（她的感冒似乎都治不好）。

◇ **clamp down on...：**
clamp（v.）意為「夾住（某物）」，clamp down on... 為口語用法，意為「取締……；嚴格壓制……」，例如：The government intends to clamp down on soccer hooliganism.（政府擬採取措施嚴禁在足球賽中鬧事。）

◇ **from then on：**
then（adv.）是「那時；當時」，from then on 是「從那時起」，例如：They had a fight a year ago, and they didn't talk to each other from then on.（他們一年前吵了架，從此以後就不再跟對方說話）。

◇ **the distinction between...：**
distinction（n.）是「區別；辨別」，the distinction between... 是

「……與……的區別」，例如 the distinction between right and wrong 是「對與錯的區別」、the distinction between black and white 就是「黑與白的區別」。

◇ **push for... :**

push(v.)是「推」，push for... 是「催促從事……」，例如：They are pushing for reform.(他們在催促改革)。

◇ **make up for... :**

make up 是「彌補；賠償」，make up for... 則是「因……彌補；因……賠償」，例如：She doesn't have a natural talent, but she makes up for it with hard work.(她天資並不聰穎，但她靠後天的努力來彌補)。

◇ **be infested with... :**

infest(v.)是「大批孳生；充斥」，此字常用被動語態，後面的介系詞用 with。文章中的 be infested with... 是「充滿了……；充斥著……」之意，例如：This house is infested with rats.(這房子老鼠橫行)。

句型分析 ▶

1. Aside from offering a compensation to the victims and their families, the government is also helping to restore the reputation of those defamed in the incident.

   ♦ 這句話的主詞是 the government，主要動詞是 is helping。句首的 Aside from... 是「除此之外……」，這裡的 Aside from offering a compensation 是「除了提供補償金」。

♦ compensation (n.) 通常當不可數名詞，意為抽象的「補償」，這裡用 a compensation，是將其當成可數名詞，意為「補償金」。

♦ 句中 defame (v.) 是「破壞名譽；毀謗」，句子原本是 those who were defamed，這裡省略 who were，剩下 defamed，意為「被詆毀的；被破壞名譽的」，restore the reputation of those defamed 則是「重新恢復那些被詆毀的人的名譽」。

2. Several surveys show that more than 70% of Taiwanese citizens— including relatives of the victims of the 2-28 incident— believe that we should just cast away our historical woes and live together in peace and harmony.

♦ 這句話的主詞是 several surveys，主要動詞是 show。show 後面接的 that 子句則描述調查的結果，可將句子省略為：surveys show that more than 70% of Taiwanese citizens... believe that...(調查結果顯示，超過七成的民眾相信……)，民眾相信的事情有兩件，由「對等連接詞」and 連接：(1)we should just cast away our historical woes (2)we should live together in peace and harmony。

♦ 句中由——隔離中的字是形容詞，形容前面的 citizens 包含哪種特性，這裡是 including relatives of the victims of the 2-28 incident(包括親人經歷過二二八事件者)。

♦ 句中 cast (v.) 是「拋擲；投」，cast away... 是「拋開……；丟掉……」，這裡的 cast away historical woes 是「拋開歷史傷痛」。

造句練習 ▶

1. 台灣在日本殖民統治下度過50年。（Japanese colonial rule）

------

2. 政府正在取締毒品販賣者。（clamp down / drug pusher）

------

3. 私煙正被秘密地運送到鄰近的國家。（contraband cigarette / transport）

------

4. 這系統可以讓人們分辨不同的形狀。（make distinctions between...）

------

5. 我買了一些殺蟲劑，以防止蟲子在我們的花園大肆孳生。
（pesticide / prevent... from infesting...）

社會萬象

21

爆料文化
Exposé Culture

俗諺云：「人怕出名豬怕肥」。在台灣，豬太肥會被奉為（或被罵成）「神豬」，雖然風光一時，最終逃不了被宰殺的命運。在台灣，太紅的人的遭遇也差不多，雖然可以風光一時，最終也難逃被狗仔宰殺的命運。

台灣的爆料文化始於談話性節目，這些節目特愛邀請所謂的 buckraker（撈錢記者），大談各種八卦聳動的話題。如果今天節目講的是如何買賣外匯，那這些 buckrakers 便全部化身為財經專家，滿口投資理論；如果今天節目講的是某間大樓發生火災，那這些 buckrakers 又全部搖身一變，成為公共危險專家兼風水師；又如果今天節目講的是蔣家興衰，則這些 buckrakers 絕對每個都對蔣家歷史如數家珍，好像他前輩子就在蔣家幫傭一般！

好玩的是，台灣不只狗仔會爆料，連政治人物都會彼此爆料，當然，政客爆完料，其之前所捲入的弊案就被轉移焦點。反正弊案這麼多，誰有空去理會呢？倒不如在被人捉到把柄時置之不理，繼續加碼爆對方的料，先報先贏，不報不贏，反正民眾的記憶是短暫的，這年頭誰還在乎「溫柔敦厚」、「為國為民」、「鞠躬盡瘁、死而後已」這些唱高調的東西？

Exposé Culture (CD2-3)

From the **occurrence** of the foreign worker **riot** and the **KRTC** scandal to the **gambling** of the "two Chens" and the **legitimacy** of TVBS's capital, Taiwan has been engulfed in a **flurry** of exposé culture. ❶

Taiwan was once a place where people were simple, **decent**, and **magnanimous**. But now a **newfound** culture is **overtaking** the island. It started when TV **talk shows** began revealing **gossip** about **entertainment celebrities**. These talk shows eventually led to the rise of **political shows** which **expose** scandals related to **political figures**. Most of this is done just to boost **ratings**.

Such exposé culture gets even more out of control when elections are **impending**. Not only do **civil representatives** start to expose scandals, but other officials and even the president himself jump on the bandwagon as well. **Paparazzi** are to the entertainment circle as "**Deep Throat**" is to the political circle. ❷ People now expose scandals whether they exist or not! Consequently, the general public's **contempt** for the media and political figures continues to rise, while Taiwan, in turn, continues to **sink**!

爆料文化

從外勞暴動、高捷弊案，到「雙陳」賭博、TVBS資金的合法性……，台灣已籠罩在一片爆料文化中。

曾經，台灣是個民風純樸、人心厚道的的地方。但一種新興文化卻突然降臨這個小島：電視開始出現不同的「談話性節目」，大爆影視名人的八卦。這些節目導致許多「政論性節目」的興起，大揭政治人物的的醜聞。這一切為的都是提高收視率。

尤其每次接近選舉，爆料文化就會更形猖獗。不僅民意代表開始爆料，連官員、總統也紛紛跟著爆料。娛樂圈有狗仔隊、政治圈有深喉嚨。有料亂爆、沒料也爆！結果老百姓對媒體及政治人物的不滿情緒一直向上提升；而台灣，卻一直向下沈淪！

主題句：　　　　　**單字：加黑**　　　**片語：套色**　　　**句型：❶❷**

單字例句 ▶

◇ **exposé culture** 爆料文化

◇ **occurrence**(n.)事件；發生
The occurrence of such scandals ruins the reputation of the country.
這些醜聞的發生毀了國家的名聲。

◇ **riot** [`raɪət`](n.)暴動；喧鬧
Many people were wounded in the riot.
暴動中許多人受了傷。

◇ **KRTC**(**Kaohsiung Rapid Transit Corporation**)高雄捷運

◇ **gambling**(n.)賭博
Many people lose all their money gambling.
許多人在賭博中輸了所有的錢。

◇ **legitimacy** [lɪ`dʒɪtəməsɪ`](n.)合法性
The legitimacy of the proposal is doubtful.
這份提案的合法性值得懷疑。

◇ **flurry**(n.)一陣(混亂、慌張、熱鬧)
A flurry of activities seems to erupt all at once.
一連串的活動似乎都一起發生。

◇ **decent** [`disṇt`](adj.)好的；正當的
His mother advised him to find a decent job.
他母親告誡他應去找個正當工作。

◇ **magnanimous**（adj.）慷慨大量的
The donation was a very magnanimous gesture.
這捐獻真是個慷慨大量的舉動。

◇ **newfound**（adj.）新興的；新發現的
He is devoting all his time to his newfound interest.
他將所有的時間都投入新發現的興趣上。

◇ **overtake**（v.）襲擊，突然降臨
An urge to run away overtook him.
一種想要逃跑的衝動襲捲了他。

◇ **talk show** 談話性節目
People watch talk shows on television to relax.
人們觀賞電視談話性節目來放鬆。

◇ **gossip** [ˋgɑsəp]（n.）八卦；閒談
People talk about gossip when they are trying to kill time.
人們要殺時間時便開始八卦。

◇ **entertainment**（n.）娛樂
The movie guide can be found in the entertainment section of the newspaper.
電影節目指南可以在報紙的娛樂版找到。

◇ **celebrity** [səˋlɛbrətɪ]（n.）名人
Celebrities live under the constant scrutiny of the public.
名人一直活在大眾的檢視之下。

◇ **political show** 政論性節目
Political shows are becoming more and more popular among

the public.
政論性節目越來越受到民眾的歡迎。

◇ **expose**(v.)揭露；使曝光
My friend promised not to expose my secret identity.
我朋友答應不洩漏我的秘密身分。

◇ **political figure** 政治人物
Political figures have to serve as role models for society.
政治人物必須成為社會的好榜樣。

◇ **rating**(n.)收視率
Television companies look for various ways to boost ratings.
電視公司找尋不同的方法來提高收視率。

◇ **impending**(adj.)逼近的；將發生的
Animals can sense impending danger.
動物可以感知迫近的危險。

◇ **civil representative** 民意代表

◇ **paparazzi**(n.)狗仔隊
Paparazzi are generally very persistent, making them extremely intolerable.
狗仔隊一般而言都很堅持不懈，讓人超難忍受。

◇ **Deep Throat**「深喉嚨」；爆料者
Deep Throats provide information that is not found elsewhere.
深喉嚨提供別處找不到的資料。

◇ **contempt**(n.)蔑視

Corrupt officials are held in contempt by the people.
人們對貪污腐敗的官員心存輕蔑。

◇ **sink(v.)下沈**
If you don't know how to swim, you might sink in the water.
如果你不知如何游泳,就很可能沈下水中。

片　語　▶

◇ **reveal... about... :**
reveal(v.)是「洩漏」,文章中的 reveal gossip about... 則是「洩漏有關……的八卦」,例如:He likes to reveal gossip about his co-workers.(他喜歡洩漏同事的八卦)。

◇ **out of control :**
control(n.)是「控制」,out of control 則是「猖獗;失去控制」,例如:The leader of this country is getting out of control.(這國家的領導人越來越失控了)。

◇ **jump on the bandwagon :**
bandwagon(n.)是「樂隊花車」,jump on the bandwagon 是一個慣用語,意指「一窩蜂做某事;跟隨潮流」,例如:Many students jumped on the bandwagon and protested the war.(許多學生投向這股反戰的潮流。)

◇ **contempt for... :**
contempt(n.)是「蔑視」,contempt for... 則是「對……的蔑

視」，例如：He has a great contempt for conventionality.(他非常鄙視因循苟且)。

句型分析 ▶

1. From the occurrence of the foreign worker riot and the KRTC scandal to the gambling of the "two Chens" and the legitimacy of TVBS's capital, Taiwan has been engulfed in a flurry of exposé culture.

   ♦ 這句話的主詞是 Taiwan，主要動詞是 has been engulfed。句子逗號前面的 From... to... 乃修飾全句，意為「從……到」。

   ♦ 句子的 From... to... 總共舉了四個事件，用兩個「對等連接詞」and 連接，其句型可以分析為：

   from (1) the occurrence of the foreign worker riot (2) the KRTC scandal

   to (3) the gambling of the "two Chens" (4) the legitimacy of TVBS's capital。

   ♦ engulf(v.)是「吞沒」，be engulfed in... 是「被吞噬在……」，這裡的 Taiwan has been engulfed in a flurry of... 是「台灣已被一連串的……所吞噬」。

2. Paparazzi are to the entertainment circle as "Deep Throat" is to the political circle.

♦　這裡用的句型為：... is to... as... is to...，意為「……之於……，就如同……之於……」。此句的意思為「狗仔隊之於娛樂圈，就如同『深喉嚨』之於政治圈」。

造句練習 ▶

1. 爆料文化席捲台灣媒體圈。(exposé culture)

----

2. 這議題深陷於爭議之中。(be engulfed in...)

----

3. 民意代表幫助人民說出他們所關切的東西。
   (civil representative / voice out...)

----

4. 這狗失去控制，不聽他主人的話。(out of control)

----

5. 不管何時，只要有新的趨勢，公司都會一窩蜂跟著做，以獲得利潤。(jump on the bandwagon)

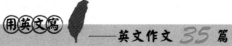

22

光碟風波
Video Hijinks

古代人要破壞別人的名譽很不簡單,靠的只有「口耳相傳」,厲害一點的可以「登高一呼」,不過傳遞效果通常有限。自從科技進步,現代人要破壞他人名譽就簡單多了,最容易的方式便是在仇家附近裝個「針孔攝影機」,將他(她)吃飯睡覺脫衣穿衣蹲廁所摳鼻孔的醜態「全都錄」,然後將片子壓一壓,隨著「伊週刊」或「水果日報」散發,保證馬上傳遍全島。如果嫌這樣的威力不夠強、速度不夠快,還可以將檔案上傳網路,保證不到兩秒鐘,「讓全世界都知道」!

在台灣,自從一個長相清純卻很倒楣的女議員被偷拍後,台灣的光碟文化便一發不可收拾。從夜市販賣的色情光碟、盜版光碟、女廁的偷拍光碟、選舉時一定會出現的「非常光碟」,到某藝人的「自慰光碟」……,令人不禁好奇下次又會有什麼更勁爆的光碟出現?

當然,攝影機也不是全然的壞。在國外就很流行所謂的 nanny-cam(奶媽攝影機),這種小到可以藏在音響裡或者 teddy bears(泰迪熊)身上的隱藏式攝影機,就是用來供家長監視自己所雇的 nanny(奶媽),確保自己的小孩沒有被偷偷虐待。可見科技的本質並不壞,壞的只有人心。

Video Hijinks (CD2-4)

A well-known **celebrity** suffered from **insomnia** and **depression** due to **mounting** pressure after being secretly **videotaped**. He eventually **resolved** his **dilemma** by holding a **press conference** and making the incident public. But video **scandals** are like a snowball rolling **downhill**, gathering **momentum** and size. This one involved not only an actress, but also a **county councilor** and several **gangsters**— definitely **livelier** than any **prime time soap opera**!

Although the "**Masturbation** CD" was less **juicy** than the "**Intercourse** CD" from a few years back that **featured** a **city councilor**, there are still lessons that may be learned from it. ❶ First and **foremost**, once videotaped, do not try to resolve the matter in private. Report the incident to the **law enforcement authorities**, no matter how **inefficient** they may seem to be. Second, do not under any circumstances ask for help from gangsters to avoid the risk of being **double-crossed**. ❷ Third, the "original copy" you paid money for will definitely not be the "original copy." And last (and most importantly), do not take Viagra or Viazome from **unknown** sources!

光碟風波

有一位知名藝人，因為被偷拍的壓力日增，搞得失眠、憂鬱症都上身。他為了解決此難題，最後只好召開記者會，將事件公諸於世。不過這個光碟醜聞有如滾雪球一般，越滾越大。涉案人士不止女藝人，還包括縣議員、黑道人士……，簡直比任何八點檔連續劇還精彩！

這次的「自慰光碟」的精彩度與幾年前某市議員演出的「性愛光碟」相比，雖然遜色不少，不過我們仍可從中學習教訓。首先，若遭偷拍，絕不可私了，一定要求助警察伯伯，儘管他們的辦案效率可能很差。第二，任何情況下都不可找黑道幫忙解決，不然會有被黑吃黑的風險。第三，付錢拿到的「母帶」絕非「母帶」。最後(也是最重要的)，絕不吃來歷不明的威而剛或威而柔！

主題句：░░░░　　單字：**加黑**　　片語：套色　　句型：❶❷

單字例句 ▶

◇ **hijinks** [ˈhaɪˌdʒɪŋks] (n.) 胡鬧；狂歡作樂

◇ **celebrity** (n.) 名人
Celebrities are frequently followed around by reporters and fans.
名人通常有記者與粉絲到處追隨。

◇ **insomnia** [ɪnˈsɑmnɪə] (n.) 失眠症
More and more people suffer from insomnia because of too much stress.
因為壓力太大，越來越多的人為失眠症所苦。

◇ **depression** (n.) 消沈；憂鬱症
People who suffer from depression are most likely to commit suicide.
為憂鬱症所苦的人最可能自殺。

◇ **mounting** (adj.) 逐漸增加的
He waited with mounting impatience for the waiter to bring him his hamburger.
他越來越沒耐性地等著服務生送來他點的漢堡。

◇ **videotape** (v.) 錄影
My parents used to love to videotape us when we were kids.
當我們還小時，我爸媽很喜歡替我們錄影。

◇ **resolve** (v.) 解決

The teacher told us to resolve our problems outside the classroom.

老師叫我們在課堂外解決我們的問題。

◇ **dilemma** (n.)左右為難的狀況

The boy was in a dilemma as to whether to tell his mother the truth or not.

這男孩左右為難，不知該不該告訴他媽媽實話。

◇ **press conference** 記者會

◇ **scandal**(n.)醜聞

Some magazines pride themselves on exposing scandals.

有些雜誌以揭露醜聞為豪。

◇ **downhill**(adv.)向下地；走下坡地

I like riding my bike downhill more than riding uphill.

我喜歡騎腳踏車下坡勝過上坡。

◇ **momentum** [moˋmɛntəm](n.)衝勁；動量

The bike gained momentum as it slid down the hill.

腳踏車滑下坡時增加了動能。

◇ **county councilor** 省議員

◇ **gangster**(n.)幫派份子；歹徒

Gangsters are said to treat one another like brothers.

幫派份子據說彼此以兄弟相待。

◇ **lively** [ˋlaɪvlɪ](adj.)精彩的；活潑的

The girls performed a lively dance number.

女孩們表演了精彩的舞蹈曲目。

◇ **prime time soap opera 黃金時段連續劇**

◇ **masturbation（n.）手淫**
Students are taught in sex education class that masturbation is an acceptable act.
學生在性教育課上學到手淫是可以接受的行為。

◇ **juicy（adj.）精彩的；有趣的**
Some magazines include the juicy details of the affairs of the rich and famous.
有些雜誌包含了有錢人及名人的外遇精彩細節。

◇ **intercourse（n.）性交**
The politician was caught having intercourse with his secretary.
這政治人物被逮到與秘書發生性關係。

◇ **feature（v.）以……為號召；由……演出**
This movie features five of the most famous actors in the world.
這部電影由5位世界上最知名的演員演出。

◇ **city councilor 市議員**

◇ **foremost（adv.）首先**
The man thought of himself first and foremost as a father, and not a lawyer.
這男人認為自己的首要角色是父親，而非律師。

◇ **law enforcement authorities**（多用複數）執法當局

◇ **inefficient**（**adj.**）效率低的；無能的
The construction company is very inefficient; they spent a month just moving the bricks.
這建築公司超沒效率；他們花了一個月的時間只搬了磚頭。

◇ **double-cross**（**v.**）黑吃黑；出賣；欺騙

◇ **unknown**（**adj.**）未知的；不熟悉的
This author is fairly unknown, and her books are not selling very well.
這位作者不太知名，且她的書也賣得不太好。

片　語　▶

◇ **suffer from... :**
suffer（v.）是「經歷；蒙受」，suffer from... 則是「遭受……；受……煎熬」，後面通常接不好的事情，例如：I used to suffer from extreme poverty.（我曾經遭逢極端的貧窮）。

◇ **make... public :**
public（adj.）是「公眾的；公開的」，make... public 則是「將……公開」，例如：He made his friend's scandal public.（他將朋友的醜聞公諸於世）。

◇ **first and foremost :**
first and foremost 是個習慣用法，意思是「首先；第一」，例

如：Food is, first and foremost, something to be enjoyed.(首先，食物就是用來享受的)。

◇ **in private：**

private(adj.)是「私人的；不公開的」。in private 與 in public(公開地)剛好相反，是「私底下；祕密地」之意，例如：Let's talk in private later.(我們等會兒私下再談)。

◇ **no matter how...：**

no matter 是「不論……」，not matter how 則是「不論怎麼樣……」，例如：You'll never beat me, no matter how hard you try.(不管你怎樣努力，都贏不了我)。

句型分析 ▶

1. Although the "Masturbation CD" was less juicy than the "Intercourse CD" from a few years back that featured a city councilor, there are still lessons that may be learned from it.

   ♦ 這句話的主、動詞是 there are(there 為形式主詞，指的真正主詞是動詞後的 lessons)。這句話的主要子句是 there are still lessons that may be learned from it。逗號前面的 although... 是「副詞子句」，功能為講述本句的情況。

   ♦ from a few years back 的 back 是口語的用法，意思為「過去；從前」，from a few years back 就是「從幾年前的……」。

   ♦ feature(v)意為「以……為號召的；由……演出的」，後面接的則是演出的人員：a city councilor(市議員)。

2. Second, do not under any circumstances ask for help from gangsters to avoid the risk of being double-crossed.

♦ 這句話是「祈使句」，省略主詞 you。

♦ under any circumstances 是「在任何情況下……」，do not under any circumstances... 則是「在任何情況下都不可……」。ask for help from... 則是「向……求援」。

♦ risk(n.)是「危險；冒險」，to avoid the risk of... 意思是「避免冒……的危險」，危險的東西接在後頭：being double-crossed(被黑吃黑)。

造句練習 ▶

1. 大學生活通常讓人和自由與狂歡享樂聯想在一起。(be associated with... / hijinks)

----

2. 這位政治人物召開記者會宣布退休。(hold a press conference / retirement)

----

3. 這位市議員計畫再競選下一任。(the city councilor / run for another term)

----

4. 老闆叫我們私下解決這件事。（in private）

----

5. 老闆炒了這個出賣公司的傢伙魷魚。（double-cross）

寶島台灣！
Formosa Taiwan!

　　台灣好，台灣妙，台灣呱呱叫！大家都知道，台灣的夏天很濕熱、冬天很濕冷，有些巷弄的確又髒又亂；但是台灣也是個人情味濃厚、人民勤奮、混亂中見秩序、傳統中見現代的好所在。

　　很多去國多年的台灣人，雖然常愛在公眾場合高聲批評台灣，但不管承不承認，其內心卻很清楚，只有在自己的國家才能真正昂首闊步，理直氣壯。許多生活在台灣、對台灣有認同感的外籍人士，也愛極了台灣的擁擠喧鬧、五光十色、甚至人與人之間的摩肩擦踵，因為在這片土地上，「生活」的感覺更實在、「快樂」的感受也更強烈！

　　本來嘛，全世界還有什麼地方，大夥可以在夏天挨肩擦背地窩在一起吹冷氣吃火鍋、看到水族箱裡的金魚時互相討論該用「清蒸」還是「紅燒」、自己開在高速公路的「路肩」還笑其他人不懂得利用這多出來的「好康」車道、連與朋友去餐廳吃飯，都可以為了搶付帳而反目成仇、更誇張的還有一輛「小綿羊50」擠5個人的特技表演，以及會唱完整首「兩隻老虎」的汽車喇叭聲……。不管你同不同意，台灣是我的家，我愛台灣！

Formosa Taiwan! (CD2-5)

The previous week saw the year's strongest **cold front**, marking the end of the most **bizarre** "3-in-1" elections in history. A **hubbub** of voices can be heard from within **hot pot** restaurants. Meanwhile, **ginger ducks** are selling like crazy at **night markets**... Yes, the year is coming to an end!

The year 2005 does not appear to have been a good year for many Taiwanese. According to **statistics**, there were more than 3,000 **suicides** this year, while the number of AIDS patients **surpassed** the 10,000 **mark** for the first time. ❶ One in eight persons have varying degrees of **melancholia**, and for the first time, the average **starting salary** of **inexperienced** masters' graduates has dropped to less than NT$30,000.

But despite it all, there is some **encouraging** news. The total number of international tourists visiting Taiwan reached 3 million this year. The tourists said **unanimously** that Taiwan is naturally **abundant** in its tourism resources, and the **lure** of the local **delicacies** and **snacks** is **irresistible**. ❷ Most importantly, Taiwanese people are **hospitable** and very **welcoming**! Without a doubt, Taiwan's stunning **landscape**, as well as the people's **friendliness** and **creativity**, may well be Taiwan's best asset in promoting future development!

寶島台灣！

上個星期來了一個今年最強的冷鋒，結束了一個有史以來最詭譎的「三合一」選舉、火鍋店的人聲鼎沸、夜市賣得嚇嚇叫的薑母鴨……，是的，年底將屆！

2005年對許多台灣人而言，似乎不是一個好年。據統計，今年全國有3000多人自殺，愛滋病患首次超過一萬人，每8人便有一人罹患輕重不等的憂鬱症，而沒經驗的碩士畢業生平均起薪首次跌到3萬元以下。

儘管如此，還是有令人鼓舞的消息。台灣今年的外國觀光客到達300萬人。這些人不約而同的說，台灣天然觀光資源豐富、美食小吃魅力無法擋；最重要的，台灣人好客、人情味超濃！的確，台灣的好山好水，以及人民的友善及創造力，便是台灣促進永續發展的最佳資產！

主題句：　　　　　單字：**加黑**　　　片語：套色　　　句型：❶❷

單字例句 ▶

◇ **Formosa**（n.）福爾摩沙；台灣

◇ **cold front** 冷鋒

◇ **bizarre** [bɪˋzɑr]（adj.）古怪的，滑稽可笑的
His performance turns from serious to bizarre.
他的表演由嚴肅變成滑稽可笑。

◇ **hubbub**（n.）嘈雜；喧囂
The hubbub of voices drowned out the host's voice.
嘈雜的聲音淹沒了主人的聲音。

◇ **hot pot** 火鍋

◇ **ginger duck** 薑母鴨

◇ **night market** 夜市

◇ **statistics**（n.）統計資料
Statistics show a steep rise in unemployment.
統計資料顯示失業（率）急速上升。

◇ **suicide**（n.）自殺
More and more students are considering suicide as a means of resolving their problems.
越來越多學生認為自殺是解決問題的方法。

◇ **surpass**（v.）超過
The total sales figures finally surpassed their projected goal.

全部的銷售數字總算超過他們預估的目標。

◇ **mark**(**n.**)記號；標記
The temperature is expected to reach the 35 degree mark in the next few days.
接下來的幾天氣溫預計會到達三十五度的標記。

◇ **melancholia / depression**(**n.**)憂鬱症
People suffering from melancholia generally like to be alone.
患有憂鬱症的人一般喜歡獨處。

◇ **starting salary** 起薪

◇ **inexperienced**(**adj.**)沒有經驗的
The young man was inexperienced in using a hammer, so he hit himself in the thumb.
這年輕人沒有使用鐵鎚的經驗，因此捶到自己的拇指。

◇ **encouraging**(**adj.**)鼓舞人心的
The teacher gave each of the students an encouraging smile.
老師給每位學生一個激勵人心的微笑。

◇ **unanimously** [juˋnænəməslɪ](**adv.**)全體一致地
The class decided unanimously to go on a field trip.
全班同學一致決定去戶外教學。

◇ **abundant**(**adj.**)豐富的；充裕的
Taiwan is abundant in tourist attractions.
台灣有很多吸引觀光客的地方。

◇ **lure**(**n.**)魅力；吸引力

He is not mature enough to resist the lure of alcohol and drugs.
他還沒成熟到可以抵抗酒與毒品的吸引力。

◇ **delicacy** [ˋdɛləkəsɪ] **(n.)** 美食；佳餚
Taiwan is known for its mouth-watering delicacies.
台灣以令人垂涎的美食聞名。

◇ **snack**(**n.**)小吃；零食
He went downstairs to buy some snacks for the party.
他下樓去買些舞會要吃的零食。

◇ **irresistible**(**adj.**)無法抵抗的
The cookies she makes are irresistible!
她做的餅乾魅力無法檔！

◇ **hospitable**(**adj.**)好客的
The visitor was well taken care of by his hospitable hosts.
這訪客受到好客的主人很好的招待。

◇ **welcoming**(**adj.**)真誠的；熱心的
Children are very welcoming by nature.
小孩的本性是很真誠的。

◇ **landscape**(**n.**)風景
The tourists went to the mountains to admire the landscape.
旅客們到山上欣賞風景。

◇ **friendliness**(**n.**)友善
She is very popular in school because of her friendliness.
她因為很友善，在學校廣受歡迎。

◇ **creativity** [ˌkrieˈtɪvətɪ] (**n.**) 創造力
Artists rely on their creativity to make a living.
藝術家倚賴創意維生。

片　語 ▶

◇ **(sell) like crazy：**
crazy (adj.) 是「瘋狂的」，like crazy 是口語用法，意為「猛烈
地；拼命地」，故文中 sell like crazy 為「賣得嚇嚇叫」。其他
如 run like crazy 則是「拼了老命地跑」。

◇ **come to an end：**
end (n.) 為「終止」，come to an end 是「到達終點」，例如：
My training course here has come to an end, and it is time for me to
leave. (我在這裡的訓練課程已結束，是該離去的時候了)。

◇ **varying degrees of...：**
varying (adj.) 是從 vary (v.)「改變；變更」而來，意思是
「不同的；變化的」，varying degrees of... 則是「不同程度
的」，例如：He faced varying degrees of opposition from his
supporters. (他面臨了支持者不同程度的反對)。

◇ **despite it all：**
despite 是介系詞，意為「儘管；雖然」，despite it all 為「儘管
上述所有的一切……」，例如：They fight a lot, but despite it all,
they are still deeply in love. (他們常吵架，不過儘管如此，他們
仍深深相愛)。

◇ **without a doubt：**

doubt(n.)為「懷疑」，without a doubt 就是「毫無疑問地，確實地」，例如：This is without a doubt the stupidest thing I've ever seen.(這毫無疑問是我見過最蠢的事情)。

句型分析 ▶

1. According to statistics, there were more than 3,000 suicides this year, while the number of AIDS patients surpassed the 10,000 mark for the first time.

   ◆ 這句話的主、動詞是 there were。句子逗號後的 while 是連接詞，意為「當……的時候；與……同時」，因此there were more than 3,000 suicides, while the number of AIDS patients... 意為「自殺的人數超過3,000人，在此同時，患有愛滋病的人數……」。

   ◆ 句中的 mark 為名詞，意為「記號，標記」，surpassed the... mark 是「超過……的標記」之意。

2. The tourists said unanimously that Taiwan is naturally abundant in its tourism resources, and the lure of the local delicacies and snacks is irresistible.

   ◆ 這句話的主詞是 the tourists，主要動詞是 said。that 後面接的是子句，說明「遊客說」的內容，總共包括兩大項，以「對等連接詞」and 連接：(1)Taiwan is naturally abundant in its tourism resources(2)the lure of the local delicacies and snacks is irresistible。

◆ 句中的unanimously 為副詞，用來形容動詞 said，意為「異口同聲地說」。

◆ 句中 the lure of... 是「……的誘惑力」，the lure of the local delicacies and snacks 便是「當地美食及小吃的吸引力」。abundant in... 是「富於……」，因此 abundant in tourism resources 便是「富含旅遊資源」。

造句練習 ▶

1. 台北遭受另一道冷鋒。(cold front)

----

2. 人們在冬天喜歡吃火鍋。(hot pot)

----

3. 台灣以夜市聞名。(be famed for... / night market)

----

4. 人們帶著不同的興奮程度來參加活動。(varying degrees of...)

----

5. 這公司提供他一年65萬的起薪。(starting salary)

24

媒體亂象
Chaos in the Media

　　說到台灣媒體的亂象，還真不是三天三夜可以說得完的！自從台灣開放媒體以來，這個小島上每天發生的屈指可數的小事，便成為各家電視新聞媒體24小時反覆播放的大事。

　　媒體數量過份膨脹的結果，也導致從業人員專業素質大幅下降，君不見電視上一大堆看起來無厘頭的記者，天天報著無厘頭的新聞：「今天稍早之前一點的時候呢……」唉，可憐的記者小時候沒好好念書，不知道「稍早」就是「之前」、「稍」就是「一點」，整句話根本可以簡省為「稍早」兩字！還有記者喜歡說：「最後呢終於呢完成了呢這樣的一個呢舉動……」，其實「最後」就是「終於」，「完成一個舉動」是西式語法，整句中文其實就是「完成」，何必囉囉嗦嗦，莫名其妙？

　　當然，電視台也有苦衷。台灣新聞頻道數量過多，廣告不足，為了生存競爭，「只好」造假炒作，將沒的說成有的，將白的炒成黑的。況且台灣就這個小島，哪有那麼多「獨家」可跑，因此貓跑到樹上是「獨家」，狗掉進水溝也是「獨家」，管他全球暖化、美伊戰爭、金磚四國崛起……，反正「給我收視率，其他一切免談」！

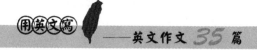

Chaos in the Media　(CD2-6)

Two people have committed suicide recently, both acting out of fear that the media would focus on their suspected wrongdoing. This is part of the reason why the "media" is now considered one of "Taiwan's Three Harms," placing third just after "**black gold**" and "politicians."

How serious has the chaos in the media become? A murderer approaches the media to arrange an **exclusive interview** only to let out a **spate** of **nonsense**. A small-scale typhoon is reported as "a **raging** thunderstorm that **sweeps** over Taiwan." A mother who **abandons** her child is touted as "a person of **high society**." An **unconfirmed** report about a celebrity is splashed across the headlines. What's more, people who have just lost their loved ones are **pestered** with questions as "how are you feeling now?" And this is just the tip of the iceberg. Other examples include the **commercialization** of news programs, the **proliferation** of sex and violence, the **deluge** of scene **simulations**, and the abuse of on-the-scene reporting. ❶ It's no wonder that the Taiwan media has been dubbed as a "**fabricator**," "**abuser**," and "**butcher**."

Naturally, the Taiwanese media is not completely devoid of **merit**. In fact, news reporters usually reach a scene faster than the police. Such a spirit is worth **emulating**. Cases that render prosecutors and investigators helpless are picked up by the media, with reporters **piecing** the evidence together and **staging** acts deserving of awards like "Best **Screenplay**" and "Best Actor!" ❷ What's more, the **balderdash** the reporters utter when reporting may help inject laughter into the lives of generally **gloomy** Taiwanese people!

媒體亂象

最近接連兩起民眾自殺事件，原因都與害怕媒體專注其可能的罪行有關，這也使得「媒體」繼「黑金」及「政客」之後，名列「台灣三害」之一。

台灣媒體的亂象有多嚴重？殺人犯可以找媒體作專訪，大放厥詞；一場小颱風可以變成「狂風暴雨橫掃全台」；一個拋棄女兒的媽媽可以被捧成「上流社會人士」；未經證實的藝人消息可以「榮登」頭條新聞；更有甚者，剛失去親人的家屬必須不斷被追問「現在心情如何？」。這些只是冰山一角。其他媒體亂象如新聞廣告化、暴力色情氾濫、模擬場景充斥、現場連線浮濫等等，難怪有人要戲稱台灣媒體是「製造業」、「修理業」，與「屠宰業」了！

當然，台灣媒體也不是一無是處。君不見每次發生重大事件，記者總是比警察更早到達現場，其精神值得大家學習。對於檢調單位束手無策的案件，記者們也都可以自行拼湊證據，甚至自導自演，「最佳編劇」、「最佳演員」當之無愧！而記者們無厘頭的亂報，更可替苦悶的台灣人提供茶餘飯後的笑料呢！

主題句：　　　　　單字：加黑　　　片語：套色　　　句型：❶❷

單字例句 ▶

◇ **chaos**[ˋkeɑs]**(n.)**混亂
Chaos erupted when a kid punched another and other kids joined in.
當其中一個小孩打了另一個小孩，而其他小孩跟進時，混亂就爆發了。

◇ **black gold** 黑金

◇ **exclusive interview** 專訪

◇ **spate(n.)**大量；一連串
Her day was filled with a spate of bad luck.
她今天運氣超差。

◇ **nonsense(n.)**胡說八道
Do not believe everything you read; some of it may be nonsense.
別相信你所讀到的每件事；有些是胡說八道的。

◇ **raging(adj.)**劇烈的
The woman is suffering from a raging headache.
這女人被劇烈的頭痛所苦。

◇ **sweep(v.)**掠過；橫掃
Another Hello Kitty craze is sweeping over Taiwan.
另一波的 Hello Kitty 狂熱正橫掃台灣。

◇ **abandon**(**v.**)拋棄

Unwanted babies are sometimes abandoned on other people's doorsteps.

沒人要的小嬰兒有時會被遺棄在別人家門前。

◇ **high society** 上流社會

She is trying her best to act and dress like those in high society.

她盡其所能在行為舉止及穿著上像那些上流社會的人士。

◇ **unconfirmed**(**adj.**)未經證實的

Unconfirmed reports of the scandal are plastered all over the headlines.

未經證實的醜聞占據了所有新聞報紙的頭條。

◇ **pester**(**v.**)糾纏；不斷打擾

The boy pestered his mother for a new toy gun.

這男孩一直纏著他媽媽買新的玩具槍給他。

◇ **commercialization**(**n.**)商業化

The commercialization of charitable events makes such events seem less believable.

慈善活動的商業化使得這些活動看來較不可信。

◇ **proliferation** [prəˌlɪfəˈreʃən](**n.**)快速增加

The proliferation of scams has made it difficult for people to trust others.

詐騙的激增使得人們很難相信他人。

◇ **deluge** [ˈdɛljudʒ] (n.) 大量氾濫

People receive a deluge of spam mail every day.

人們每天收到一拖拉庫的垃圾郵件。

◇ **simulation** (n.) 模擬

This is a direct simulation of the actual crime scene.

這是個真實犯罪現場的直接模擬。

◇ **fabricator** (n.) 捏造者

He has a reputation of being a fabricator of lies.

他擁有喜歡捏造謊言的名聲。

◇ **abuser** (n.) 虐待者

The child abuser is appearing in court today.

這個虐童者今天上法庭。

◇ **butcher** [ˈbutʃɚ] (n.) 嗜殺者

The heartless man who kills babies in their sleep is considered by many as a butcher.

對許多人而言，這個沒心肝、殺害熟睡嬰孩的男人就像個屠夫。

◇ **merit** (n.) 優點

She has a lot of merits worth praising.

她有許多值得稱讚的優點。

◇ **emulate** [ˈɛmjəˌlet] (v.) 熱心學習

We should emulate the optimistic outlook of children.

我們應該向小孩的樂觀態度學習。

◇ **piece**(**v.**)拼湊
They tried to piece the puzzle pieces together.
他們試著將拼圖的碎片拼湊起來。

◇ **stage**(**v.**)上演；表演
Weeks, or even months of rehearsal are needed before a play can be staged.
在一齣戲可以上演之前，幾個星期、甚至幾個月的排練是必要的。

◇ **screenplay**(**n.**)電影劇本
The screenplay is very well written.
這電影劇本寫得很好。

◇ **balderdash**[ˋbɔldɚˌdæʃ](**n.**)胡言亂語
The woman passed his remarks off as balderdash.
這女人讓別人覺得他說的話是胡言亂語。

◇ **gloomy**(**adj.**)鬱悶的
After being scolded by his father, the boy remained gloomy the whole afternoon.
被他爸爸罵了之後，這男孩整個下午都很鬱卒。

片　語 ▶

◇ **focus on... :**
focus(v.)是「集中注意力……；聚焦……」，focus on... 是「專注於……；聚焦於……」之意，例如：You should focus on your studies.(你應該專注於課業上)。

◇ **let out :**

let out 是「把……放出去；發出……；將……發出來」，例如：He let out a low whistle.(他低聲吹口哨)。

◇ **be touted as... :**

tout(v.)是「極力稱讚、推薦」之意，be touted as... 是「被吹捧為……；被推薦為……」，例如：He is being touted as the next big thing in Hollywood.(他被吹捧為好萊塢的明日之星)。

◇ **the tip of the iceberg :**

tip(n.)是「尖端」，iceberg(n.)是「冰山」，the tip of the iceberg 則是「冰山的頂端」，通常用來暗示可能出現大問題或嚴重錯誤的跡象，例如：The reported cases of domestic violence are only the tip of the iceberg.(被通報的家暴案件只是冰山的一角)。

◇ **no wonder :**

wonder(n.)是「驚異」，no wonder 則是「難怪；果然；怪不得」，例如：They had a fight; no wonder he didn't come.(他們吵架了；難怪他沒來)。

◇ **be dubbed as... :**

dub(v.)是「給(某人)取綽號；把(某人)叫做……」，be dubbed as... 是「將(某人)的綽號取做……；將……稱做……」，例如：Timmy was dubbed as "Tiny" because of his large size.(Timmy 因為身材高大而被取了「小個兒」的綽號)。

◇ **be devoid of... :**

devoid(adj.)是「缺乏的」，be devoid of... 是「缺乏……」，例如：He is devoid of a sense of humor.(他缺乏幽默感)。

◇ **inject... into... :**

inject (v.) 是「注射；注入」，inject... into... 是「將……注入……」，文章中的 inject laughter into the lives of people 是「將笑聲注入人們生活中」。

句型分析 ▶

1. Other examples include the commercialization of news programs, the proliferation of sex and violence, the deluge of scene simulations, and the abuse of on-the-scene reporting.

   ◆ 這句話的主詞是 other examples，主要動詞是 include；包含的例子有4樣，由「對等連接詞」and 連接：(1) the commercialization of news programs (2) the proliferation of sex and violence (3) the deluge of scene simulations (4) the abuse of on-the-scene reporting。

   ◆ 此句所包含的4樣東西句型結構非常工整：(1) the commercialization of... (2) the proliferation of... (3) the deluge of... (4) the abuse of... (……的商業化，……的激增；……的氾濫；……的濫用)。

2. Cases that render prosecutors and investigators helpless are picked up by the media, with reporters piecing the evidence together and staging acts deserving of awards like "Best Screenplay" and "Best Actor!"

   ◆ 這句話的主詞是 cases，主要動詞是 are picked up (被拿去；

被撿去)。

♦ 句首 Cases 後面接的 that... 子句是用來形容前面的 cases 有何種性質，這裡的 render... helpless 是「讓……感到無助；使……束手無策」。因此逗號前的句子 Cases that render prosecutors and investigators helpless are picked up by the media 是「讓檢調單位束手無策的案件被媒體撿去用」。

♦ 句子逗號後面的 with... 當形容詞用，修飾逗號前的句子。「對等連接詞」and 連接 reporters 做的兩件事：(1) piecing the evidence together (2) staging acts...。piecing 的原形是 piece (v.)「拼湊」，staging 的原形是 stage (v.)「上演；表演」，表示這些記者們愛「將證據拼湊在一起」，也喜歡「表演節目」。

♦ 句末的 deserving of... 為 which is deserving of... 的縮寫，修飾前面的 acts (表演)，意為「這些表演值得……」。值得的東西為後面的 awards (獎)，這裡舉出兩個獎項，以 like (例如) 帶出：(1) Best Screenplay (2) Best Actor。

造句練習 ▶

1. 這記者每天打電話給市長，希望能獲得專訪。(journalist / exclusive interview)

   ----

2. 這政客因為與黑金有來往而入獄。(black gold)

   ----

3. 她的臉缺乏任何溫暖及幽默。(be devoid of...)

   ----

4. 他一直試著將新的想法注入到討論中。(inject... into...)

   ----

5. 舞會中大家都玩得很高興，笑聲滿盈。(laughter)

25

為富不仁的台灣
Taiwan, Land of Wealth and Cruelty

　　台灣人超喜歡將其他國家分等級：美國、日本等屬於「最高級」，韓國、香港等則與台灣「同等級」，而東南亞及非洲國家等便屬於「最低級」！究其原因，等級的高低與國家的富有程度有「正相關」，且既有等級，就有隨之而來的差別待遇與態度。

　　近十年來，外籍新娘在台人數日漸增多。可憐的東南亞新娘離鄉背景、遠嫁至台灣，誰知來到寶島後，不僅被台灣人貼上「落後」、「愛錢」、「沒知識」的負面標籤，還要背負不肖人士加諸的「生出遲緩兒」、「製造社會問題」、「教養下一代不力」、「體內有餘毒」等沈重罪名，真是情何以堪！根據統計，外籍新娘的平均年齡只有22歲，在這個大部分台灣女孩還在求學、工作、玩樂的年紀，她們卻已經背負「服侍公婆、操持家務、照顧丈夫、生養下一代」的多重身分，儘管她們選擇默默接受，很多時候還是要面對社會大眾對她們歧視的眼光。

　　其實，絕大多數的外籍新娘善良勤奮，都懷有強烈「融入」台灣當地社會的希望，對於台灣的文化也採取積極認同的態度，這也是為什麼大多數的外籍新娘都十分積極地學中文。她們的努力應該得到肯定及善意的回應！捫心自問，換成咱們離鄉背井，是否也能像她們一般，任勞任怨、樂天知命？

Taiwan, Land of Wealth and Cruelty ⏎CD

The "Country Reports on Human Rights Practices" **released** by the US Department of State in March clearly identifies the problem of "**abuse** of foreign workers" in Taiwan. The report also includes a detailed account of the massive riot **staged** by Thai workers at the Kaohsiung mass rapid transit project. And only a few weeks earlier, the **contractor** involved in the **exploitation** of the workers filed a **civil lawsuit** against them.

Taiwan has had its share of **poverty**. Members of the former generation can still vividly recall the hard times when there was no food to eat and no shoes to wear. Taiwanese have become **affluent** over the past few decades, but have yet to become richer at heart. Some households that employ foreign **maids** force these workers to work overtime; some even give their children free rein to order the maid around. **Human trafficking groups** have also been conniving with **unscrupulous** companies to fool women from **impoverished** nations into the sex industry. Moreover, **matchmaking agencies** openly advertise such **disgraceful** claims as "**guaranteed** a virgin," "**fertile** or your money back," or "comes with a one-year **warranty**." ❶

Most Taiwanese are **benevolent** by nature, and they often claim their country is "a nation founded on **human rights**." However, now that they have **accumulated** wealth, people have begun to treat people from poor nations with **atrocity**. ❷ If the rich displays a lack of "benevolence," then of course the poor can also display a lack of "**righteousness**." Taiwan's future prospects are worrisome indeed!

為富不仁的台灣

今年3月美國國務院公布的「世界人權報告」中,明確指出台灣有「虐待外國勞工」的問題,報告中並詳述高雄捷運外勞暴動事件。而就在前陣子,當初涉及剝削泰勞的人力仲介公司,向泰勞們提出了民事訴訟。

台灣曾經貧窮過,上一代的人還能細數那段沒有東西吃、沒有鞋子穿的苦日子。這些年台灣人富裕了,然而內心卻沒有跟著富裕起來。一些雇有外傭的家庭,常強迫外傭超時工作,甚至放任小孩對外傭大呼小叫。人蛇集團也常與不肖業者勾結,詐騙貧窮國家的女孩來台賣淫。更有甚者,婚姻仲介業者大辣辣掛起「保證處女」、「不生包退」、「一年保固」的可恥招牌……。

多數台灣人民本性善良,也常自稱「人權立國」,卻在累積了財富之際,如此不堪地對待貧窮國家的人民。只是富者可以不「仁」,貧者當然也可以不「義」,台灣的前景真令人堪憂!

主題句:　　　　單字:加黑　　片語:套色　　句型:❶❷

單字例句 ▶

◇ **release**(v.)發表；公布
The newspaper released the results of a recent survey.
報紙公布了最近一個調查的結果。

◇ **abuse**(n.)虐待；濫用
The policeman's abuse of power is very unethical.
這警察濫用權力是非常不道德的。

◇ **stage**(v.)籌畫；發動
The students staged a protest against the school administration.
學生們發動一場抗議學校行政單位的活動。

◇ **contractor** ['kɑntræktɚ](n.)承包商；立約者
Have you chosen a contractor to build your house?
你選了建造你房子的承包商了嗎？

◇ **exploitation**(n.)剝削
The exploitation of nature will not bring any positive results.
對大自然的剝削不會帶來任何好結果。

◇ **civil lawsuit** 民事訴訟

◇ **poverty**(n.)貧窮
Poverty may have caused the increase in the crime rate.
貧窮很可能造成了犯罪率的增加。

◇ **affluent** ['æfluənt](adj.)富裕的

It is not safe for such an affluent person to walk around the city like this.
這位有錢人如此這般的在城市裡趴趴走是不安全的。

◇ **maid**(n.)女傭
The maid is very diligent in cleaning the house.
這女傭清掃房子時很勤快。

◇ **human trafficking group** 人蛇集團

◇ **unscrupulous**(adj.)沒有道德的；無恥的
I refuse to be with such an unscrupulous person!
我拒絕跟這種無恥的人在一起！

◇ **impoverished**(adj.)貧困的
Help is urgently needed in impoverished countries.
貧困的國家迫切需要幫忙。

◇ **matchmaking agency** 婚姻仲介業者
I met my future wife at a matchmaking agency.
我在婚姻仲介所遇到未來的妻子。

◇ **disgraceful**(adj.)丟臉的；不名譽的
The way he treats his mother is disgraceful!
他對待他母親的方式真是丟臉啊！

◇ **guarantee**(v.)保證
I can guarantee that our product will last a lifetime.
我可以保證我們的產品可用一輩子。

◇ **fertile**(adj.)能生育的；富饒的

This soil is so fertile that fruits and vegetables grow rapidly.
這土地是如此的肥沃，水果與蔬菜都生長得很快。

◇ **warranty**（n.）保固；擔保
Does this product have a warranty?
這產品有保固嗎？

◇ **benevolent** [bə`nɛvələnt]（adj.）仁慈善良的
I am blessed with a kind and benevolent wife.
我很幸運有位親切且仁慈善良的妻子。

◇ **human rights** 人權
We should demand our human rights!
我們應當要求人權！

◇ **accumulate**（v.）累積
Do not allow the dust to accumulate before cleaning the room.
在清掃房間前，別讓灰塵累積。

◇ **atrocity** [ə`trɑsətɪ]（n.）惡毒殘暴（的行為）
I hope I will never experience another atrocity.
我希望別再經歷另一次的暴行。

◇ **righteousness** [`raɪtʃəsnɪs]（n.）正義
Righteousness brings peace.
正義帶來平安。

片　語 ▶

◇ **an account of... :**
account(n.)是「事件等的報告；依事件先後順序所做的敘述」，這個片語通常為 give an account of...，意為「敘述……的始末」，例如：This document gives a firsthand account of the war.(這份文件為戰爭作了第一手的敘述)。

◇ **file a lawsuit against... :**
file(v.)是「申請；提出」，lawsuit(n.)是「訴訟」，file a lawsuit against... 為「對……提出訴訟」，例如：He filed a lawsuit against the bank.(他對銀行提出訴訟)。

◇ **has... share of... :**
share(n.)是「部分；所持有的份」，has... share of... 就是「有……的一份」，例如：He has had his share of luck.(他過去的運氣可真不錯)。

◇ **give... free rein :**
rein(n.)是「行為的自由；掌控權」，give... free rein 是「讓……發揮；讓……自由」，例如：The teacher gives free rein to her students' imagination.(老師讓她的學生自由發揮想像力)。

◇ **order... around :**
order(v.)是「命令；指揮」，order... around 則是「任意地下命令驅使……；指使(人)做這做那」，例如：He likes to order people around.(他喜歡差使別人)。

❖ **connive with... :**

connive [kə`naɪv](v.)是「串通；勾結」，connive with... 是「與……密謀(犯罪)」之意，例如：They connived with John to deceive me.(他們與 John 共謀騙我)。

❖ **by nature :**

nature(n.)是「自然，本質」，by nature 是「生來；天生；生就」，例如：She is artistic by nature.(她生來就具有藝術氣息)。

句型分析 ▶

1. Moreover, matchmaking agencies openly advertise such disgraceful claims as "guaranteed a virgin," "fertile or your money back," or "comes with a one-year warranty."

   ◆ 這句話的主詞是 matchmaking agencies，主要動詞是 advertise。句中用到片語 such as...(例如……)，這裡所舉的例子有三個，用「對等連接詞」or 連接：(1)"guaranteed a virgin"(2)"fertile or your money back"(3)"comes with a one-year warranty"。

   ◆ 句中 openly(adv.)為「公開地」，這裡用來修飾動詞 advertise，意為「公開地登廣告」。claim(n.)為「宣稱；主張」，其前面的 disgraceful 為形容詞，意為「丟臉的；不名譽的」，因此 disgraceful claims 是「可恥的宣傳口號」。

♦ 句中的宣傳口號 "fertile or your money back" 的 or 在這裡是「否則……」，因此這句話是「包生，否則還你錢」。另一句口號 "comes with a one-year warranty" 的 come with... warranty 是習慣用法，表示「附……的保固」。

2. However, now that they have accumulated wealth, people have begun to treat people from poor nations with atrocity.

♦ 這句話的主詞是 people，主要動詞是 have begun。逗號前的 now that... 是「現在既然……」，這裡的意思是「現在累積越來越多的財富後，人們開始……」。

♦ 句中 treat people with... 是「用……對待人們」，這裡的 treat people with atrocity 則是「用殘酷的方式對待別人」。

造句練習 ▶

1. 你應該對你老闆的惡意對待提出告訴。(file a complaint against...)

----

2. 他太太昨天提出民事訴訟。(civil lawsuit / file)

----

3. 人蛇集團應該被判終身監禁。(human trafficking group / life in prison)

----

4. 他從小就愛指使朋友。(order... around)

----

5. 警察發現這店員與強盜勾結。(connive with...)

26

兩性關係及性教育
Inter-gender Relationships and Sex Education

　　相信許多人都還有印象，國中老師教到「健康教育第14章」時，不是藉口跳過，便是含糊其詞。台灣很多人的第一次性教育，便是在一種說不出、也不知為何的羞恥與嫌惡中度過。

　　前陣子國中性教育自學手冊「青春達人」中因為出現了「靠」、「屌」、「AV女優」及「RU486」等名詞而被某些衛道人士罵到臭頭，他們怕台灣善良的社會風氣因此敗壞，也怕台灣純潔的國中生會因為看了這本手冊就從此不再純潔。但事實是，現今台灣性教育的最大問題並不在於教材的適當與否，而在於教育當局對此問題的刻意忽略及淡化。這種鴕鳥心態以為，只要不告訴我們的國中生有關「性」的一切，他們便永遠不會知道，也永遠不會有興趣，當然也就不會「做」，那麼援交、墮胎、性侵的事情便會從社會上絕跡。問題在於我們的國中生並不是活在彩色泡泡球裡面的玩具熊。

　　至於「性教育」的內涵也遠非「性交教育」而已，它尚包含兩性教育、情感教育。這些在很多國家從國小就實施的教育，台灣明顯落後許多。這也難怪校園感情糾紛事件頻傳、「9月墮胎潮」越演越烈，甚至連大學研究所都不時上演校園情殺……。光是撻伐「青春達人」，有用嗎？

Inter-gender Relationships and Sex Education CD2-8

A while back, the Ministry of Education (MOE) **authorized** the production of a sex education **pamphlet** for junior high school students called "The Youth Expert." This **handbook** has been heavily criticized by some **legislators** for its **seemingly** "**vulgar** choice of words and **daring** content." It was also around this time that a male student from a "famous senior high school" seriously **wounded** a female student because of relationship problems.

Both incidents point towards a need for improvement of inter-gender relationships and sex education of students in Taiwan. According to reports, **approximately** 70 percent of senior high school students in Taipei City have previously been in a relationship with someone of the **opposite sex**. The **trend** is becoming more **evident** among the students, with sexual relations occurring at a younger age and at a higher rate. ❶ Such being the case, is there a need to **deprive** the youth of their right to learn about sex just because the wording used in "The Youth Expert" is closer to the language used by the youth **subculture**, and because the content **vividly** reflects the actual life of our youth? ❷

In addition, for a long time now in Taiwan, homes and schools have been placing too much attention on academic performance and **overlooking** the development of **morality** and **interpersonal relationships** of students. Given this, how can we expect our youth to be capable of solving life's problems? Having a high IQ does not **guarantee** a high EQ. A healthy personality and good relations with the opposite sex cannot be achieved **overnight**. Making a fuss over nothing or running away is definitely not the solution!

兩性關係及性教育

　前陣子，教育部委託編撰的國中性教育手冊《青春達人》，因為看似出現「不雅的用詞與大膽的內容」，遭到某些立委強烈批評。就在前些時候，一位「明星高中」的男學生因感情問題，重傷一名女同學。

　這兩個事件顯示，台灣學生的兩性關係及性教育有待加強。據報導，台北市有七成左右的高中生曾與異性交往，其中發生性關係的有年齡下降、比例升高的趨勢。既然如此，我們為何要因為《青春達人》用詞貼近年輕人的次文化語言、內容傳神表達年輕人的現實生活，就剝奪青少年們學習性知識的權利？

　另外，長久以來，台灣的家庭及學校過度注重課業成績，忽略學生品德與人際關係的培養。既然如此，我們又怎能期待青少年具備解決人生的能力？高智商不等於高情緒商數，健全的人格及良好的兩性關係更不是一蹴可及，大驚小怪或一味逃避絕不是解決之道！

主題句：　　　　單字：加黑　　　片語：套色　　　句型：❶ ❷

單字例句 ▶

◇ **inter-gender relationships / relations with the opposite sex** 兩性關係
We should learn how to improve our relations with the opposite sex.
我們應學習如何增進我們的兩性關係。

◇ **sex education** 性教育
Sex education courses are offered at my school.
我的學校有提供性教育課程。

◇ **authorize**(v.)授權；委任
No one is authorized to enter this room except the manager.
除了經理，沒有人被授權進入這個房間。

◇ **pamphlet**(n.)小冊子
We were given these pamphlets on gender equality.
有人給我們這些有關性別平等的小冊子。

◇ **handbook**(n.)手冊
Please read the handbook carefully to avoid confusion.
為免誤解，請小心閱讀此手冊。

◇ **legislator**(n.)立法委員
Legislators passed a bill yesterday allowing freedom of speech.
立法委員昨天通過法案，允許言論自由。

◇ **seemingly**（**adv.**）看起來；表面上
She conquered a seemingly incurable disease.
她戰勝了一個看起來無可救藥的疾病。

◇ **vulgar** [ˋvʌlgɚ]（**adj.**）不優雅的；粗俗的
He got into trouble because of his vulgar behavior.
他因粗俗的舉止惹上麻煩。

◇ **daring** [ˋdɛrɪŋ]（**adj.**）大膽的
I never knew you were that daring until now.
我直到現在才知道你這麼大膽。

◇ **wound**（**v.**）傷害
She accidentally wounded her finger while chopping vegetables.
她切菜時不小心傷到手指頭。

◇ **approximately**（**adv.**）大約
There are approximately 200 guests at the banquet.
這場宴席大約有兩百個賓客。

◇ **opposite sex** 異性

◇ **trend**（**n.**）趨勢
Can you tell me what the latest trend in fashion is?
你可否告訴我最新流行的時尚趨勢？

◇ **evident**（**adj.**）明顯的
It is very evident that he made a mistake.
很明顯的，他犯了錯。

◇ **deprive**(**v.**)剝奪;使喪失
We will never deprive you of your desires and needs.
我們永遠不會剝奪你的渴望與需要。

◇ **subculture**(**n.**)次文化
A new subculture is emerging among the youth.
年輕人間出現了一個新的次文化。

◇ **vividly**(**adv.**)逼真地
The painting depicts the woman's emotion so vividly.
這幅畫很逼真地描述了這女人的情緒。

◇ **overlook**(**v.**)忽視
Do not overlook any sudden changes in the stock market.
別忽略股票市場的任何突發變動。

◇ **morality**(**n.**)道德;品行
Morality has not been emphasized in school curricula.
道德品行在學校課程中一直不是很被強調。

◇ **interpersonal relationships**(多用複數)人際關係

◇ **guarantee**(**v.**)保證
Please guarantee that you will be back after an hour.
請保證你會在一小時後回來。

◇ **overnight**(**adv.**)一夜間;突然地
Changes cannot be made overnight.
改變不能突然發生。

片　語 ▶

◇ **place attention on...：**

place(v.)是「安放」，place attention on...「將注意力放在……」，例如：When exercising, place your attention on your breathing.(運動時，將注意力放在你的呼吸)。

◇ **be capable of...：**

capable(adj.)是「有能力的」，be capable of... 是「能做得出……」，例如：Kevin is a man capable of doing anything.(Kevin 是個什麼事都做得出來的人)。

◇ **make a fuss over...：**

fuss(n.)是「大驚小怪；忙亂」，make a fuss over... 是「對……無事自擾；對……小題大作」，over 後面接的是「事件」，例如：Don't make a fuss over a small error.(不要對小失誤大驚小怪)。

◇ **run away：**

run away 是「跑走」，引申有「逃避」之意，例如：You can't just run away from your responsibilities.(你不能就這樣逃避責任)。

句型分析 ▶

1. The trend is becoming more evident among the students, with sexual relations occurring at a younger age and at a higher rate.

   ◆ 這句話的主詞是 The trend，動詞是 is becoming。逗號後的 with... 當形容詞用，修飾逗號前的句子。

   ◆ evident (adj.) 是「明顯的」，is becoming more evident 是「益發明顯」。句中 occurring 的原形是 occur (發生)，由 which are occurring 省略而來。

   ◆ 句中 at... rate 是「按……的比率；以……比例」，at a higher rate 則是「以較高的比例」。

2. Such being the case, is there a need to deprive the youth of their right to learn about sex just because the wording used in "The Youth Expert" is closer to the language used by the youth subculture, and because the content vividly reflects the actual life of our youth?

   ◆ 這句話的主、動詞是 there is (there 為形式主詞，指的真正主詞是動詞後的 a need)。

   ◆ 這句話可以簡省為：Is there a need... just because..., and because...? (有必要……只因為……，且因為……嗎？)

   ◆ 句中用到片語 deprive... of... 是「剝奪……」之意，這裡的 deprive the youth of their right to learn 是「剝奪年輕人學習的權利」。

♦ be closer to... 是「較接近……」之意，這裡的 is closer to the language used by the youth 是「較接近年輕人用的語言」。

♦ reflect(v.)是「反射；反應」之意，句中 reflects the life of our youth 是「反應我們年輕人的生活」。

造句練習 ▶

1. 我已委託他在我出國期間處理我的工作。(authorize... / take care of...)

   -

2. 他有能力犯下任何罪。(be capable of...)

   -

3. 他對異性總是很害羞。(the opposite sex)

   -

4. 很明顯的，他是個騙子。(it is evident that...)

   -

5. 發展厚實的人際關係可以促進個人的成長。
   (interpersonal relationships / personal growth)

   -

27

狗屎與環保
Dog Feces and Environmental Protection

　　台灣的流浪狗多，路上狗屎也多，多到日本人中村夫婦決定捲鋪蓋回家。有人說，狗屎算什麼？人家義大利跟法國也處處是鴿糞，走在街頭踩到是運氣、不踩到是奇蹟！唉，偏偏我們不是義大利與法國，人家的鴿糞想起來就浪漫，我們的狗屎想起來就噁心。

　　偏偏台灣人又超愛養狗，帶狗出去大便時又常忘了隨身攜帶撿拾工具，就算帶了撿拾工具，也常在愛犬「解放」時忘了隨手撿拾……，這就是為什麼台灣街頭到處有狗屎。當然，有人說台灣的狗屎主要來自於骯髒討厭又愛攻擊人的流浪狗，不過這些人忘了，台灣的流浪狗都不是「自願」的，都曾經是人見人愛的「家犬」，變成了流浪犬，台灣人恐怕要負大部分的責任。不信？

　　君不見台灣的流浪犬有「流行性」：前前陣子電影「可魯」大賣時，幾個月後台灣街頭忽然多了許多「可魯流浪狗」。前陣子名模林志玲的「咖啡」大紅特紅後，這陣子街頭也多了幾隻「咖啡流浪犬」。這就是台灣人的養狗文化：不是因為有愛心，而是為了趕流行。一旦流行退燒，或者發現可愛的小狗原來會長大，便棄如敝屣。你說，台灣怎會沒有狗屎問題？

Dog Feces and Environmental Protection (CD2-9)

A while back, a Japanese couple who had planned to take part in a "long stay" program in Taiwan decided to opt for the "no stay" choice. They complained that the environment around Puli was below standard, and was especially **dotted** with an **excessive** amount of dog waste. Recently, the Environmental Protection Administration (EPA) decided to strictly **implement** the clearing up of dog feces and establish a **penalty** system.

Taiwan is filled with **hospitality** and **humanity**; people in general are especially concerned with the **well-being** of family and friends. However, people are **indifferent** to **public morals**. In addition to the issue of dog feces, some people also like running the red lights or **jaywalking**, while some do not even think twice about talking on their cell phones or discussing the **plot** while in a movie theater. ❶ There are also people who cut in line, take up public space, or belt out Karaoke songs at home or outdoors. ❷ Moreover, there are people who make a lot of noise in public, or give their kids or pets free rein in public. The worst **offenders** are the people who **litter**, spit **phlegm** or **betel nut juice**, or throw their cigarette butts everywhere, turning "Hehuan Mountain" into "Waste Mountain!"

In recent years, some people are starting to become worried that Taiwan's environment is taking a turn for the worse. These people have become "**conservation volunteers**." Some of the volunteers sort out trash for **recycling**, while some pick up trash while hiking. Some even help plant trees. In fact, all you really need is a desire to help; you can help **preserve** the beauty of Taiwan just by carrying your own environmentally-friendly **tableware**. What are you waiting for?

狗屎與環保

前陣子，一對原本想來台灣「長住」的日本夫婦最後決定「不住」。他們抱怨埔里地區環境不佳、尤其狗屎太多。這陣子，環保署決定嚴格執行清理狗屎的活動，並訂定罰則。

台灣有濃濃的人情味；一般人對親朋好友尤其關心，但對於公共道德，卻漠不關心。除了狗屎問題，有些人喜歡闖紅燈、橫過馬路，有人則超愛在看電影時講手機、討論劇情。還有些人喜歡插隊、占用公共空間、在家中或戶外大唱卡拉OK。另外有些人愛在公共場所大聲喧嘩，或者放任小孩與寵物趴趴走。更可惡的，有些人還喜歡亂丟垃圾、隨地吐痰或檳榔汁、亂扔煙蒂，將「合歡山」搞成「垃圾山」！

這幾年，社會上已有人開始對惡質的台灣環境感到憂心，紛紛當起「環保志工」。這些志工有的將垃圾分類回收，有的一邊健行一邊撿拾垃圾，有的甚至植樹成林。其實只要有心，即使只是隨身攜帶環保餐具，也可以為維護美麗的台灣盡一份心力。你還在等什麼？

主題句： 　　　　　單字：加黑　　　片語：套色　　　句型：❶❷

單字例句 ▶

◇ **feces** [ˋfisiz] (n.) (複數) 糞便；排泄物
The general medical exam requires samples of your feces and urine.
一般健康檢查需要你的糞便及尿液樣本。

◇ **environmental protection** 環境保護

◇ **dot** (v.) 散布；點綴
The dance floor was dotted with litter from last night's party.
這舞池散布著從昨晚舞會留下來的垃圾。

◇ **excessive** (adj.) 過度的；過多的
Excessive usage of alcohol is detrimental to your health.
過度飲酒對你的健康有害。

◇ **implement** [ˋɪmpləˌmɛnt] (v.) 實行
When will they implement the new set of rules and regulations?
他們何時會實施新的規則及法令？

◇ **penalty** (n.) 處罰
Penalties will be given to those who do not follow the rules.
不遵守規則的人將會受到處罰。

◇ **hospitality** (n.) 殷勤招待；好客
The couple's hospitality earned their neighbors' appreciation.
這對夫婦的熱情好客使他們贏得鄰居的好感。

◇ **humanity** (n.) 人情

The small town is renowned for its humanity.

這小鎮以人情味著稱。

◇ **well-being**(n.)幸福；健康

He is always concerned about the well-being of others.

他總是關心其他人的福利。

◇ **indifferent**(adj.)漠不關心的；不感興趣的

Please be patient with customers who are indifferent.

對沒有興趣的顧客請有耐心。

◇ **public morals** 公德心

◇ **jaywalk**(v.)橫越馬路

I jaywalked this morning because I was running late.

我今早因為快遲到了，所以橫越馬路。

◇ **plot**(n.)劇情；情節

It has been said that the plot of this movie is extraordinary.

據說這部電影的情節很特別。

◇ **offender**(n.)違法者

Offenders will be immediately reported to the presiding officer.

違法者會馬上被舉報給審裁官。

◇ **litter**(v.)亂丟垃圾

The children littered trash all over the place.

小孩子們到處亂丟垃圾。

◇ **phlegm** [flɛm](n.)痰

Cough out all your phlegm to reduce the itching in your throat.

將你的痰都吐出來，以免喉嚨癢。

◇ **betel nut juice 檳榔汁**

Spots of betel nut juice dot the road.

檳榔汁散布路上。

◇ **conservation volunteer 環保志工**

◇ **recycling(n.)回收**

Recycling should be taught to children at an early age.

孩子從很小的時候就應該被教導回收(的概念)。

◇ **preserve(v.)維持；防護**

The police preserved all the evidence in the crime scene.

警察保留著犯罪現場所有的證據。

◇ **tableware(n.)餐具(總稱)**

Do not forget the tableware for our picnic.

別忘了我們野餐的餐具。

片　語　▶

◇ **take part in... :**

take part in...是個常見片語，指「參加……；貢獻於……」，例如：They all took part in the fundraising event.(他們全都參加了募款的活動)。

◇ **opt for... :**

opt(v.)是「選擇」，後面常接 for 或 to，例如：Many students have opted to take her class.(許多學生選修了她的課)。

◇ **be concerned with... :**
concerned(adj.)是「關心的；擔心的」，be concerned with...是「認為……很重要」，例如：Many politicians are more concerned with power than with the good of the people.(許多政客較關心權力，而非人民的利益)。

◇ **sort out :**
sort(v.)是「把……分類；揀選」，sort out 是「把…從中分開；挑出……；歸類」，例如：He sorted out his winter clothes.(他將冬天的衣服挑出來)。

句型分析 ▶

1. In addition to the issue of dog feces, some people also like running the red lights or jaywalking, while some do not even think twice about talking on their cell phones or discussing the plot while in a movie theater.

   ◆ 這句話的主詞是 some people，主要動詞是 like(喜歡)。句首的 In addition to... 用來形容整句，意為「除了……之外」。

   ◆ 這句話舉了四件人們平常喜歡做的事：(1)running the red lights (2)jaywalking(3)talking on their cell phones while in a movie theater(4)discussing the plot while in a movie theater。run 這

裡當「闖越」解。

◆ 本句出現兩個 while，第一個 while 意為「另一方面……；而」，指的是「有些人喜歡……，另一方面，有些人喜歡……」。第二個 while 是「當……的時候；與……同時」，指的是「在看電影的同時，喜歡……」。

2. There are also people who cut in line, take up public space, or belt out Karaoke songs at home or outdoors.

◆ 這句話的主、動詞是 There are(there 為形式主詞，指的真正主詞是動詞後的 people)。句中列出了三個人們喜歡做的事：(1)cut in line(2)take up public space(3)belt out Karaoke songs at home or outdoors。句中的 who 為關係代名詞，代替前面的 people。

◆ 句中的 cut in.. 是「插進……」，cut in line 便是「插隊」；take up 是「占用(時間、空間)」，take up public space 便是「占用公共空間」；belt out...是口語的「大聲唱出……」。

造句練習 ▶

1. 他決定參加今年的演講比賽。(take part in...)

----

2. 我欽佩環保團體所做的努力。(environmental protection group)

----

3. 試著將這些檔案依主題歸類。(sort out...)

----

4. 不論到哪裡，千萬別忘了你的公德心。(public morals)

----

5. 我週末擔任環保志工。(conservation volunteer)

28

火星文來了！Orz！
Here Comes the Martian Language! Orz!

在台灣的中學教育裡，「國文」一直不是個重要的話題，因為它既沒有數學及理化的有「錢」景，也沒有英文的國際化。不過現在情況改變了！

自從許多學者專家出面痛批現在學子的中文程度每下愈況後，學校國文課的時數到底要增要減、「基測」到底要不要考作文、國文教材到底要有多少比例的白話文與文言文等等，都成了熱門話題。中文如此火紅，難怪連安親班、補習班都開始招募學生補國文、補作文。

現今令學者專家頭痛的另一個中文問題，便是「火星文」的大舉登陸台灣。發展至今，「火星文」的創意已到了匪夷所思的地步，令老師緊張（因為不知道同學上課傳的紙條到底寫些什麼東東）、讓家長抓狂（因為不知道孩子手機簡訊到底寫些什麼東東），連外星人看了都彼此搖搖頭，互瞪眼，嘆為觀止。

說了半天，到底什麼是 Orz？別問我，也別問火星人，因為我們都不是今年「學測」的國文科命題委員！

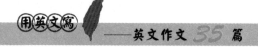
Here Comes the Martian Language! Orz! (CD2-10)

An exam question using the "Martian language" caused quite a **stir** in this year's college **scholastic exam** and **triggered** a heated **debate**. ❶ Many believe that this sort of test question not only proves that there is a serious "**urban-rural gap**" in Taiwan; it also encourages the **proliferation** of the already-widespread Martian language!

What exactly is the Martian language? According to the Martians themselves, it is a **hybrid** writing system which **incorporates** Chinese, English, Taiwanese, numbers, Mandarin **phonetic symbols**, and special computer symbols. Originally, this term was used to **accommodate** "netizens" in their online chatting sessions. Later, the term became part of the daily writing vocabulary of our youth.

Language is, in essence, **evolving**. Modern language **variations** usually come and go **swiftly**, so we need not worry that Taiwan will be **consumed** by these Martian words. Besides, if we look at this issue from another perspective, the young people who are **proficient** in the Martian language might one day be able to create a **coded** language that would be impossible to **comprehend** from the outside. Eventually, these young people may become Taiwan's foremost **intelligence agents**! But one thing that is on everyone's mind now is that if even the adults at the Ministry of Education make mistakes writing **elegiac couplets**, then Taiwan's language education is truly in big trouble! ❷

火星文來了！Orz！

今年大學學測出現了令人爭議的「火星文」考題，引發熱烈討論。許多人認為這種題目不止證明了台灣有嚴重的「城鄉差距」，更助長了已經氾濫的「火星文」！

「火星文」到底是啥？據火星人自己說，這是一種結合了中文、英文、台語、數字、注音符號、以及特殊電腦符號而成的混合字。這東西原本是為了順應「網路族」線上聊天方便之用，後來變成年輕人平日書寫時的用詞。

其實語言本來就會演變；新時代語言的變體通常來得快、去得也快，因此大人們不用太擔心火星文會大舉占領台灣。而且換個角度想，這些擅長「火星文」的年輕人未來還可能創造出無人能懂得語言密碼，成為台灣最厲害的情治人員呢！不過現在大家比較擔心的是，如果連「教育部」裡面的大人都會寫錯輓聯，台灣的語文教育可能真的出了大問題！

主題句：　　　　單字：**加黑**　　片語：套色　　句型：❶❷

單字例句 ▶

◇ **Martian** [ˋmɑrʃɪən] **language** 火星文

◇ **stir**(n.)騷亂
The controversial book caused quite a stir.
這本受爭議的書造成了不少騷動。

◇ **scholastic** [skəˋlæstɪk] **exam** 學力測驗

◇ **trigger**(v.)促使；引起
We must be very careful not to trigger the alarm.
我們要很小心，不要觸動警鈴。

◇ **debate**(n.)辯論；爭論
After a whole day of debate, a decision has still not been reached.
經過一整天的辯論，還是沒有達成決議。

◇ **urban-rural gap** 城鄉差距

◇ **proliferation**(n.)快速增加；繁殖
The proliferation of information was boosted by the introduction of satellites.
衛星的引進更擴大了資訊的快速繁殖。

◇ **hybrid** [ˋhaɪbrɪd](adj.)混血的；混合的
These are hybrid roses.
這些是混種的玫瑰。

◇ **incorporate**(v.)結合；混合
We have to find a way to incorporate more features in our product.
我們必須找出方法讓我們的產品結合更多的特色。

◇ **phonetic symbol** 語音符號
It is often useful to learn how to read phonetic symbols.
學習如何念語音符號通常是很有用的。

◇ **accommodate**(v.)順應……；照顧……；容納……
We've made every effort to accommodate your point of view.
我們已經盡其所能順應你的觀點了。

◇ **netizen**(n.)網路族
Anyone with a computer and an Internet connection can become a "netizen."
任何有電腦及網路連線的人都可以成為「網路族」。

◇ **evolving**(adj.)進化的；演變的
Technology is constantly evolving to provide for the needs of humanity.
科技不間斷的演變，提供人性的需求。

◇ **variation**(n.)變體；變異
Adding a little variation to things will make them more interesting.
在事情上加點變化會讓它們更有趣。

◇ **swiftly**(adv.)迅速地
The marathon runner moved swiftly across the finish line.

馬拉松跑者快速跑過終點線。

◇ **consume**(v.)吞噬；食盡

The apartment building was consumed by a fire.

這公寓被火吞噬。

◇ **proficient**(adj.)精通的；擅長的

She is very proficient in computer languages and programming.

她很精通電腦語言及程式設計。

◇ **coded**(adj.)有密碼的

The two good friends communicate using a coded language.

這兩個好朋友用密碼語言溝通。

◇ **comprehend**(v.)理解

This book is very difficult to comprehend.

這本書十分難以理解。

◇ **intelligence agent** 情治人員

You need to be very smart and quick-witted to qualify as an intelligence agent.

要成為一個情治人員，你必須非常聰明且機智。

◇ **elegiac** [ˌɛləˈdʒaɪək] **couplet** 輓聯

He wrote a poem composed of elegiac couplets for his mother.

他為母親寫了一首輓聯詩。

片 語 ▶

◇ **in essence：**

essence(n.)是「(東西的)本質；精髓」，in essence 是「大體上；本質上；基本上」，例如：In essence his message was very simple.(他的訊息本質上很簡單)。

◇ **come and go：**

come and go 是「來來去去；變化不定」，引申為一個事情或現象的快速崛起及消逝，例如：Money will come and go.(財富會來來去去)。

◇ **look at... from another perspective：**

perspective(n.)是「觀點；角度」，look at... from another perspective 是「從另一個觀點看……」，例如：A good teacher can take a current international issue and have students look at it from another perspective.(一個好的老師可以拿一個國際時事，然後要學生從另一個角度來看此事件)。

句型分析 ▶

1. An exam question using the "Martian language" caused quite a stir in this year's college scholastic exam and triggered a heated debate.

   ♦ 這句話的主詞是 an exam question，動詞是 caused...(and)

triggered；兩個動詞由 「對等連接詞」and 連接：
(1) caused quite a stir in this year's college scholastic
exam (2) triggered a heated debate。

♦ 句中的 using 原本是由關係代名詞 which 所引導的 which
was using，這裡省略 which was。

2. But one thing that is on everyone's mind now is that if even
the adults at the Ministry of Education make mistakes writing
elegiac couplets, then Taiwan's language education is truly in
big trouble!

♦ 這句話的主詞是 one thing，主要動詞是 is。one thing 後面
由 that 引導的 that is on everyone's mind now 是修飾 thing，
意為「現在存在每個人心中的一件事」。因此本句第二個
出現的 is 才是主要動詞。其後面接 that... 是另一個子句，
句中用到 if..., then...(如果……，那麼……)的條件句。

♦ 句中由if 所領導的條件句可以簡省為：if even the adults...
make mistakes..., then Taiwan's language education is... in...
trouble(如果連大人都……犯錯……，那台灣的語言教育
就……有麻煩)。

♦ in trouble 是「有麻煩」，句中的 in big trouble 則是「有大
麻煩」。

造句練習 ▶

1. 年輕人在網路聊天時喜歡用火星文。(be fond of... / Martian language)

_____

2. 學生每天讀書準備學力測驗。(scholastic exam)

_____

3. 就生活方式而言，台灣有非常明顯的城鄉差距。(urban-rural gap / lifestyle)

_____

4. 就本質而言，音樂被認為是國際語言。(in essence)

_____

5. 一種情況可以從幾個不同的觀點來看。(situation / perspective)

_____

29

禽流感恐慌
The Avian Flu Scare

曾經有位病理學家說過:「人類的歷史即疾病的歷史」,的確,人類有歷史以來,似乎一直逃不過疾病肆虐的宿命。而且這些大型疾病似乎都在每隔一段時間後伺機爆發,讓人類恐懼不已。例如中世紀以來、已經發生過至少三次的黑死病(the Black Death,又稱「鼠疫」 plague)、十六世紀的天花(smallpox)、黃熱病(yellow fever),二十世紀的腦炎(encephalitis)、霍亂(cholera)、瘧疾(malaria),以及蔓延快速的愛滋(AIDS)……。

值得注意的是,在人類與各式各樣傳染病抗戰的漫長歷史中,「流行性感冒」(influenza,簡稱 flu)聽起來雖然不像黑死病、愛滋病、天花等那麼恐怖,事實上,它帶給人類文明與社會的衝擊,卻絲毫不遜色!根據傳染病流行史,人類早在西元前四世紀就有流行性感冒流行的記載,而1918年發生在西班牙的流感,更奪去了五千多萬人的性命,連其國王也不能倖免,果真浩劫一場!

台灣這幾年也一直被不同傳染病所困擾,從SARS、腸病毒(Enterovirus)到現在人人聞之色變的「禽流感」。雖然有人責怪媒體「嚇死人」,不過我們在「剉著等」的同時,還是要在下一場瘟疫爆發之前,做好準備!

The Avian Flu Scare (CD2-11)

With the emergence of avian flu in Asian **poultry**, along with seasonal changes causing the **H5N1 strain** to spread to other **continents**, the whole world is **engulfed** in a **frightening atmosphere**. ❶ Many experts predict that **once** a human-to-human bird flu **transmission** breaks out, its speed and scale would far surpass that of SARS from a few years back.

Tamiflu, made by the Swiss **pharmaceutical** company Roche, is currently the most effective drug in treating bird flu. However, owing to the problem of **obtaining** a **patent**, **mass production** of the drug requires further discussion. This has also sparked international concern.

In Taiwan, no one **dares** to feed the **pigeons** at Chiang Kai-Shek Memorial Hall **square** or buy poultry in the market because of bird flu. People have also switched to ordering pork when eating out. Consequently, pigeons **suffer**, geese and chickens **rejoice**, and pork producers **reap** the benefits. ❷ An avian flu **episode** has not yet hit Taiwan, but it has already created quite a **commotion**!

禽流感恐慌

　　自從亞洲的禽鳥出現禽流感，並隨著季節遷移將 H5N1 型病毒散播到其他大陸後，全球就籠罩在一片恐慌中。很多專家預言，一旦爆發「人對人」的禽流感疫情，其蔓延速度之快及規模之大，將遠遠超過前幾年的 SARS。

　　目前只有瑞士羅氏藥廠生產的「克流感」，是治療禽流感最為有效的藥物。不過因為取得專利權的問題，量產此藥需進一步討論。這也引起世界各國的關切。

　　在台灣，因為禽流感的關係，中正紀念堂廣場的鴿子因此沒人敢餵，大家上菜市場時也不敢買雞鴨，外食時也紛紛改吃豬肉。到頭來，瘦了鴿子，樂了雞鴨，肥了豬肉商。一場尚未到來的禽流感，在台灣已經造成不小的震撼！

主題句：　　　　　　單字：**加黑**　　片語：套色　　句型：❶❷

單字例句 ▶

◇ **avian flu / bird flu** 禽流感

◇ **poultry**（n.）家禽
Poultry is no longer allowed on public transportation.
大眾交通工具上已不容許帶家禽上車。

◇ **H5N1 strain：H5N1型**（病毒）

◇ **continent**（n.）大陸
The businessman has to travel from one continent to another.
商人必須旅行於不同的大陸間。

◇ **engulf**（v.）吞沒
In a matter of minutes, the whole building was engulfed in flames.
幾分鐘內，這棟建築物就被火舌吞沒。

◇ **frightening**（adj.）引起恐懼的
The earthquake was a frightening experience for everyone in the town.
地震對鎮裡的每個人而言都是可怕的經驗。

◇ **atmosphere**（n.）氣氛；環境
People enjoyed the relaxing atmosphere at the beach.
人們喜歡海灘輕鬆自在的氣氛。

◇ **once**（conj.）一旦

◇ **transmission**(n.)傳播；輸送
The doctors tried to prevent the transmission of the disease.
醫生們試著避免這疾病的傳播。

◇ **surpass**(v.)超過
His performance has surpassed expectations.
他的表現超過預期。

◇ **Tamiflu**(n.)「克流感」

◇ **pharmaceutical** [͵fɑrməˋsjutɪkl̩] (adj.)製藥的；藥學的
Pharmaceutical companies must balance concern for public welfare with the need to operate profitably.
藥廠必須在關心大眾福利與獲得利潤間求取平衡。

◇ **obtain**(v.)獲得
It's expected that our company will obtain permission to produce the drug.
我們公司預計會取得生產此藥的許可。

◇ **patent**(n.)專利；專利權
The inventor is applying for a patent to prevent people from making cheap imitations.
這發明者申請專利，以避免其他人製造便宜的仿造品。

◇ **mass production** 大量生產；量產
Machines are usually used for the mass production of products.
機器的使用通常是為了大量生產產品。

◇ **dare**(v.)敢於……

The boy does not dare to tell his mother lies.
這男孩不敢跟他媽媽撒謊。

◇ **pigeon** [ˋpɪdʒɪn] (**n.**) 鴿子
People feed the pigeons in the park with scraps of food.
人們用食物殘渣餵食公園的鴿子。

◇ **square / plaza** (**n.**) 廣場
Couples stroll around the square and enjoy the beautiful weather.
情人們漫步於廣場，享受美好的天氣。

◇ **suffer** (**v.**) 受苦
Other people suffered for his mistakes.
旁人因他的錯誤受苦。

◇ **rejoice** (**v.**) 感到高興；充滿喜悅
They rejoiced at the birth of their second child.
他們因第二個孩子的誕生充滿喜悅。

◇ **reap** (**v.**) 獲得；收割
He reaped the benefits of having bilingual parents.
他因擁有說雙語的父母而獲得好處。

◇ **episode** (**n.**) 插曲，情節
He tried to forget the episode by the lake.
他試著忘記發生在湖邊的插曲。

◇ **commotion** (**n.**) 騷動
The police came to investigate the cause of the commotion.
警察跑來調查這起騷動的原因。

片　語 ▶

❖ **break out：**

break out 是「（火災、戰爭、暴動、流行病等的）突然爆發」，例如：A fire broke out in a neighboring store.(鄰近的一家商店發生了一場火災)。

❖ **owing to... ：**

owing to... 當介系詞用，是「由於……；起因於」的意思，例如：Owing to careless driving, she had an accident.(由於不小心駕駛，她出了車禍)。

❖ **spark concern：**

spark(v.)是「激起……；刺激」，spark concern 是「引起關切」，例如：A crack in the wall of the dam has sparked concern among neighboring communities.(水壩牆上的裂縫已引起附近社區的關切)。

❖ **switch to... ：**

switch(v.)是「轉換；改變」，通常的用法是 switch... to... 意思是「由……轉換為……」，例如：We switched from coal to gas.(我們由煤炭改用瓦斯)。

句型分析 ▶

1. With the emergence of avian flu in Asian poultry, along with seasonal changes causing the H5N1 strain to spread to other continents, the whole world is engulfed in a frightening atmosphere.

   ◆ 這句話的主詞是 the world，動詞是 is engulfed。句子一開頭的 With... to other continents為形容詞，修飾整句話，意為「隨著……到其他大陸」。

   ◆ 句中 With... , along with... 是「隨著……，伴隨著……」，提到的東西有兩樣：(1) the emergence of avian flu in Asian poultry(亞洲禽鳥出現禽流感)(2) seasonal changes causing the H5N1 strain to spread to other continents(季節遷移導致 H5N1 型病毒散播到其他大陸)。

   ◆ engulf(v.)是「吞沒」，be engulfed in... 是「被吞噬在……」，這裡的 the world is engulfed in a frightening atmosphere 是「全球被一片恐慌所吞噬」。

2. Consequently, pigeons suffer, geese and chickens rejoice, and pork producers reap the benefits.

   ◆ 句首的 Consequently 是副詞，修飾全句，意為「結果……」。

   ◆ 這句話中用了「對等連接詞」and連接三個小句子：(1) pigeons suffer (2) geese and chickens rejoice (3) pork producers reap the benefits。

   ◆ 整句話直譯的意思是：「結果，鴿子受苦，鵝與雞高興，

豬肉生產商獲得利益。」

造句練習 ▶

1. 全世界的人都擔心禽流感的傳播。(bird flu)

   -

2. 他一旦開始哭，就很難有辦法讓他停下來。(once...)

   -

3. 醜聞一爆發，記者們馬上就聚集到這演員的家。(scandal / break out)

   -

4. 她青少年時期皈依不同的宗教。(convert to... / religion)

   -

5. 這事件很嚴重，足以激起廣泛的關切。(spark concern)

   -

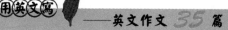

志工旅遊
Volunteer Vacationing

　　台灣是個島國，加上地小人稠，大家因此對島外的世界充滿好奇，也因此許多台灣人都「身經百戰」，旅遊經一籮筐。不過玩到一種極限後，大家關注的可能已不再是「旅遊國家數目」的多寡，而是「實際旅遊收穫」的多寡；看重的也不再是「去哪裡玩」，而是「如何玩」。

　　也因此，目前已有許多新型的旅遊方式被開發出來，例如「志工旅遊」(volunteer vacationing)。這種「一邊度假、一邊當義工」度假方式，在國外其實已盛行了好一段時間，現在也慢慢被國內一些旅遊者所接受。

　　除此之外，有些人會在假期報名參加各種夢想課程，例如學習開賽車、當廚師、耍特技、扮特務等。想想看，一趟旅程結束後，自己忽然有了另一項專長，的確很令人心動！

　　還有這幾年國外流行「慢食運動」(slow food movement)。slow food 是相較於 fast food(速食)而創的新詞，指的是一種食物生長及飲食的方式。此運動強調傳統的、有機的農業生長方式，以及欣賞美食與酒的生活態度；目的無非希望人們能在忙碌的生活中，撥出時間烹煮當地農人種的食材，享受與家人朋友相聚的快樂時光。影響所及，現在有人提出「慢遊」，認為這樣的旅行方式才能玩得深刻，你認為呢？

Volunteer Vacationing (CD2-12)

Office workers in Taiwan are frequently **rushing** to use up their **annual leave** before the end of each year. **Employees** of **foreign-based companies** also have their major vacation during the New Year holidays. This time of year is therefore the **peak season** for the **tourism** industry.

Taiwanese people work very **diligently** year in and year out, and it is only right that they make use of the New Year holidays to travel. But the thing is, people are so **worn out** from a year of **toil** that even when they decide to travel with a tour group, the only thing they do is to "get on the bus and sleep, get off the bus and **pee**, take some pictures, buy some **pills**, and end up with nothing at all." ❶

Elsewhere in the world, more and more people are **opting** for a different kind of vacation: "**volunteer vacationing**." These **vacationers** make use of their weekends or longer holidays to go to **remote** schools and participate in after-school **tutoring** or **volunteer** in hospitals. ❷ Those who are better off **financially** might even go abroad to participate in **disaster relief** and in **construction** of **underdeveloped countries**. Indeed, "It is more **blessed** to give than to receive." After having experienced a **spiritually-void** tour group, why not go on a tour where you can enjoy your holiday in a **meaningful** way?

志工旅遊

在台灣，許多上班族會趕在每年年底前休完年假，而外商公司的員工也通常在新年期間休長假，因此這段期間是旅遊業的旺季。

台灣人民一年到頭勤奮工作，理應利用新年假期從事旅遊。只不過因為大家平日實在太辛勞了，因此就算決定跟團旅遊，也經常發生「上車睡覺，下車尿尿，拍照買藥，什麼都不知道」的情況。

在國外，有越來越多的人選擇另一種度假方式：「志工旅遊」。這些度假者利用週末或更長的休假，到偏遠的學校參與學生課後輔導，或者到醫院做義工。較有錢的甚至到海外參與救災及落後國家的建設。的確，「施比受更有福」，在參加過心靈空虛的旅行團後，你何不也試試這種有意義的度假方式？

主題句： 單字：加黑 片語：套色 句型：❶❷

單字例句 ▶

- ❖ **rush**（**v.**）趕；匆促行事
  People in Taipei are always rushing from one place to another.
  台北人通常匆匆忙忙地從一個地方趕到另一個地方。

- ❖ **annual leave** 年假

- ❖ **employee**（**n.**）員工
  He was selected as employee of the month.
  他被選為當月最佳員工。

- ❖ **foreign-based company** 外商公司

- ❖ **peak season** 旺季
  The cost of a plane ticket reaches its highest during the peak season.
  旺季時，機票的價格達到最高。

- ❖ **tourism**（**n.**）旅遊業
  Tourism is one of the most flourishing industries.
  旅遊業是最富榮景的行業之一。

- ❖ **diligently** [ˈdɪlədʒəntlɪ]（**adv.**）勤奮地
  After working diligently for several years, he was finally promoted to manager.
  勤奮工作了幾年之後，他終於被升為經理。

- ❖ **wear out** 疲倦；耗損

◇ **toil**(**n.**)辛勞；苦工
His body bore the marks of a lifetime of toil.
他的身體顯示著他一生的辛勞。

◇ **pee**(**v.**)(俚語)小便；尿尿
"Pee" is an indecent word.
「尿尿」是不禮貌的字眼。

◇ **pill**(**n.**)藥丸
Taking a sleeping pill can help you fall asleep easier.
吃安眠藥可以助眠。

◇ **elsewhere**(**adv.**)在別處
I plan to travel elsewhere.
我計畫到別處旅行。

◇ **opt**(**v.**)選擇
I decided to opt for a better place to live.
我決定選擇較好的地方居住。

◇ **volunteer vacationing** 志工旅遊

◇ **vacationer**(**n.**)度假者
I like to watch vacationers wandering on the beach.
我喜歡看度假者在海灘漫步。

◇ **remote**(**adj.**)偏遠的；偏僻的
I want to be a teacher in remote area to help children in need.
我希望到偏遠地區當老師，幫助需要的小朋友。

◇ **tutoring**(**n.**)教學；輔導

Tutoring is necessary, especially for children with learning disabilities.

個別輔導是有必要的，尤其對於有學習障礙的小朋友而言。

◇ **volunteer**(v.)志願；做義工

I volunteered to clean all the sickrooms in the hospital.

我志願打掃醫院的所有病房。

◇ **financially**(adv.)財務上地

This program is not financially attractive.

這方案在財務上並不吸引人。

◇ **disaster relief** 災難救助

Some African leaders called for disaster relief from rich countries after the earthquake struck the area.

在當地發生地震後，一些非洲領導人請求富有國家提供災難救助。

◇ **construction**(n.)建築；建設

The hotel is currently under construction.

這旅館目前正在施工中。

◇ **underdeveloped country** 低度開發國家

◇ **blessed**(adj.)幸福的；受祝福的

Their marriage was blessed by both their families.

他們的婚姻受到雙方家庭的祝福。

◇ **spiritually-void** 心靈空虛的

This novel consoles every spiritually-void heart.

這本小說撫慰了每個空虛的心靈。

◇ **meaningful（adj.）有意義的**
Helping people is one of the most meaningful things in life.
助人是人生中最有意義的事情之一。

片　語　▶

◇ **use up：**
use（v.）是「用；使用」，use up 則是「耗盡；用光」之意，例
如：I have used up all my energy.（我已耗盡了所有的精力）。

◇ **year in and year out：**
此片語也可寫成 year in, year out，意指「歲歲年年；不斷地；
始終」，例如：Year in, year out, my work never changes.（我的
工作年復一年都沒改變）。

◇ **make use of...：**
use（n.）是「使用」，make use of...是「利用……；使用……」，
例如：You must make good use of your time.（你必須善用時間）。

◇ **be better off：**
better（adj.）更好的，be better off 是「更富裕；處境更佳」之
意，例如：You would be better off living somewhere else.（你住
在其他地方會過得更好）。

◇ **Why not...?：**
Why not...? 意為「為何不……？」，是口語的用法，表示「提
議某事」，後面接原形動詞，例如：Why not try it again?（何不

再試一次？）

句型分析 ▶

1. But the thing is, people are so worn out from a year of toil that even when they decide to travel with a tour group, the only thing they do is to "get on the bus and sleep, get off the bus and pee, take some pictures, buy some pills, and end up with nothing at all."

   ♦ 這句話的主詞是 people，主要動詞是 are。句中用到的句型為：so... that...（太……以致於……）。

   ♦ wear out 是「耗損」，be worn out from... 是「因……而累壞了」。tour group 是「跟團旅遊」，travel with a tour group 則是「跟旅遊團一起旅遊」。

   ♦ 句中 the only thing they do is...是「他們唯一做的事是……」，這裡列出了五件事，用「對等連接詞」and 連接：(1)get on the bus and sleep(2)get off the bus and pee(3)take some pictures(4)buy some pills(5)end up with nothing at all。

2. These vacationers make use of their weekends or longer holidays to go to remote schools and participate in after-school tutoring or volunteer in hospitals.

   ♦ 這句話的主詞是 these vacationers，主要動詞是 make use of

   ♦ 句中的 and 與 or 當「對等連接詞」，連接主詞 these

vacationers 利用週末及長假所做的兩個主要動作：(1)go to remote schools and participate in after-school tutoring (2)volunteer in hospitals.

◆ 句中的 make use of... 是「利用……；使用……」。after-school 是「課後的」。

造句練習 ▶

1. 他的美國之旅花光了他所有的積蓄。(use up)

----

2. 人們應該好好利用年假放鬆個幾天。(annual leave)

----

3. 她希望在外商公司工作。(foreign-based company)

----

4. 這份累人的工作將會讓你累壞了！(wear out)

----

5. 在非洲有許多低度開發國家。(underdeveloped country)

31

別做卡奴！
Don't Be a Credit Card Slave!

　　記得幾年前，台灣還是個用cash（現金）的老實社會，大家不論買菜、註冊、上餐廳，甚至買車、買房子，都是現金交易，銀貨兩迄，誰也不欠誰。在那個民風純樸的時代，民眾有錢便買東西，沒錢便看東西，單純得很。

　　但時代不同了。打開現代台灣人的皮夾，那真是卡片滿天飛！除了一般的credit card（信用卡）、cash card（現金卡）、debit card（簽帳卡）及ATM card（提款卡）、IC卡，還有各餐廳、百貨公司、商店核發的 VIP card（貴賓卡）、discount card（折扣卡）、membership card（會員卡）……，台灣已堂堂邁入 plastic money（塑膠貨幣）的時代！

　　不過伴隨著卡片而來的，便是許多人的過度消費，以及「卡奴」的快速成長。「卡奴」的問題如此嚴重，搞到現在幾乎天天都有卡奴上電視哭訴，卡奴自殺的消息也屢見不鮮。究竟誰該為「卡奴現象」負責？有人認為貪得無厭的銀行該負責，也有些人認為不管事的政府該負責。其實不管誰該負責，或者到最後有沒有人負責，「解鈴還需繫鈴人」，卡奴們還必須痛定思痛、自立自強，「喬治與瑪麗」的光鮮亮麗終究只存在電視廣告中！

Don't Be a Credit Card Slave!

"George and Mary" sing and dance on television, all **festive** and without a care in the world. A middle-aged actor looks into the camera and says with **sincerity**, "Borrowing money is a noble act"... You may wrongfully assume that the television is presenting a concert or a **civics class**. In fact, these **commercials** that you can't make head nor tail of are there for one reason alone: to entice you into applying for a credit card or **cash card**!

Over the past few years, banks have been trying to **boost** their performance by **issuing** cards in droves. Then came the super-low **minimum monthly payment** and the super-high "**revolving credit**" that gave rise to 500,000 "credit card slaves" in Taiwan. Legislators, the Bankers Association of the ROC, and other related organizations are presently studying and drafting **debt relief plans** in the hope of freeing these credit card slaves from their **misery**. ❶

On the other hand, these "credit card slaves" are not all **ignorant** youths and office workers that are in need of cash for **domestic expenses**. Many of these **cardholders** overspend and end up having to apply for a new card to **transfer** the **balance** from another card. It is said that some credit card slaves have more than 20 credit cards and cash cards combined! If these "credit card slaves" do not change their **attitudes** and consumption habits, no amount of **bail-out measures** can keep them from getting deeper and deeper into a **rut**! ❷

別做卡奴！

　　電視裡「喬治與瑪麗」唱唱跳跳，氣氛歡樂，了無煩憂；中年男藝人對著鏡頭，誠懇的道出「借錢是高尚的行為」……。你以為電視正在播放演唱會或公民課嗎？其實這些令人摸不著頭緒的廣告只有一個目的：誘使你申辦信用卡及現金卡！

　　這幾年各家銀行為了自身的業績，發卡浮濫。接著以超低的「每月最低應繳金額」與超高的「循環利息」，替台灣創造了高達50萬的「卡奴」。對此立委、銀行公會及相關單位正在研擬債務減輕方案，希望能將卡奴們從痛苦中解放出來。

　　不過話說回來，這些「卡奴」也非全是無知的青少年或急需家用的上班族。許多持卡人過度消費，到頭來只好以卡養卡，以債養債。據說有些卡奴甚至擁有高達20多張的信用卡及現今卡呢！如果「卡奴」的心態及消費行為不改，再多的解套方案，恐怕只會使這些人越陷越深！

主題句：　　　　單字：加黑　　　片語：套色　　　句型：❶❷

單字例句 ▶

◇ **credit card slave** 卡奴

◇ **festive**(adj.)歡樂的
The atmosphere is very festive during the New Year.
新年期間的氣氛是非常歡樂的。

◇ **sincerity**(n.)真誠；誠摯
I don't doubt her sincerity, but I think she's got her facts wrong.
我不懷疑她的真誠，不過我認為她的資料有誤。

◇ **civics class** 公民課

◇ **commercial**(n.)電視廣告
This car commercial boasts of the car's superior horsepower.
這汽車電視廣告誇耀車子優越的馬力。

◇ **cash card** 現金卡
More and more people are applying for cash cards.
越來越多的人申請現金卡。

◇ **boost**(v.)提高
Their improving performance has boosted investor confidence.
他們越來越進步的表現提高了投資者的信心。

◇ **issue**(v.)發(卡)
The bank set up a table outside the supermarket to issue

credit cards.
銀行在超市外面設置桌位發行信用卡。

◇ **minimum monthly payment 每月最低應繳金額**
The minimum monthly payment has been reduced to an all-
time low.
每月最低應繳金額已被減到有史以來最低。

◇ **revolving credit / rate 循環利息**
The revolving credit is implemented every quarter.
循環利息每季都實施。

◇ **debt relief plan 債務減輕方案**

◇ **misery(n.)痛苦；悲慘**
Losing a loved one is the greatest misery in life.
失去至愛是人生最大的痛苦。

◇ **ignorant(adj.)無知的**
The man insisted that he was ignorant of the crime.
這人堅持他對這犯罪毫無所知。

◇ **domestic expenses 家用**
As lifestyles change, domestic expenses change also.
生活方式改變，家用也隨之改變。

◇ **cardholder(n.)持卡人**
Only cardholders are allowed to purchase that product.
只有持卡人可以買那產品。

◇ **transfer(v.)轉移**

He transferred his money from one bank account to another.
他將他的錢從一個銀行帳號轉移到另一個。

◇ **balance**(n.)餘額
He went to an ATM to check the balance on his card.
他到自動櫃員機查他卡片的結餘。

◇ **attitude**(n.)態度
A positive attitude about life eases stress.
正面積極面對人生的態度可減輕壓力。

◇ **bail-out measures**(多用複數)解套方案
When the economy becomes oppressed, certain bail-out measures may be undertaken.
當經濟不好時,可以執行某些解套方案。

◇ **rut**(n.)常規;老習慣
You mustn't get yourself stuck in a rut.
你千萬不可墮入常規。

片　語　▶

◇ **cannot make head nor tail of... :**
head(n.)是「頭」,tail(n.)是「尾」,cannot make head nor tail of... 就等於 can make neither head nor tail of...,意思是「對……莫名其妙;根本不了解……」,例如:I can't make head nor tail of what she said.(我根本搞不清楚她說什麼)。

◇ **entice someone into... :**
entice(v.)是「誘惑」，entice someone into... 是「誘惑某人……；慫恿某人……」，例如：Jack holds the man's medicine to entice him into revealing more secrets.(Jack 握有這人的藥，以誘使他揭露更多的祕密)。

◇ **apply for... :**
apply(v.)是「申請」，apply for... 是「申請……」，例如：In order to go abroad, I need to apply for a visa.(要出國，我必須申請簽證)。

◇ **in droves :**
drove(n.)是「大批移動的畜群或人群」，in droves 則是「成群結隊；絡繹不絕」，例如：Tourists come in droves to see Taipei 101.(旅客絡繹不絕地來觀看台北101大樓)。

◇ **give rise to :**
rise(n.)是「升起，增加」，give rise to... 是「引起(不好的事)；導致……」，例如：Privilege often gives rise to abuses.(特權常會造成弊端)。

◇ **in need of... :**
need(n.)是「需要」，in need of... 是「需要……」，例如：He is in need of money.(他需要錢)。

◇ **end up :**
end(v.)是「結束」，end up 是「以……結束；最終……」，後面接動詞時，用的多是 by + V-ing，且介系詞 by 多省略，例如：He ended up winning the race.(他最終贏得比賽)。

句型分析 ▶

1. Legislators, the Bankers Association of the ROC, and other related organizations are **presently** studying and drafting **debt relief plans in the hope of freeing these credit card slaves from their misery.**

   ♦ 這句話的主詞比較長，是 Legislators, the Bankers Association of the ROC, and other related organizations，由「對等連接詞」and 連接。主要動詞為 are studying and drafting，一樣由「對等連接詞」and 連接。

   ♦ 句中 in the hope of... 是「希望……；冀望……」，所希望的東西接在 of 後，這裡是 free these credit card slaves from their misery(將卡奴從悲慘中解放出來)。free... from... 是「將……從……解放出來」。

2. If these "credit card slaves" do not change their attitudes and consumption habits, no amount of bail-out measures can keep them from getting deeper and deeper into a rut!

   ♦ 這句話的主詞是 no amount of bail-out measures，主要動詞是 can keep... from...。句首用到由 If 引導的條件句，意為「如果……」。這裡的 do not change their(1)attitudes(2)consumption habits 是「不改變他們的(1)態度(2)花錢方式」。

   ♦ 句中的 keep...from... 是「防止……發生」，這裡的 keep them from getting... 是「防止他們變成…」；加上前面的主

詞 no amount of... can keep them from getting... 則是「沒有任何數量的……可以防止他們變成……」，引申為「再多數量的……也無法防止他們變成……」。

造句練習 ▶

1. 如果你不想成為卡奴，你就不應該花超過你賺的。(credit card slave)

----

2. 上公民課就如同上其他學科一樣重要。(civics class / subject)

----

3. 我們特價的目的是引誘人們來購買。(special offer / entice)

----

4. 遊客絡繹不絕地來看無尾熊。(in droves / koala)

----

5. 債務減輕方案將要施行，以幫助那些身負巨債的人。(debt relief plan)

32

黑心食品又來了！
The Return of Adulterated Food Products!

　　台灣黑心商人多、黑心食品也多。其中有些較不嚴重，有些卻很嚴重。例如前兩年發生過許多出家人賴以維生的「素食」，被不肖商人加入肉類成分的事件，這對於台灣超過兩百萬的素食者而言，簡直是心中永遠的痛！

　　又例如前陣子爆發的台糖案，搞得台灣不管哪個年代的人都很鬱卒。因為大家從小吃到大的、或者曾買給下一代吃的台糖「健素糖」，竟然從十三年前開始使用劣質的酵素粉為原料。對於那些吃著豬飼料卻一直被蒙在鼓裡的大人、小孩而言，真是情何以堪啊！這件「健康食品」的案例，不只消費者受害，台糖公司也蒙羞；而且再次印證了商人不只無祖國，也沒有良心！

　　不過話說回來，在這次事件中，據說一些英文程度不錯的台糖員工在好幾年前便發現公司進口的原料袋上印有「動物飼料」、甚至在進口的報關單上寫有「不可食」字樣，因此早已偷偷警告周邊親朋好友拒吃自家產品。由此可知，處於這凡事「黑心」的社會，民眾要自保，除了必須處處睜大眼睛外，還必須加強自個兒的英文能力！

The Return of Adulterated Food Products! (CD2-14)

The New Year holiday is a time to eat, drink, and be **merry**, but with the **inundation** of "adulterated food products" in recent years, people have become **apprehensive** when they should really be enjoying reunion dinners or traditional New Year snacks.

Adulterated food products can be found by the dozen in Taiwan: adulterated **vegetarian** foods, adulterated **mushrooms**, adulterated **black moss**, adulterated milk powder, etc. Some of the adulterated food products are **padded** with **soybeans** or **starch** for **ingredients** and then sold at a high cost. ❶ Many of these ingredients neither **benefit** nor harm the human body, so they are more or less considered as "**conscientious**" adulterated food products. Some adulterated food products contain dangerous amounts of **preservatives** or **bleach**, meat made from **diseased** pigs, or ingredients beyond their **expiration date**. ❷ These harmful food products are known to be **carcinogenic** or even **deadly**!

In point of fact, Taiwan does not only have adulterated food products, but also adulterated **mattresses**, adulterated televisions, adulterated gasoline, and so on and so forth. Apparently, to **combat** this **unscrupulous** world, we have no **alternative** but to uphold the "Four No's Plus One Without" **strategy**: no eating, no drinking, no sleeping, no leaving the house, and without alternatives!

黑心食品又來了！

過年是快樂吃喝的好時機，不過這些年因為「黑心食品」充斥，搞得大家不管是吃團圓飯或是傳統的年節點心，都變得憂心忡忡。

說起台灣的黑心食品，那真是多得數不完：黑心素食、黑心香菇、黑心髮菜、黑心奶粉……。有些黑心食品價格超貴，卻用大豆或澱粉充當原料，這些東西對人體沒啥益處，卻也沒有危害，因此多少算是有「良心」的黑心食品。有些黑心食品則含有過量的防腐劑或漂白劑，甚至含有病死豬肉、過期的原料，這些有害的食品不僅可能致癌，更有致命的危險！

其實不只黑心食品，台灣還有黑心床墊、黑心電視、黑心汽油等等。看來為了對付這個黑心的世界，我們只好使出「四不一沒有」技倆：不吃、不喝、不睡、不出門、沒有辦法！

主題句：　　　　　　單字：**加黑**　　　片語：套色　　　句型：❶❷

單字例句 ▶

◇ **adulterated** [əˋdʌltəˏretɪd] **food product** 黑心食品

◇ **merry**（adj.）歡樂的
His only wish is to live a merry life.
他唯一的希望是過著快樂的生活。

◇ **inundation**（n.）氾濫；滿盈
The inundation of spam mail is a cause for great concern.
垃圾郵件的氾濫引來強烈的關切。

◇ **apprehensive**（adj.）憂慮不安的
She is very apprehensive and cannot calm down.
她很憂慮，無法冷靜下來。

◇ **vegetarian**（adj.）素食的
Let's find a vegetarian restaurant for lunch!
我們找家素食餐廳吃中飯吧！

◇ **mushroom**（n.）香菇
My mother gave me another spoonful of mushrooms.
我媽又給我滿滿一匙的香菇。

◇ **black moss** 髮菜

◇ **pad**（v.）填塞
He padded his shirt with tissue paper to make his chest look broader.
他在襯衫裡塞了些衛生紙，好讓他的胸部看起來寬闊些。

- **soybean**(n.)大豆
  Soybeans are very important to a child's diet.
  大豆是小孩子很重要的食物。

- **starch**(n.)澱粉
  He used too much starch in this dish.
  他這道菜裡用了太多的澱粉。

- **ingredient**(n.)原料；成分
  She placed all the ingredients in a bowl and mixed them together.
  她將所有的原料放進碗中，混合在一起。

- **benefit**(v.)有益於
  Vitamins and minerals benefit the body.
  維他命及礦物質有益身體。

- **conscientious** [ˌkɑnʃɪˈɛnʃəs](adj.)有良心的；謹慎盡責的
  You must be conscientious in doing your work.
  你工作時一定要謹慎盡責。

- **preservative**(n.)防腐劑

- **bleach**(n.)漂白劑
  She poured some bleach to help remove the stains.
  她倒了一點漂白劑以去除污點。

- **diseased**(adj.)患病的；有病的
  He cut away the diseased branches from the trees.
  他把有病害的樹枝剪除。

◇ **expiration date** 有效期限

◇ **carcinogenic** [kɑrˋsɪnəˋdʒɛnɪk] (**adj.**) 致癌的
Foods that are carcinogenic should be avoided at all costs.
可能致癌的食物無論如何千萬要避免。

◇ **deadly** (**adj.**) 致命的
The doctors are trying to contain the deadly virus.
醫生們試著抑制這致命的病毒。

◇ **mattress** (**n.**) 床墊
The mattress was so soft that he fell asleep as soon as his head touched his pillow.
這床墊是這麼的軟，以致於他的頭一碰到枕頭就睡著了。

◇ **combat** (**v.**) 與⋯戰鬥
Having a healthy diet is the best way to combat diseases.
健康的飲食是對抗疾病最好的方式。

◇ **unscrupulous** (**adj.**) 不講道德的；肆無忌憚的
Unscrupulous people do not care about the well-being of others.
沒道德的人不關心旁人的福祉。

◇ **alternative** (**n.**) 替換物；可選擇之事物
He chose his college because it was the best alternative available to him.
他選這所大學，因為這是他可以選擇之中最好的。

◇ **strategy** (**n.**) 策略；計謀
The company is trying to develop a new marketing strategy.

這家公司正試著要發展一個新的市場行銷策略。

片 語 ▶

⟡ **by the dozen :**
dozen(n.)是「一打；十二」之意，by the dozen 是「很多地；數以打計地」。

⟡ **be considered as... :**
consider(v.)是「仔細考慮；認為」，be considered as... 為被動語態，意思是「被認為是⋯⋯」，例如：He is considered one of the best actors of our time.(他被認為是當代最好的演員之一)。

⟡ **more or less :**
more or less 是「或多或少；有些；差不多」，例如：He is more or less drunk.(他差不多醉了)。

⟡ **be known to... :**
know(v.)是「知道」，be known to... 是「為⋯⋯所知的」，例如：He is known to the police.(他為警察所知曉)。

⟡ **so on and so forth :**
so on and so forth 等於 and so on及 and so forth，例如：They called him a liar, hypocrite and so on and so forth.(他們稱他做騙子、偽善者等等)。

句型分析 ▶

1. Some of the adulterated food products are padded with soybeans or starch for ingredients and then sold at a high cost.

   ♦ 這句話的主詞是 some of the adulterated food products，主要動詞是 are padded...(and then)sold...，以「對等連接詞」and 連接。

   ♦ pad(v.)是「填塞」，be padded with... 為被動語態，意為「被填以……」。

   ♦ cost(n.)是「價格」，a high cost 是「高價」，be sold at a high cost 則是「被以高價售出」。

2. Some adulterated food products contain dangerous amounts of preservatives or bleach, meat made from diseased pigs, or ingredients beyond their expiration date.

   ♦ 這句話的主詞是 some adulterated food products，主要動詞是 contain，其所包含的東西有三種，以「對等連接詞」or 連接：(1)dangerous amounts of preservatives or bleach (2)meat made from diseased pigs (3)ingredients beyond their expiration date。

   ♦ 句中 beyond 當介系詞，意為「超過範圍；出乎……之外」，beyond their expiration date 為「超出它們的有效期限」。

造句練習 ▶

1. 台灣各地都可以發現黑心食品。(adulterated food product)

   ----

2. 我們今晚的晚餐吃了些髮菜。(black moss)

   ----

3. 對我而言，他或多或少像個兄弟。(more or less)

   ----

4. 防腐劑對我們的健康有害。(preservative / harmful)

   ----

5. 這產品的有效期限寫在盒子的下方。(expiration date)

詐騙之島
Fraud Island

　　記得在不太久遠的年代，「馬路」還是個挺安全的地方。如果迷路了，隨便找個人問路，一般人都會好心報路，甚至親自帶你走一趟。曾幾何時，民眾再也不能安心走在路上。如果有人靠過來，現在一般人的本能反應是趕快閃開，因為誰知道這個人是不是金光黨、會不會強拉人推銷化妝品、或者假借賣「愛心筆」敲詐、趁機下迷藥，甚至綁架！

　　不止「馬路」不安全，連上館子吃飯也不得安寧。有時飯吃到一半，便有打著殘障人士旗號的人在一旁強力推銷口香糖等產品。如果不買，對方會賴著不走，一旦買了，才知道現在物價飆漲，兩條抹布一百五、一條「青箭」竟然要50塊台幣！

　　在外不安全，在家也好不到哪裡去。電話五通有一通是詐騙電話，難怪正派做市調的公司要感嘆生意作不下去，因為現在台灣人只要聽到陌生人的聲音，第一反應一定是掛電話！

　　說來悲哀，太多的詐騙事件讓善良的台灣人個個成為驚弓之鳥，而應對之道則是板起臉來面對所有身邊的人事物。也因此，現在真正想問路的反而常遭白眼，而真正需要幫忙的人求救時反而被人冷眼相待！

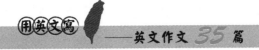

Fraud Island (CD2-15)

These past few years, if you ask Taiwanese people what their worst **collective** experience has been, people will reply: "**Telephone fraud!**" **Fraudulent** companies have utilized **random** calls, or so-called "**reckless** shooting," to create one of Taiwan's most **profitable** industries! ❶

There is hardly anyone in Taiwan who has not received a single **scamming** phone call. Beginning with earlier **rackets** of informing individuals they have won a prize or received a **tax return**, to later **schemes** of faking credit card theft, posing as friends or relatives in need, or faking **kidnappings**, to the latest tactic of pretending to be a **judicial institution**, Taiwanese telephone fraud has exhibited a vast **repertoire** of **maneuvers**, an abundance of creativity, and a world-class speed of "**internationalization**." ❷ This type of fraud is really worthy of mention in the Guinness Book of World Records!

Poor Taiwanese are now reminded of telephone fraud each time their phone rings, and afraid of picking up any calls that do not show up on **caller ID**. In addition, it is becoming harder for people to judge the **truthfulness** of anything. How can people be sure they have really received a call for **ransom** or when they can claim a prize they have **rightfully** won? Even more **tragic** is when people are certain that the call is fraudulent and still have to keep themselves from blurting out any four-letter words. The reason is that if they let themselves go, alas, they might just receive a **truckload** of unordered pizza at their doorstep the very next day!

詐騙之島

這幾年，問到台灣人最差的共同經驗為何，大家都會說：「詐騙電話」！而詐騙集團靠著隨機打電話，「亂槍打鳥」，也成為台灣最賺錢的行業之一！

在台灣，幾乎沒有人沒接過詐騙電話。從早期的通知民眾中獎、退稅，之後的偽稱信用卡被盜刷、親友急難、假綁架等陰謀，到現在的偽裝成司法機構，台灣詐騙電話的花招之多、創意之豐富，以及「國際化」的速度之快，簡直可以列入金氏世界紀錄！

可憐的台灣人，現在只要聽到電話鈴聲就會以為是詐騙電話，沒有「來電顯示」的電話更不敢接。大家越來越難判斷事情的真實性。人們如何確定是否接到的贖金電話，或者何時可以真的去領獎？更慘的是，有時民眾明明知道是詐騙電話，卻還不能向對方罵「三字經」，因為若如此，隔天可能就會收到一拖拉庫不請自來的披薩。嗚呼哀哉！

主題句：　　　　　單字：**加黑**　　片語：套色　　句型：❶❷

單字例句 ▶

- **collective**(adj.)集體的；共同的
  The audience heaved a collective sigh when the hero in the movie died.
  當電影裡的英雄死掉的時候，觀眾一起發出了嘆息聲。

- **telephone fraud** 詐騙電話

- **fraudulent** ['frɔdʒələnt](adj.)欺騙性的
  I am worried that you might be involved in fraudulent activities.
  我擔心你被捲入了詐欺的活動。

- **random**(adj.)胡亂的；隨機的
  To be fair, I will make the choice random.
  為了公平起見，我會讓選擇變成隨機的。

- **reckless**(adj.)魯莽的；不計後果的
  Reckless drivers' driver's licenses should be confiscated.
  魯莽駕駛的駕駛執照應該被沒收。

- **profitable**(adj.)有利可圖的；賺錢的
  I am glad this is such a profitable venture.
  我很高興這是個這麼有利可圖的投資。

- **scam**(n.)(v.)詐欺
  Be careful not to be trapped by a scam.
  小心別落入詐欺的陷阱。

◇ **racket**(n.)（俚語）騙局；非法勾當

Whatever you do, don't get involved in the drug dealing racket.

不管你做什麼，千萬別涉入毒品買賣的非法勾當。

◇ **tax return 納稅申報單**

◇ **scheme** [skim]（n.）陰謀

There are many promising schemes that are deceiving.

許多看起來大有可為的計畫其實是騙人的。

◇ **kidnapping**(n.)綁架；誘拐

Kidnappings are rampant in some countries.

綁架在有些國家十分猖獗。

◇ **judicial** [dʒuˋdɪʃəl] **institution 司法機構**

◇ **repertoire** [ˋrɛpɚˏtwɑr]（n.）全部項目

The clown amazed the crowd with his repertoire of tricks.

這小丑的翻箱把戲讓觀眾驚奇不已。

◇ **maneuver** [məˋnuvɚ]（n.）策略；花招；動作

To get a pilot's license, you must be able to perform certain basic maneuvers.

要拿到飛機駕駛執照，你必須能夠表演某些基本的動作。

◇ **internationalization**(n.)國際化

The internationalization of security forces is an astounding feat.

安全部隊的國際化是項令人驚奇的成就。

- **caller ID 來電顯示**
  Aren't you glad we have caller ID on our cellular phones?
  手機有來電顯示不是很棒嗎？

- **truthfulness（n.）真實性**
  We always uphold truthfulness in our research.
  研究時，我們總是堅持真實性。

- **ransom（n.）贖金**
  The kidnappers demanded a huge amount of ransom.
  綁架者要求很高的贖金。

- **rightfully（adv.）合法地；應該地**
  We should fight for what is rightfully ours.
  我們要爭取我們應該擁有的東西。

- **tragic（adj.）悲慘的**
  The novel has a very tragic yet exciting ending.
  這小說有個非常悲慘但令人激動的結局。

- **truckload（n.）一貨車之量**
  The manager ordered a truckload of books for the grand opening.
  為了開幕，經理叫了一拖拉庫的書。

片　語　▶

❖ **be worthy of... :**

worthy(adj.)是「值得」之意，後面接名詞。be worthy of... 是
「值得……」之意，例如：He is a teacher who is worthy of
respect.(他是一位值得尊敬的老師)。

❖ **remind of... :**

remind(v.)是「提醒」，remind someone of something 是「提醒
某人某事；令某人想起某事」，例如：The girl reminds me of
myself when I was her age.(這女孩令我想起我在她這個年紀時
的情景)。

❖ **blurt out :**

blurt out 是「不經思索脫口而出」之意，例如：He blurted the
news out before we could stop him.(在我們可以阻止他之前，他
不經思索地將消息說了出來)。

❖ **let oneself go :**

let oneself go 是「完全放鬆；不在意……」，例如：He has
really let himself go since his wife died.(他太太去世後，他就完
全不修邊幅了)。文章中的 if they let themselves go... 是「如果
他們豁出去了……」之意。

句型分析 ▶

1. Fraudulent companies have utilized random calls, or so-called "reckless shooting," to create one of Taiwan's most profitable industries!

    ◆ 這句話的主詞是 companies，主要動詞是 have utilized。句首的 fraudulent(adj.)為「欺騙性的」，修飾主詞 companies，意為「詐騙公司；詐騙集團」。

    ◆ 句中逗號與逗號間的 or so-called "reckless shooting," 是逗號前 random calls 的同位語。

2. Beginning with earlier rackets of informing individuals they have won a prize or received a tax return, to later schemes of faking credit card theft, posing as friends or relatives in need, or faking kidnappings, to the latest tactic of pretending to be a judicial institution, Taiwanese telephone fraud has exhibited a vast repertoire of maneuvers, an abundance of creativity, and a world-class speed of "internationalization."

    ◆ 這句話的主詞是 Taiwanese telephone fraud，主要動詞是 has exhibited。句首的 Beginning with..., to later..., to the latest...(從一開始的……，到後來的……，到最後的……)是形容詞，目的是提供整句話所言的背景。這裡總共提到了五種詐騙方式：(1)informing individuals they have won a prize or received a tax return (2)faking credit card theft (3)posing as friends or relatives in need (4)faking kidnappings (5)pretending to be a judicial institution。

♦ 這句話的主、動詞 Taiwanese telephone fraud has exhibited... 意為「台灣的詐騙電話顯現了⋯⋯」，顯現出的東西有三項，以「對等連接詞」and 連接：(1)a vast repertoire of maneuvers (2)an abundance of creativity (3)a world-class speed of "internationalization"，直譯為「全副武裝的策略秘笈、豐富的創意、世界級的全球化速度」。

造句練習 ▶

1. 詐騙電話讓人對人性懷疑。(telephone fraud / humanity)

- -

2. 這女人讓我想起我的小學老師。(remind of...)

- -

3. 我何時要申報我的所得稅？(tax return)

- -

4. 這國家的司法機構非常值得信賴。(judicial institution)

- -

5. 在盛怒下，他脫口說出祕密。(blurt out...)

- -

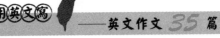

34

寒假打工
Part Time Jobs Over the Winter Break

　　現在的大學生鮮少有人不打工的。說實在，打工的好處多多，既不用成為「伸手牌」，又可以增加社會歷練、拓展人脈。很多學生也因為這種「職前訓練」，找到自己的就業方向，省去了畢業後的跌跌撞撞。

　　不過在大學裡，也有學生雖不缺錢，卻為了滿足消費慾望而身兼數職。這些學生將工作當成正職，把念書看成副業，打工時精神抖擻，上課時則哈欠連連。

　　只不過世風日下，人心不古，許多聽起來頗像一回事的工作其實都不是那回事，讓人不禁為單純的打工族捏一把冷汗。例如有些公司應徵名為「理財人員」的工讀生，卻要他們去跟還很健朗的家人推銷生前契約及靈骨塔，嚇得家人哇哇叫；有些公司假裝應徵兼職模特兒，卻逼工讀生繳費拍一拖拉庫醜到斃的宣傳照，連送人避邪都沒人要；還有些公司應徵「美容專業人員」，卻要應徵者先購買一大堆抹了可能會毀容、吃了可能會中毒的「生技產品」，林林總總，真是既不道德又沒品格！

Part Time Jobs Over the Winter Break CD2-16

　　Each year when school starts, the first thing many students do upon their return to **campus** is to share their work experience over the winter break with their classmates. There are some who work to pay for **tuition** and **living expenses**, while there are others who work to gain experience in society. Working part time has become an experience many students share.

　　There is a wide variety of winter vacation jobs to choose from. Some students help sell **dry goods** at the Lunar New Year's shopping **bazaar**, while others work as **tutors** in **cram schools**. There are also those who choose to work part time in sunny Australia or New Zealand so that they can learn languages in a different environment while **clipping** wool or feeding horses. ❶

　　But lately, there has been an **influx** of **unscrupulous** companies that take advantage of the **naiveté** of students. These companies set up **traps** to hurt the students. When working part time, **beware**! Do not hand over your **ID card freely**, do not sign **contracts** freely, and do not pay for fees that are not clearly listed. You should also make clear the **specifications** of the job to prevent **misfortunes** from happening, such as working as a **babysitter** instead of a tutor, becoming part of a **pyramid scheme** after being hired as an **assistant**, or posting **flyers** and being **fined** for **violating** the law. ❷

寒假打工

　　每年開學，許多學生回到校園的第一件事，便是與同學交換寒假的打工經驗。有些人打工為了賺取學費、生活費，有些則是為了增加社會歷練。「打工」已成了許多學生共同擁有的經驗。

　　寒假打工的種類眾多；有人到年貨大街賣乾貨，有人到補習班當輔導老師，也有人選擇到陽光普照的澳洲、紐西蘭打工，一邊剃羊毛、餵小馬，一邊在不同的環境學習語言。

　　不過近來有許多不肖業者利用學生的單純，設下打工陷阱。因此打工時必須注意：不隨便將身分證件交給他人、不隨便簽合約、也不繳交名目不清的費用。另外還要搞清楚應徵的職務項目，以免發生應徵家教變成保母、應徵助理變成「老鼠會」一員、或者張貼傳單反而違法被罰款的倒楣事！

主題句：　　　　**單字：加黑**　　**片語：套色**　　**句型：❶❷**

單字例句 ▶

◇ **part time job** 打工工作

◇ **winter break** 寒假
I am planning to spend the winter break with my family.
我寒假打算和家人一起度過。

◇ **campus**(n.)校園
University campuses are ideal places for socializing with friends.
大學校園是與朋友社交的好場所。

◇ **tuition**(n.)學費
Parents worry about rising tuition rates.
父母們擔心高漲的學費。

◇ **living expenses**(多用複數)生活費

◇ **dry goods** 乾貨
I bought this dried fish from the dry goods store.
我在乾貨店買了魚乾。

◇ **bazaar** [bəˋzɑr](n.)市場；市集
The bazaar will hold its annual summer sale this weekend.
這市集會在週末舉辦年度的夏日拍賣。

◇ **tutor**(n.)輔導老師(或稱 **guidance teacher**)
Tutors help students improve their learning.
輔導老師幫助同學增進學習。

◇ **cram school** 補習班
Most high school students have to go to cram school after school every day.
大部分的高中生每天下課後都必須上補習班。

◇ **clip**(**v.**)修剪
It is a good habit to clip your nails regularly.
定期修剪指甲是好習慣。

◇ **influx**(**n.**)湧入
This small town has a large influx of tourists in the summer.
這個小鎮在夏天有大批旅客湧入。

◇ **unscrupulous**(**adj.**)不講道德的；肆無忌憚的
Your unscrupulous behavior at work is very unfavorable to our organization.
你毫無廉恥的舉止對我們組織而言是很不利的。

◇ **naiveté** [nɑˋivte](**n.**)天真無邪
Many companies take advantage of students because of their naiveté.
許多公司利用學生的天真無知占他們便宜。

◇ **trap**(**n.**)陷阱
I will set up this trap to finally catch the mouse.
我要設下這陷阱，最終逮到那隻老鼠。

◇ **beware**(**v.**)小心；注意
Beware of people who might take advantage of you.
注意那些會占你便宜的人。

◇ **ID card 身分證**
Citizens are required to apply for the new ID card.
國民必須申請新的身分證。

◇ **freely（adv.）隨意地**
Information is freely available on the Internet.
網路上的資訊可以隨意取得。

◇ **contract（n.）合約**
You need to sign this contract before you can start working.
在可以開始工作之前，你必須簽這合約。

◇ **specifications（n.）（多用複數）規格；明細表**
To avoid accidents, read all safety specifications of the machine before using it.
為避免意外，在使用這機器之前要閱讀所有的安全規定明細。

◇ **misfortune（n.）不幸事故；災難**
He bore his misfortunes bravely.
他勇敢地忍受著苦難。

◇ **babysitter（n.）保母**
We need a babysitter to take care of the children while we're away.
我們不在時，需要一個保母來照顧孩子們。

◇ **pyramid scheme [ˈpɪrəmɪdˈskim]老鼠會**
Many people are attracted to pyramid schemes because they promise high income.
很多人被老鼠會所吸引，因為它承諾高的收入。

◇ **assistant**(n.)助理

I need an assistant to help me finish all the work in the office.

我需要一位助理來幫我完成辦公室的所有工作。

◇ **flyer**(n.)傳單

He received a flyer advertising real estate.

他拿到一張房地產的廣告傳單。

◇ **fine**(v.)罰款

Follow all road rules and regulations to avoid being fined.

遵守所有的道路規則和法令，以避免被罰款。

◇ **violate**(v.)侵犯；妨害

He was sent to prison for violating the law.

他因為違反法令而被關到監獄。

片　語　▶

◇ **upon someone's return :**

此片語也寫作 on someone's return，意思為「回來……」，例如：Upon his return from the US, he joined the army.(從美國回來後，他加入軍隊)。

◇ **a variety of... :**

variety(n.)是「多樣性；種類」，a variety of... 是「(同種中)的種類」，of 後面的名詞通常是單數且不用冠詞，例如：This is a new variety of rose.(這是新品種的玫瑰)。

◇ **take advantage of… :**
advantage (n.) 是「優勢」，take advantage of... 則是「占……便宜」，例如：Don't try to take advantage of me!(別想占我便宜)。

◇ **set up :**
set up 有許多意思，這裡是「設下(陷阱)；設置……」，例如：They've set up road blocks around the city.(他們在城市周圍設置路障)。

◇ **hand over :**
hand (v.) 是「交給」，hand over 是「交出；提交；移交；讓渡」，例如：He handed the book over to me.(他將書遞給我)。

句型分析 ▶

1. There are also those who choose to work part time in sunny Australia or New Zealand so that they can learn languages in a different environment while clipping wool or feeding horses.

   ◆ 這句話的主、動詞是 There are。there 為形式主詞，指的真正主詞是動詞後的 those(那些人)，後面的 who 是關係代名詞，代替前面的 those。句中的 so that... 是「所以……」。

   ◆ 句中的 while 是連接詞，意為「當……的時候；與……同時」，learn languages while clipping wool or feeding horses 就是「一邊學語言，一邊剪羊毛或餵馬」。

2. You should also make clear the specifications of the job to prevent misfortunes from happening, such as working as a babysitter instead of a tutor, becoming part of a "pyramid scheme" after being hired as an assistant, or posting flyers and being fined for violating the law.

♦ 這句話的主詞是 you，主要動詞是 should make clear。逗號後面的 such as...是補充說明前面的 misfortunes（不幸的事），這裡列出了三個事件，用「對等連接詞」or 連接：(1)working as a babysitter instead of a tutor(2)becoming part of a "pyramid scheme" after being hired as an assistant(3)posting flyers and being fined for violating the law。

♦ 句中 make clear... 是「將……的事情搞清楚」，要搞清楚的東西放在 clear 之後，這裡接的是 specifications of the job（工作的職務項目）。

♦ 第一個逗號前出現一個常見用法：prevent... from...（避免……發生），這裡是 prevent misfortunes from happening（避免不幸的事發生）。

♦ 句中的 instead of... 是「而非……」，a babysitter instead of a tutor 是「保母而非家教」。fine(v.)是「罰款」，這裡的 be fined 是被動語態，意為「被罰款」，be fined for... 是「因……被罰款」。

造句練習 ▶

1. 你為何不兼差賺點錢？（part-time job）

----

2. 近幾年的生活費漲了。（living expenses / go up）

----

3. 在熱帶國家，經年可以看到各式各樣的水果。（a variety of... / tropical country）

----

4. 別借他們車子──他們是在占你便宜！（take advantage of...）

----

5. 電話遞過來，好讓我和她說話。（hand over...）

35

李安與斷背山
Ang Lee and Brokeback Mountain

　　李安導演的「斷背山」不僅在今年的各大國際獎項發光發熱，其電影中的「同志」議題，更引發各界熱烈的討論。有人說，「斷背山」之所以得不到奧斯卡的「最佳影片」，乃受其「同志」議題所累，畢竟照一般世俗標準來看，「同性戀」確實稱不上是 politically correct（政治正確）！

　　世界上的許多事，或許都有道理可講，偏偏感情這檔事，毫無理由可言。「小王子」縱使身入玫瑰園，也不能阻擋他迷戀家鄉那朵既高傲又自私的玫瑰花。「別人眼中的糞土，是另一個人眼中的黃金」，愛情這種事，真真沒個準！

　　偏偏這世界上的許多人，就愛吃飽撐著，管他人閒事，連諾貝爾獎得主娶了個小他數十歲的妻子，都要被罵成「老牛吃嫩草」、「臨老入花叢」、「晚節不保」。其實人家生活快不快樂，自己知道就好了，何必向大家報告呢？還有些人，一會兒歧視「同性戀」，一會兒嘲笑「姊弟戀」，一會兒批評人家「鮮花插牛糞」……。唉，大家各自過各自的日子，何必管其他人閒事呢？

Ang Lee and Brokeback Mountain CD2

Applause has been given to "Brokeback Mountain," a movie directed by **internationally acclaimed** Taiwanese director Ang Lee, ever since its **premiere**. The film has also won Lee the Best Director at this year's **Academy Award**. Lee's achievements are a source of pride to us. Even more **admirable** is the way he has **challenged** the traditional concepts and **values** of **gender**.

First off, as everyone knows, Lee was only able to **concentrate on** moviemaking during his six-year "**struggle**" in the United States because his wife had worked hard to **make ends meet**. ❶ During this period, the couple took no notice of the public's **judgmental** glare, **overthrew** the traditional **mindset** of "men outside, women inside," and **exemplified** that love does indeed **conquer** all. ❷

"Brokeback Mountain" goes beyond being a **mere homosexual** movie to **transcend stereotypes**. The film is a love story that describes the real essence of human nature. The deep and **profound** emotions between the couple **illustrate** that love is by no means **constrained** by gender.

Lee and "Brokeback Mountain" teach us that when love finds you, tradition, gender, and the judgment of others will no longer be **significant**. After all, your life is your business and no one else's!

李安與斷背山

　　「斷背山」由享譽國際的台灣導演李安執導，上映以來佳評如潮；這部戲也替李安在今年的奧斯卡金像獎贏得「最佳導演獎」。李安導演的成就令我們驕傲，而他本人及這部影片所挑戰的傳統性別觀，則更令人欽佩。

　　先說李安導演。眾所周知，他在美國「奮鬥」時，有六年的時間都靠妻子努力維持家計，才能專心於電影創作。這段時間李安夫婦不顧外界眼光，顛覆「男主外，女主內」的傳統觀念，證明了真愛可以戰勝一切。

　　「斷背山」超越單純的同性戀電影，跳脫刻板印象。這部電影描繪真實的人性及情感深刻的愛情故事，顯示真愛可以超越性別。

　　李安及「斷背山」告訴我們：當愛降臨時，傳統、性別、社會眼光都不再重要。畢竟要過生活的還是自己，關他人啥事呢！

主題句：　　　　單字：**加黑**　　片語：套色　　句型：❶❷

單字例句 ▶

◇ **applause**(n.)稱讚；鼓掌；喝采
After the movie, the audience gave a loud round of applause.
電影過後，觀眾給予熱烈的掌聲。

◇ **internationally acclaimed** 享譽國際的

◇ **premiere** [prɪˋmɪr](n.)首映
The premiere of this movie drew a big crowd.
這部電影的首映吸引大批觀眾。

◇ **Academy Award** 奧斯卡金像獎

◇ **admirable**(adj.)令人欽佩的
Her public speaking skills are extremely admirable.
她的公眾演講技巧完全令人佩服。

◇ **challenge**(v.)挑戰
His ideas were challenged by other team members.
他的想法被其他隊友挑戰。

◇ **value**(n.)價值觀
Our values change time and again.
我們的價值觀隨時間不斷改變。

◇ **gender**(n.)性別
Gender equality has always been a debatable issue.
性別平等一直是個受爭論的議題。

◇ **concentrate on...** 專注於……

◇ **struggle**（n.）奮鬥；掙扎
After many struggles in his life, he finally succeeded.
他的人生經過許多掙扎奮鬥，終於成功。

◇ **make ends meet** 餬口；養家活口

◇ **judgmental**（adj.）帶有評判性的
You should not be judgmental about people and their differing sexual preferences.
你不該批判別人及他們不同的性向偏好。

◇ **overthrow**（v.）推翻
The protesters aim to overthrow the government.
這些抗議者的目的在推翻政府。

◇ **mindset**（n.）心態；思考傾向
Different people have different mindsets.
不同人有不同的思考傾向。

◇ **exemplify**（v.）成為例證
Their life together has exemplified the endlessness of love.
他們在一起的生活證明了愛的永無止盡。

◇ **conquer** [ˈkɑŋkɚ]（v.）戰勝；克服
After visiting the Empire State Building, she conquered her fear of heights.
造訪過帝國大廈後，她克服了她的懼高症。

◇ **mere**（adj.）僅僅的

She finished the job in a mere few minutes.
她幾分鐘就完成工作了。

◇ **homosexual**（**adj.**）同性戀的
Homosexual people are often discriminated against.
同性戀者通常受到歧視。

◇ **transcend** [træn`sɛnd]（**v.**）超越；凌駕
His qualifications transcend the requirements for the job.
他的資格超過這個工作所需要的。

◇ **stereotype** [`stɛriəˌtaɪp]（**n.**）刻板印象
We should not judge people according to stereotypes.
我們不該根據刻板印象評斷別人。

◇ **profound**（**adj.**）深刻的
Mozart's music is profound and overwhelming.
莫札特的音樂既深刻又令人無法抗拒。

◇ **illustrate**（**v.**）顯示
Love may be illustrated in different ways.
愛情可以用不同方式顯示。

◇ **constrain**（**v.**）束縛；壓制
Don't be constrained by what other people say.
別被別人所說的東西束縛住。

◇ **significant**（**adj.**）重要的；顯著的
She achieved significant success in a very short time.
她在很短的時間內便達到顯著的成功。

片 語 ▶

◇ **go beyond... :**

beyond 是介系詞，意思是「越過……；超過範圍」，go beyond... 是「超越……」，例如：Their relationship had gone beyond friendship.(他們的關係已超越友誼)。

◇ **by no means :**

by no means 是「決不……；絕非……」，例如：It is by no means easy to satisfy Alan.(要滿足 Alan 絕非易事)。

◇ **no longer :**

no longer 與 not... any longer 一樣，是「不再……」，例如：She could no longer wait for him.(她不能再等他了)。

◇ **after all :**

after all 用於字首是「畢竟」，例如：After all, we are still friends.(我們畢竟還是朋友)。

◇ **no one else's business :**

business(n.)是「事務；職責」，no one else's business 是「不關其他人的事」，例如：People can believe or disbelieve in God, and it's no one else's business.(人們可以相信或不相信上帝，而這不關其他人的事)。

句型分析 ▶

1. First off, as everyone knows, Lee was only able to concentrate on moviemaking during his six-year "struggle" in the United States because his wife had worked hard to make ends meet.

   ◆ 這句話的主詞是 Lee，主要動詞是 was able to...。句中另有一副詞子句 because his wife had worked hard to make ends meet，用來解釋主要子句，這裡用的動詞 had worked hard to... 是「過去完成式」。

   ◆ 句中 concentrate on 為「專注於……」，所專注的事接在 on 後面，這裡是 moviemaking(電影製作)。

   ◆ 句首之 First off 意為「先從第一點來說」。之後的 as everyone knows 為插入語，意為「大家都知道……」，因此不能算是此句的主詞及動詞。副詞子句中的片語 make ends meet 是「餬口；養家活口」之意。

2. During this period, the couple took no notice of the public's judgmental glare, overthrew the traditional mindset of "men outside, women inside," and exemplified that love does indeed conquer all.

   ◆ 這句話的主詞是 the couple，主要動詞則有三個，由「對等連接詞」and 連接：(1) took... (2) overthrew... (3) exemplified...。

   ◆ take notice of... 是「注意到……；留意……」，句中的 take

no notice of... 則是「不在意……」，這裡不在意的事是 the public's judgmental glare（一般大眾的批判眼光）。

◆ 句中 overthrow the mindset on... 是「顛覆……的心態」，這裡顛覆的是"men outside, women inside"（「男主外，女主內」）。

◆ 句尾的 does 是「強調語氣」用法，意為「的確；絕對」。

造句練習 ▶

1. 她贏得今年奧斯卡金像獎的最佳女配角獎。(Academy Award)

- -

2. 專注於你的工作，準時完成。(concentrate on... / on time)

- -

3. 中國草藥一直享譽國際。(internationally acclaimed)

- -

4. 我父母常需要非常努力工作才能養家活口。(make ends meet)

- -

5. 口音會加強負面的刻板印象。(accent / negative stereotype)

- -

造句解答

01. 新年新願望

1. What are your New Year's resolutions?
2. Her life is plagued with many problems.
3. The terrorist attacks caused widespread alarm.
4. The flood took away numerous lives.
5. The fireworks display is an amazing blend of shapes and colors.

02. 吃尾牙囉！

1. The police rewarded the man who turned in the money he found on the street.
2. The man aimed the arrow at the bull's-eye.
3. The job-hopping craze is one of the biggest problems in businesses.
4. We usually stay home and watch variety shows on TV during the weekend.
5. The actress tried to keep a low profile.

03. 農曆新年

1. Students usually stay up late to prepare for an examination.
2. The terrorist threatened to set off the bomb if the government doesn't cooperate.
3. People gather with family during the Lunar New Year holidays for a reunion dinner.
4. He is shy and quiet by nature.
5. The dog tried to scare away the strangers.

04. 青年節與草莓族

1. March 29 is Youth Day, and the government holds many activities on this day.
2. The strawberry generation is said to be very vulnerable and inattentive.
3. The spy was branded as a traitor by his comrades.
4. Her advice pertains to people of all generations.
5. As a police officer you need to uphold the law.

05. 清明掃墓節

1. We show our respect towards our ancestors on Tomb Sweeping Day.
2. The new president immediately imposed some new policies.
3. The children were excluded from participating in their parents' conversation.
4. Alcohol is strictly forbidden in Saudi Arabia.
5. Let's take advantage of today's good weather!

06. 情人節

1. Couples enjoy a candlelit dinner on Valentine's Day.
2. Rumor has it that she's a liar, but I don't believe it.
3. Teenagers are always obsessed with pop idols.
4. He had a wonderful love affair with his wife before they married.
5. You can see the rage from his face.

07. 快樂母親節

1. An old saying goes, "You can't judge a book by its cover."
2. I celebrated this year's Mother's Day by taking out mom to a five-star restaurant.

3. Fortunately we are blessed with good health.
4. Single-parent families are now becoming more common.
5. She is suing the company for sex discrimination.

08. 端午節

1. People who commit suicide do not realize the promise of the future.
2. People enjoy rice dumplings on the Dragon Boat Festival.
3. Dragon boat racing is always intense and exciting.
4. People performed a ritual trying to drive away evil spirits.
5. Please remove the dead mouse from the house.

09. 月圓人團圓

1. He's halfway from completing his work.
2. In many countries, it is customary that the groom must not see the bride before the wedding.
3. The little girl asks her mother to keep her company because she is afraid of sleeping in the dark.
4. Young children sometimes fantasize about meeting cartoon characters in person.
5. The Consumers' Foundation warns against using bleach-treated chopsticks.

10. 教師感嘆的教師節

1. The author dedicated his last book to his daughter.
2. This report aims to highlight the disciplinary problems that teachers regularly face.
3. They held a concert to pay tribute to their teachers.
4. The school proposed that the teachers be paid in accordance with

the students' performance.

5. Military personnel enjoy great benefits, even through retirement.

11. 雙十國慶

1. This law was enacted by the then Labour Party.
2. People gathered around to watch the military review ceremony.
3. Kids especially enjoy watching the fireworks display because of its beautiful colors.
4. There is an ongoing debate on the issue of abortion.
5. There is a group of angry demonstrators shouting slogans on the street.

12. 行憲紀念日與聖誕節

1. December 25th is ROC's Constitution Day.
2. The national flag is raised on special occasions.
3. The over-commercialization of holidays distorts the true meaning of holidays.
4. Holidays are the time of year when businesses rake in the dough.
5. The event was postponed due to foul weather.

13. 色彩繽紛的台灣選舉

1. The contenders met the day before for a warm-up battle.
2. People are very concerned with the results of the presidential election.
3. She marked the page she had been reading and closed the book.
4. Their chance of winning the competition is 50-50.
5. Many countries fight to preserve their independence.

14. 馬屁文化

1. The newspapers were full of negative reports about the politician.
2. Everything was shrouded in mist and raindrops.
3. I always associate the boss with Hitler because of his cruelty.
4. People gather to see the troop formation performance in the square.
5. A good leader should not be a grudge holder.

15. 凱子外交

1. The government was harshly criticized for its cash-for-friendship diplomacy.
2. The manager is under pressure to increase sales numbers.
3. The boy tried to defend himself from the dog with a stick.
4. This new law enables European banks to gain entry into new markets.
5. Don't make a fuss about unimportant things.

16. 政治酬庸

1. The government is again criticized for handing out political compensation.
2. His father makes a lot of money on stock bonuses.
3. She blew a fuse when she found out that her son skipped school.
4. Charitable organizations look for ways to raise money for people in need.
5. Linda has been offered an executive post and a very handsome pay.

17. 熊貓來台灣！

1. They round off the talks following weeks of successful debates.
2. Pandas are considered to be one of the greatest national treasures of China.

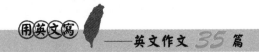

3. The suspects were held in captivity until they face the court.
4. Please try to see things from other people's standpoint.
5. She had to pay extra to speed up the application process.

18. 外資、港資、中資？

1. The police suspected that he is involved in the crime.
2. The government shut down the company for producing illegal medicine.
3. The company is a big success and rakes in large amounts of money.
4. He's been working poorly because he's preoccupied with family problems.
5. We have to tackle the problem at hand and worry about other things later.

19. 走開，損友！

1. He provided his services in exchange for a fee.
2. I went to the mountains during the weekend in the company of five.
3. Taiwan tries to maintain as many diplomatic ties as possible.
4. Alas, all that is done cannot be undone!
5. We expect our allies to come to our aid in time of need.

20. 需要和平的和平紀念日

1. Taiwan has spent 50 years under Japanese colonial rule.
2. The government is clamping down on drug pushers.
3. Contraband cigarettes were secretly being transported to nearby countries.
4. This system allows people to make distinctions between shapes.
5. I bought some pesticide to prevent bugs from infesting our garden.

21. 爆料文化

1. An exposé culture sweeps over the Taiwanese media.
2. The issue is engulfed in controversy.
3. Civil representatives help people voice out their concerns.
4. The dog is out of control and would not listen to its owner.
5. Whenever there's a new trend, companies jump on the bandwagon and try to reap the benefits.

22. 光碟風波

1. College life is usually associated with freedom and hijinks.
2. The politician held a press conference to announce his retirement.
3. The city councilor is planning to run for another term.
4. The boss told us to settle the issue in private.
5. The boss fired the man who double-crossed the company.

23. 寶島台灣

1. Taipei is hit by another wave of cold front.
2. People enjoy eating hot pot during the winter.
3. Taiwan is famed for its night markets.
4. People came to the activity with varying degrees of excitement.
5. The company offered him a starting salary of NT$650 thousand per year.

24. 媒體亂象

1. The journalist called the mayor daily, in hopes of scoring an exclusive interview.
2. The politician is sent to jail for dealing with black gold.
3. Her face is devoid of any warmth or humor.

4. He's been trying to inject new ideas into the discussion.

5. Laughter filled the air as people enjoyed themselves at the party.

25. 為富不仁的台灣

1. You should file a complaint against your boss for his ill treatment.

2. A civil lawsuit was filed yesterday by his wife.

3. Human trafficking groups should be sentenced to life in prison.

4. Even as a boy he was always ordering his friends around.

5. The police found out that the clerk connived with the robbers.

26. 兩性關係及性教育

1. I have authorized him to take care of my job while I am abroad.

2. He is capable of any crime.

3. He has always been shy to the opposite sex.

4. It is evident that he is a liar.

5. Developing strong interpersonal relationships promotes personal growth.

27. 狗屎與環保

1. He decided to take part in this year's speech contest.

2. I admire the efforts made by environmental protection groups.

3. Try to sort out these files according to topic.

4. Never forget your public morals wherever you may go.

5. I spent my weekend as a conservation volunteer.

28. 火星文來了！ORZ！

1. The youth is fond of using the Martian language when chatting online.

2. Students study daily for the scholastic exam.

3. There is a very obvious urban-rural gap in Taiwan in terms of

lifestyle.

4. In essence, music is considered an international language.

5. A situation may be seen from several different perspectives.

29. 禽流感恐慌

1. People all over the world are worried about the spread of bird flu.

2. Once he starts crying, it will be very hard to make him stop.

3. The reporters flocked to the actor's residence as soon as the scandal broke out.

4. She converted to a different religion when she was a teenager.

5. The matter is serious enough to spark widespread concern.

30. 志工旅遊

1. He used up all his savings for his trip to the United States.

2. People should make use of their annual leave to relax for a few days.

3. She wants to work in a foreign-based company.

4. This tiring job will wear you out!

5. There are many underdeveloped countries in Africa.

31. 別做卡奴！

1. If you do not wish to become a credit card slave, you should not spend more than you earn.

2. Attending civics class is as important as other subjects.

3. Our special offers are intended to entice people to buy.

4. Tourists come in droves to see the koala.

5. A debt relief plan will be implemented to help those in heavy debts.

32. 黑心食品又來了！

1. Adulterated food products can be found everywhere in Taiwan.
2. We had some black moss for dinner tonight.
3. He is more or less like a brother to me.
4. Preservatives are harmful to our health.
5. The expiration date of the product is written under the box.

33. 詐騙之島

1. Telephone frauds make people doubtful of humanity.
2. This woman reminds me of my elementary school teacher.
3. When shall I file for my income tax return?
4. The judicial institution in this country is very credible.
5. In his rage he blurted out the secret.

34. 寒假打工

1. Why don't you get a part-time job to earn some money?
2. Living expenses have gone up in recent years.
3. Throughout the year, a wide variety of fruits may be found in tropical countries.
4. Don't lend them the car—they are taking advantage of you!
5. Hand over the telephone so I could talk to her.

35. 李安與斷背山

1. She won the Best Supporting Actress at this year's Academy Award.
2. Concentrate on your work to finish it on time.
3. Chinese herbal medicine has always been internationally acclaimed.
4. My parents often had to work very hard to make ends meet.
5. Accents can reinforce a negative stereotype.

Linking English
用英文寫台灣：英文作文35篇

2006年8月初版　　　　　　　　　　　　定價：新臺幣360元
有著作權・翻印必究
Printed in Taiwan.

著　　者　黃　玟　君
發行人　林　載　爵

出版者　聯經出版事業股份有限公司
台北市忠孝東路四段555號
編輯部地址：台北市忠孝東路四段561號4樓
叢書主編電話：(02)27634300轉5227
台北發行所地址：台北縣汐止市大同路一段367號
　　　　電話：(02)26418661
台北忠孝門市地址：台北市忠孝東路四段561號1-2樓
　　　　電話：(02)27683708
台北新生門市地址：台北市新生南路三段94號
　　　　電話：(02)23620308
台中門市地址：台中市健行路321號
台中分公司電話：(04)22312023
高雄門市地址：高雄市成功一路363號
　　　　電話：(07)2412802
郵政劃撥帳戶第0100559-3號
郵撥電話：26418662
印刷者　文鴻彩色製版印刷有限公司

叢書主編　何　采　嬪
校　　對　Nick Hawkins
　　　　　林　慧　如
封面設計　古　其　創　意

行政院新聞局出版事業登記證局版臺業字第0130號

本書如有缺頁，破損，倒裝請寄回發行所更換。　ISBN　13：978-957-08-3051-4（平裝）
聯經網址：www.linkingbooks.com.tw　　　　ISBN　10：957-08-3051-4（平裝）
電子信箱：linking@udngroup.com

國家圖書館出版品預行編目資料

用英文寫台灣：英文作文 35 篇 ／
黃玟君著 . 初版 . 臺北市：聯經，2006 年
（民 95）；408 面；14.8×21 公分 .
（Linking English）
ISBN 978-957-08-3051-4（平裝）

1.英國語言-作文

805.17 　　　　　　　　　　95015637

紐約時報英文解析

透過優質文章 建構聽、說、寫的能力

本書特色

1. 精選跨領域的代表性文章——提昇英文程度；大開現代知識眼界。
2. 詳盡的生字解釋與例句。
3. 清晰的文法結構分析。
4. 完整而充分的文章解析與導讀。
5. 提供最可信賴、即時的國際性英語閱讀範本。
6. 合輯附贈2片CD，增進英文聽力。

紐約時報英文解析(I) 定價320元
紐約時報英文解析(II) 定價350元
紐約時報英文解析(III) 定價380元

最堅強解析團隊

李振清：世新大學人文社會學院院長、前教育部國際文教處處長
胡耀恆：世新大學英語系客座教授、前國立台灣大學外文系教授兼系主任
彭鏡禧：國立台灣大學外文系及戲劇系教授
梁欣榮：國立台灣大學外文系副教授、前外交部駐外人員翻譯教師
李文肇：美國舊金山州立大學外文系副教授、國立台灣師範大學翻譯研究所特約兼任副教授
賴慈芸：國立台灣師範大學翻譯研究所助理教授
奚永慧：國立台灣大學外文系助理教授

推薦者

李家同：《紐約時報》自許替世界寫歷史，讀紐時，可擴大國際視野與關懷。
彭蒙惠：《紐約時報》選材多元，值得精讀。
陳文茜：《紐約時報》是人類文化精品店，教導讀者面對這個世界的態度。
陸以正：《紐約時報》值得細細品味。

美國最新口語 American Idioms for Chinese Speakers

懷中◎著　定價：380元

掌握口語，掌握文化之鑰。

作者旅美40年，網羅美國社會常用的最新口語，書中除了口語、片語、俚語之外，特別從中國人的觀點出發，整理出我們容易弄錯的口語；最後還附有中國成語的美語說法。書中每個口語都有英英、英漢解釋；同時附上多句例句，讓每一個口語展現更多面向，讀起來更透徹。

如果您要找的是一本講求實際、蒐羅完整的口語書，This is it!

美國《世界日報》連載8年最受歡迎英語學習專欄

美國常用生活會話
Conversational English for Chinese Speakers

懷中◎著　定價：380元

懷中的《美國常用生活會話》共有七大篇，分別就文化、法律、生活、娛樂、醫療和職場各方面，詳盡書寫可能發生的情境對話，並融合文化方面的說明。讀者練習實用會話之際，可以明瞭美國人的生活概況、風俗習慣和法律規定，以免與外國人相處時冒冒失失或發生誤解，對於美國人的思維模式也有更清楚的洞察。

美國《世界日報》連載8年最受歡迎英語學習專欄

學到美國人怎麼說話；也知道他們怎麼想的……

中國人常說「忠言逆耳」，美國人卻認為要盡量使用「正向語言」。前者是一片好心，但有時會傷害感情；後者則非常悅耳，但有時也讓人覺得不夠真誠。例如美國人常先來個「恭維」、再來個「不過」：

I can see your point, but I have to think about it.

（我明白你的觀點，不過得讓我想想看）。

I would love to go with you, but I have had a previous appointment.

（我真想跟你出去，但我預先有約了）。

所以，當美國人跟你說："Let me think about it."；"Let me think it over."，他們真正的意思，是和緩的推辭用語，我們千萬不要忠心耿耿的等著他們考慮後的答案才好。

聯經出版公司信用卡訂購單

信用卡別： □VISA CARD □MASTER CARD □聯合信用卡
訂購人姓名： _____
訂購日期： _____年_____月_____日
信用卡號： _____ _____ _____ _____
信用卡簽名： _____(與信用卡上簽名同)
信用卡有效期限： _____年_____月止
聯絡電話： 日(O)_____夜(H)_____
聯絡地址： □ □□_____
訂購金額： 新台幣_____元整
（訂購金額 500 元以下，請加付掛號郵資 50 元）

發票： □二聯式 □三聯式
發票抬頭： _____
統一編號： _____
發票地址： _____
如收件人或收件地址不同時，請填：
收件人姓名： □先生
_____ □小姐
聯絡電話： 日(O)_____夜(H)_____
收貨地址： _____

・ 茲訂購下列書種・帳款由本人信用卡帳戶支付・

書名	數量	單價	合計
		總計	

訂購辦法填妥後

直接傳真 FAX：(02)8692-1268 或(02)2648-7859

洽詢專線：(02)26418662 或(02)26422629 轉 241

網上訂購，請上聯經網站： www.linkingbooks.com.tw